T0144860

BLOOD
KNIFE

BLOOD KNIFE

DEATH SMITH BOOK ONE

Joost Lassche

aka Osirium Writes

Podium

To my favorite wife and our two daughters,
who were my true inspiration for writing a book about monsters.

Copyright © 2023 by Joost Lassche

Cover design by Jason Nathaniel Artuz

ISBN: 978-1-0394-4417-1

Published in 2023 by Podium Publishing, ULC
www.podiumaudio.com

Podium

BLOOD
KNIFE

Prologue

[You have finished forging an item]
[You have combined and retrieved an item]

While life outside went on as normal, within flat 23-B, there lingered an uncomfortable silence that was only broken by the dripping of water from a nearby faucet.

Two figures were sitting on the couch next to one another, where mere moments ago there had been only one. Of the two, one was heavily injured. A mixture of dried-up blood and dirt covered most of his left side. Torn clothes stuck to his bloody skin. Next to him sat another male, unmoving and with an unnatural grayness to his features. The pale figure sat perfectly still and stared in front of him with a thousand-yard stare like a mannequin or a corpse might do.

The wounded man flicked open the lighter and produced a small flame, gazing into it for a moment before lighting a cigarette. After bringing it to his mouth, he inhaled deeply before placing it between the lips of the pale figure, securing it in place.

"There we go," the wounded man said, groaning as he leaned back into his couch with his eyes aimed upwards. He stared at the ceiling as if that might hold answers to whatever he was feeling at that moment. A few minutes passed like that, still and silent, the occasional bit of ash falling off the cigarette and piling up in a single spot. The ash was identical in colour to the pale figure's unnatural gray skin.

"You know smoking is going to get you killed one day," the wounded man said, forcing his gaze away from the ceiling and towards his companion. He noticed the cigarette was barely in place, trapped between unmoving lips. The sight might have looked funny, if not for the strange complexion of his companion and the fact that he had created it.

Instead, only anger lingered that evening. A type of silent and unstable anger that might undo a person if one wasn't careful. The man's hands turned white from clenching his fist so firmly despite his injuries, as he swore an oath right there while looking at his pale companion.

"No matter what, I'll get justice for you."

CHAPTER ONE

Heroes and Hounds

Seven months ago
August, 13 AR
Lance's flat
London, England

LANCE

With a groan, the young man woke to the sound of his alarm clock. Each buzz only intensified his suppressed yawn. He rose from his bed, running his hand through his short brown hair, knowing full well that whatever energy he could conjure up now would wither in the next few hours. He made his way to the bathroom, nearly tripping over his clothes and his hospital ID-badge with his name, Lance Turner, displayed on it. Lance studied himself in the mirror, his hazel eyes surrounded by dark bags, before getting into the shower.

As the water pelted his skin, Lance scrubbed away the exhaustion of the previous day. Stepping out afterwards, he pulled on a pair of worn jeans and a comfortable T-shirt. Despite his tall stature, courtesy of his Dutch heritage, his frame was slender. He glimpsed himself again in the mirror, wishing he had a bit more muscle. Thoughts of laundry and sleep flooded his mind as he reminded himself to do the former. In all honesty, he already knew that he was going to hit his bed immediately after his hospital shift.

Two shifts left, Lance thought as he sighed, his mind consumed with the fear of a call from work. He had come to expect them, always asking for him to cover someone else's shift. He knew all too well that he'd say yes, despite his weariness. After all, he still had a mortgage to pay since his mother's passing.

Lance snatched his backpack, shoving in everything he needed for work and a breakfast to go. As he filled a mug with steaming coffee, his gaze landed on the television, still displaying the movie he had stayed up late to watch. He couldn't help but let out a sarcastic groan. "*The Rift Apocalypse: Part 3*," he muttered, feeling a twinge of embarrassment for having watched the first two movies too. Rifter movies were always so cheesy and over the top.

"Life-altering, that's what they say about becoming a Rifter," Lance mused, his mind wandering to the battles these brave souls fought within the Rifts and the monsters they encountered. Rifts were massive black spheres of unnatural energy that could suddenly form on Earth. Some Rifts were as small as a truck, others large enough to consume entire apartment complexes. No corner of the world was immune, with new Rifts appearing regularly. Most people had either witnessed one up close or seen the footage on the news.

Lance recalled the news about the first Rifts that appeared some time around November, thirteen years ago. The first Rifts had caused hundreds of people to disappear, only to have a handful of them return weeks later, scarred by tales of the horrors they'd encountered. Some spoke of deserts overrun by feral beasts, others of forests shrouded in darkness or freezing wastelands illuminated by several moons in the night sky.

The military's attempts to enter or destroy the Rifts proved futile as the strange black energy vaporized both organic and inorganic matter upon entry. The exception was for people or things that had already survived a Rift. Scientists theorized that the strange energy within the Rift had altered these survivors in some way. Luck would have it that some of these survivors stepped up to fight against the Rifts, preventing the world from descending into chaos, earning them the nickname "Rifters" from the public.

The arrival of the Rifts marked a shift in human history, referred to as the Age of Rifts by many. "Anno Rift" or "AR" became a frequent way to mark the passage of time, a testament to the profound change the Rifts brought to the world.

The roar of a motorbike outside his flat jolted Lance into action. He quickly grabbed his keys, wallet, smartphone, and earbuds from their undesignated spots before making his way to a small display case. His eyes lingered on memories from his childhood: judo medals, diplomas, and a framed photo with his best friend, Thomas Walker. Among the trinkets from his travels, a simple urn caught his eye, bearing the name of *Turner*. "See you tonight, Mom," he whispered, kissing two fingers and placing them against the urn. With a final glance around the room, Lance burst out the door, letting it slam shut behind him.

As the motorbike roared past a car, Lance felt his legs clamp onto the machine's sides. He was no enthusiast, but he couldn't help but be enamored by its power and maneuverability. But he would never confess that to Thomas, the fearless rider, who lived for these adrenaline-fueled moments.

Lance and Thomas were childhood friends, polar opposites in personality. Lance was introverted and book-smart, while Thomas was brash, athletic, and a social butterfly. The two of them had formed an unbreakable bond when Lance and his mother moved from the Netherlands to London. Their friendship had even turned into that of co-workers after both had finished school and gotten their nursing degrees.

"Another one," Thomas said, his voice crackling over the Bluetooth device as he pointed to the left while decreasing his speed. Lance followed the movement of his hand and saw what Thomas was indicating: a massive line of trucks and cranes, each marked with the GRRO logo of the Global Rift Response Organization. These were the people in charge of containing and monitoring Rifts, as well as working with those who could enter them. The police escort and the staggering amount of cargo told Lance they were on their way to a newly opened Rift. The first step the GRRO took was to secure newly formed Rifts and establish barriers and nets to keep the public safe.

"They keep popping up more and more," Lance muttered. Each newly formed Rift held the possibility of people becoming Rifters, provided they survived their first experience. Ending up in a Rift was a risk that some people took seriously, carrying backpacks filled with survival gear. Despite their precautions, the odds of it actually happening were small. Still, more Rifts formed each month, and Lance couldn't help but wonder if there was something more at play.

Thomas increased the speed again. "Just think about it," he exclaimed. "One moment you're lounging at home, the next thing you know, a Rift forms right on top of you and BAM! Afterwards you're a Rifter. Wealth, respect, and powers beyond your wildest imaginations are all yours."

"Provided you make it past the monsters, the different gravity, and dozens of other lethal combinations that could happen," Lance added, a note of sarcasm in his voice. He knew full well that Thomas would choose to ignore these inconveniences. Soon after, the two of them arrived at the hospital, changed into their uniforms, and made their way to the break room for the morning briefing. Having just done a late shift yesterday, as well as a double shift before that, Lance was already feeling his body protest as he closed his eyes for a minute.

A pungent mix of coffee, cleaning agents, and the unmistakable odor of illness clung to the air. As Lance dozed off, the other nurses made their way into the room, each with a steaming cup of coffee or tea in hand. Minutes later, it was time for the coordinator to allocate rooms to each nurse.

"Thomas, I need you in room two and three," the coordinator instructed, her voice confident. "Patient 2-A is due for surgery in a few hours, so get them prepped. Rachel, room one is yours. Tiffany, be ready to assist during rounds." She paused, adding, "And let's all hope maintenance can get that damn toilet fixed in an hour."

"Lance, rooms four and five—" the coordinator said, but her words trailed off as she caught sight of the young man in the corner. He was fast asleep, his eyes shut tight. She strode over to him, her heels clicking against the floor. "Mr. Lance Turner!" she bellowed. When he didn't stir, she threw a pen against Lance's chest to emphasize her point.

The young man jolted awake, eyes wide as he realized the coordinator's displeasure. He knew he was in trouble, this being the third time this month. Lance caught Thomas's eye and saw the amusement dancing there. As his supposed best friend, Thomas always seemed to be there with a grin whenever Lance found himself in a bind.

"Turner, I've got a new assignment for you," the coordinator said. "Seeing as you are so well rested now, you're in charge of room six." Lance let out a defeated sigh as he slumped in his seat. He knew today was going to be brutal. Room six was the go-to room for VIP patients or Rifters. Hearing Thomas giggling like a child wasn't helping his mood either.

"Thomas, since you're in such a great mood, you're going to assist Lance this morning on top of your regular duties," the coordinator said with a smile. Thomas's face turned ashen.

A few minutes later, the two nurses had introduced themselves to the patient in room six and were busy running the first tests of the morning. Lance finished measuring the blood pressure and jotted down the numbers on a piece of paper. He then placed two fingers on the man's wrist, feeling the pulse of the artery, and used his smartphone to keep track of the time. "Any further discomfort?" he asked.

Lance listened attentively as the patient recounted his symptoms, scribbling notes as he spoke. But as the conversation progressed, Lance's gaze kept straying to the man's right arm, or rather, what remained of it. *What the hell could've done this to a person, let alone a Rifter?* he wondered, disturbed.

The man Lance was treating was a Rifter by the name of Daniel Wells. He was one of the fortunate few who had lived through the experience of his first Rift, choosing to embrace his newfound identity and make a living as a Rifter. The mark of a Rift survivor, a white crystal-like shard, graced Daniel's chest. The man had worked as a Rifter for several years before he injured his arm badly. Even the combined efforts of multiple surgeons couldn't save it. "Everything appears to be in o—" Lance began to explain, before being rudely interrupted.

"Have we considered that this might just be a minor scratch, and he's milking this injury for all its worth?" Dieter Kühn asked with a cheeky smile, his guttural German accent—the thickest Lance had ever heard—emphasizing every V and Z to the point that it was hard to understand. Lance had learned that Dieter and Daniel were guild members and long-time friends.

Today, Dieter was there to graciously offer his limited medical expertise. The man, like Daniel, was an experienced Rifter. He specialized in taming and training Rift-animals, although his frame hinted at a far more melee-oriented style. Dieter's unique class allowed better cooperation with animals that had survived Rifts and to train them to fight alongside him.

With him in the room was one of Dieter's newer animal companions, a massive dog known as a Rift-hound, who was lounging on an empty bed with a curious gaze fixed on Thomas. Despite Thomas's unease, both he and Lance held a sense of awe and respect for the formidable canine, nicknamed Little Hans.

That Little Hans had a white crystal-like element embedded in the chest, like the Rifters had, only made him seem more threatening and alien. It was a rare sight for dogs and other animals to survive a Rift, so it spoke volumes about what Little Hans had been capable of in the past. The once normal-sized mastiff had grown into a formidable beast, his piercing gaze revealing a cunning intellect unrivaled by most of his kind.

Daniel apologized for Dieter's behaviour. "Dieter's got some issues," he laughed, his eyes crinkling as he glanced over at the man flipping him off. Daniel waved back with the stub of his injured right arm, still grinning. "Spends so much time with animals, he's forgotten how human interaction works. Not to mention basic decency and hygiene." Daniel's grin was infectious, making Lance and Thomas feel more comfortable. "We tried to get rid of him during one of our previous Rifts, but he's one lucky bastard," he said, shrugging his shoulders.

"There's still time," Thomas softly whispered so that only Lance could hear. To be fair to Thomas, Dieter had taken a liking to tormenting the young nurse with vivid accounts of the horrors his Rift-hound was capable of.

There were few Rifters in the world, so meeting one in person, let alone talking to two of them, was a remarkable feat. Had it not been for this hospital having a special room for Rifters, Lance and Thomas might've never met one in their lives.

Save for the more extravagant individuals, most Rifters looked quite normal. But they each bore a distinctive mark: a white crystal fragment, known as a Rift-shard, embedded in the center of their chest. That shard irradiated and infused their cells with a strange energy, allowing them to enter a Rift and grow in power when they defeated monsters. Even the weakest Rifters could hold their own against trained athletes, but as their Level increased, so did their abilities. Those in the triple-digit Levels could brush off small caliber bullets and tear off doors from a car with ease. At the highest Levels, the Rifters were capable of feats that bordered on the realm of fiction.

It was hard not to imagine what a one-armed Rifter such as Daniel could do to a room full of civilians if the man suddenly snapped. Luckily, these types of cases were infrequent and other Rifters dealt with these incidents.

"I'll get this data recorded and be back in a little while," Lance commented as he grabbed his things and smiled at Daniel, doing his best not to stare at the missing arm.

"I'm telling you, man," Thomas persisted during lunch for the fifteenth time in a row, "that dog is just not right." Lance tuned him out, tired of hearing Thomas's spiels about how ordinary people needed to be protected from Rifters. The truth was, Thomas was a hardcore Rifter buff, devouring countless articles on the topic. Only one person was more into Rifters than Thomas, and that was his little brother, Oliver.

There was just something about Dieter and his hound that unnerved Thomas. If Lance was being honest, it affected him as well. One mere look at Little Hans made you realize that there was nothing you could do to stop the dog if he lost control. But Lance was more unnerved by the displays of intelligence and how closely bonded Little Hans and Dieter were. Still, it was amusing to see a tough figure like Thomas tremble whenever the hound approached him.

Lance took another bite of bread, the rough texture scraping against his teeth as he dipped it into the bowl of tomato soup. The meal was a bizarre combination of under-seasoned and overpowering spices. *Who in their right mind classified this as soup?* Lance thought, shuddering as he tried to ignore the taste.

Lance flipped on his earbuds, drowning out Thomas's loud ranting with the beat of his music. He couldn't handle his friend's extroverted personality at times, opting instead to retreat into his own thoughts or the solace of sound. He spooned another mouthful of what he'd come to think of as Satan's liquid ashtray while scanning the bustling crowd of patients and medical staff. With his third year on the job just around the corner, he reminisced about his experiences at work. Despite the long and irregular hours, the hospital had treated him well.

He glanced at his phone to check the time and saw a text from his older brother, asking him how he was doing. The message was in Dutch. Despite having lived in the Netherlands during his early childhood, he still remembered the language fluently, thanks to his mother's encouragement to improve it alongside his English.

After his parents' divorce, she and Lance moved to England to stay with her relatives. Lance's older brother had remained in the Netherlands due to having joined the police academy and recently gotten a girlfriend. His brother had made attempts to stay in touch, even visiting a couple of times. However, the distance and the divorce had created a rift between the siblings. Rather than confront his feelings, Lance shut off his phone.

"Time to earn our pay," Lance said gruffly, interrupting Thomas as he spun him around and guided him away from several enraptured interns. Thomas had just begun holding court, regaling the group with tales of the mythical Rift-hound, but Lance was eager to move on.

CHAPTER TWO

Vacation and Monsters

Ealing Hospital
London, England

LANCE

In the background, Lance and Thomas hurried to complete their tasks while Daniel patiently listened to the doctor's grim diagnosis. The physician outlined the severity of the damage to his arm and discussed the potential need for prosthetics, as well as the ongoing threat of infection. Although antibiotics had temporarily contained it, the road to recovery was long and uncertain. Despite the devastating news, Daniel remained composed, nodding in acknowledgement while silently appraising the wreckage that had once been his arm.

"Prosthetics won't cut it unless it's made from Rift material," Dieter said, his thick German accent making his statement sound more serious. He clarified that only materials found within a Rift could survive its passage. Daniel's prosthetic, therefore, had to be made from the same material if he intended to go with it.

"It's alright, Dieter. I'm done as a Rifter. We both know that this is the case." Daniel spoke with a composed voice, signaling the end of their discussion. He looked up at the towering figure of the German beside him, only to be met with a resolute stare.

"We won't know unless you try," the man growled.

Daniel nodded in understanding at the doctor, his left hand finding its way to Dieter's shoulder in gratitude. He appreciated the sentiment, but the decision had already been made.

Daniel let out a rueful laugh, the sound hollow and bitter. "Seems I picked the wrong class," he said to his friend when the doctor had left the room. "A Mage could still sling spells with one arm."

"A Magier, huh?" Dieter scoffed, his lips curling in amusement. "You'd probably burn off your dangling bits the first time you tried to cast a fireball."

"Pffft," Daniel scoffed with a proud expression. "It would have to be a pretty big fireball to do that."

The men's laughter echoed throughout the room as the Rift-hound's tail wagged with joy. Lance and Thomas sat in the corner, heads down and focused on their reports. Just as they were about to leave, Daniel noticed Lance staring at his arm yet again. He shot a pointed look in Lance's direction and gestured him over with a flick of his head.

Lance's face flushed as he approached. "Sorry. I didn't mean to stare," he apologized.

"Yes, you did. But don't worry about it. Come have a proper look," Daniel said, waving off Lance's apology. He rolled up his sleeve, showing the scars that crisscrossed his arm. "A Skinner did this," he said, his voice devoid of emotion, while the Rift-hound let out a low growl, as if sensing the danger that the word represented.

"I've had the pleasure of meeting a pack of those little monsters," Daniel said sarcastically, his expression darkening. "Their jaws are very flexible, and once they've bitten down, they just start spinning, grinding away at your flesh until there's nothing left. It's like being ground down to the bone."

Thomas, who had been eavesdropping on the war stories, turned pale as Daniel explained the Skinner. Lance shuddered as he tried to picture the creature—a hybrid of a crocodile and a hyena. *And these Rifters battle these things for a living?* he thought, feeling a mix of awe and horror. He knew not everyone had what it took to become a Rifter, as Rift experiences traumatized or permanently maimed many of the survivors. And those that survived their first experience intact would also need the proper mindset to go back in.

"How long does it take to lose an arm like that?" Thomas inquired, earning a swift kick to the shin from Lance. His best friend shot him a look that screamed, *Are you serious right now?* Meanwhile, Daniel remained unfazed, as if he had seen injuries like this before.

Daniel mused on the topic, his gaze distant as he considered the answer. "It all comes down to size and maturity," he finally said. "A youngling could take a few minutes to sand down an arm, but an alpha . . . about ten seconds?" He turned to Dieter, curious to hear his thoughts.

"Ja, seems about right," Dieter replied, calmly weighing in as if it were a rather lighthearted topic to discuss.

Daniel then went on: "My Rifter class is that of a Ranger . . . or it was when I had both my arms. It is best to hunt a Skinner from a distance during the day. They have poor vision in daylight, and you can spot them from afar. They get more dangerous during the nighttime. That happened to me. Still, my days of wielding a bow are over."

The conversation continued, and Daniel regaled the group with stories from his latest Rifts, with Dieter chiming in with his own experiences. They reminisced about the strange creatures they had encountered and the myriad of worlds they had visited. As they spoke, they shared fascinating stories of unique Rifter classes, like Necromancers, Summoners, and even Druids, alongside more common ones like Warriors, Smiths, Rangers, and Mages.

Thomas and Lance were enthralled by their accounts, lost in tales of distant, mystical realms that existed beyond the limits of imagination. The stories were so captivating that they could have been taken straight from the pages of a novel.

Thump. Thump.

Lance strained his eyes as he checked his phone again, mentally calculating the time he had left. *One hour.* He ignored the unread text from his brother again. "You realize you don't have to keep throwing the ball, right?" he asked his friend, hoping to end the mind-numbing game.

Thump.

Thump.

Lance's eyes followed the ball's trajectory as it flew past him. He deftly shifted his weight to the side, snatching it out of the air with ease and depriving Thomas of another irritating ball toss.

"Give it back, man. You know it helps with my nerves," Thomas grumbled, shooting Lance a disapproving look of betrayal.

"Don't be nervous. The uniform looks very slimming on you," Lance said with a grin, followed by Thomas throwing a small packet of sugar towards him.

Though his athletic build didn't exactly lend itself to diplomacy, the red-haired man tried his luck anyway, his hand hovering near the bowl of sugar packets on the table. "You know what I mean," he said. "I need a smoke and I still have to wait an hour because of that bloody new rule."

"Ah, well. New policy, new rules," Lance replied, not feeling any sympathy for his friend's unhealthy habits. He had tried for years to get Thomas to quit smoking, but the man was as stubborn as an ox.

"They didn't consult me about this," Thomas said sourly, no doubt feeling the cigarette pack and lighter burning a hole in his pocket. He always had them close at hand.

Lance shot Thomas a concerned look. "You know those things are going to kill you one day, right?" Thomas just shrugged and hurled another sugar packet at him. Lance caught it and grinned. "Geez, you're such a baby," he muttered, setting the packet back on the table.

"Bite me," Thomas said, his voice somewhat irritated.

A grin twisted Lance's lips as he stood up. "You know what? Scratch that. The uniform doesn't do you any favors. It makes you look fat." With a yawn threatening to escape, he sauntered towards the remaining tasks on his check-list. The relentless work hours and added shifts had drained him. All he wanted was to slip into bed and escape from the world.

Chicken would be good . . . perhaps a taco? he thought, deciding what to have for dinner. The ache in his stomach hinted that he would need some fresh vegetables or a proper meal at some point. For now, a microwave meal would have to suffice. Not long after deciding on his meal, he noticed that his colleagues from the late shift were arriving. He knew most of them well, occasionally sharing drinks with them after work. Some were newbies or interns, too green to form an opinion on yet.

Thomas was Lance's oldest friend. He looked and acted like a stereotypical jock, with his fiery red hair and quick temper. But Lance knew that beneath the tough exterior was a man with a kind heart. Thomas was a master at whining and complaining, but in times of crisis, he was the rock everyone could count on. He stayed calm under pressure and never wavered in his loyalty to his friends.

With his shift nearly over, Lance went to check on his VIP patient, Daniel Wells. Nearly every hospital had its doors open for Rifters, but few hospitals could handle the assortment of injuries they could sustain in a Rift. These brave men and women frequently got stabbed, cut, or even bitten by strange monsters. Beyond that, there could be strange acids or poisons involved. And sometimes, they encountered things that even medical professionals couldn't fully comprehend.

While Rifters skilled in the art of healing could typically address most injuries on the spot, some wounds were simply too severe. Daniel's condition fell into this category. Even restorative potions, which could have helped him recover, were few and far between, not to mention exorbitantly expensive.

Lance knocked softly on the door before peeking inside and asking, "You got a minute?" After receiving an affirmative from Daniel, he stepped into the room and saw the man seated in a chair, scribbling notes on a stack of papers Lance had dropped off earlier.

"Hey, lad. Just jotting down some notes to get my thoughts in order," Daniel said as he looked up. Lance couldn't help but feel a little uneasy under the weight of Daniel's piercing gaze. Though his eyes projected a sense of wisdom and knowledge, they also conveyed an intense level of scrutiny.

Lance didn't feel sorry for Daniel, but he felt a profound sense of grief. Despite their popularity, there were not enough Rifters to be in every place at once. An uncleared Rift could quickly turn into an outbreak, with whatever horrors that lay beyond spilling out and forming a permanent connection to the world. *How many more people could he have rescued if he had sustained no permanent injuries?*

As more and more Rifts appeared, the threat of an outbreak grew as well. Governments took great care in monitoring Rifts and deploying armed forces and the military where they deemed it necessary. Depending on where the Rift was located, it could mean an outbreak might occur in a heavily populated area. For Lance, losing even one Rifter like Daniel would be a great loss for the world.

"Are you all right for the rest of the day?" Lance asked, waiting for an answer from the Rifter as he stepped further into the room.

Daniel had already been in surgery a few times, at first to save the arm and later to improve the condition of what remained. His current reason for staying in the hospital was to have further tests and examine the scale of the nerve damage. To make matters worse, it turned out that monsters such as a Skinner also carried nasty lingering infectious material in their saliva. Even a Rifter as durable as Daniel could still be susceptible to these types of things. This meant that he'd require frequent treatment to prevent the infection from getting worse.

"Yeah, I'm all right, lad. Thanks for checking up on me," Daniel replied, setting down his pen on the table. "Dieter's out with Little Hans and grabbing some things from my car. You almost finished with your shift for the day?"

"Almost done. Just need to grab my backpack and update the late shift," Lance replied, his smile reassuring. "Brendan or Sophia should be taking care of you tonight. They're both excellent nurses." He hesitated for a moment, thinking about his experiences helping other Rifters. Most of them had severe injuries or an aura that made them hard to approach. As an introvert, Lance didn't enjoy dealing with haughty Rifters who were idolized as heroes.

Despite being a Rifter, Daniel felt surprisingly normal to Lance. It was difficult to put into words, but there was something about the man that made him seem like just an average bloke. If Lance could ignore the crystal-like object in the center of his chest and the fact that he was missing an arm, Daniel would blend right in with any group of dads.

The man's build was the product of a lifetime of labor: compact, strong, and purposeful. His hair, once brown, was now shot through with gray, lending him an air of gravitas. But his brown eyes were lively and mischievous, defying the wrinkles that clustered around them. It was a face that spoke to experience and endurance.

Lance cleared his throat, suddenly unsure of how to proceed. "This might sound weird or inappropriate, but . . . do you think you're going to miss being a Rifter?" he asked, watching the other man's face for any sign of a reaction.

"Yes and no," the Rifter said, with a thoughtful look. "I won't miss the pain, the hardships, and the constant fear," he said with a dismissive wave of his hand when Lance appeared to be surprised by his answer. "Every Rifter is afraid, lad. Every time we step into a Rift, we know we might not come back. That kind of fear stays with you. What, did you think we were all made of steel or something?

"Don't believe everything you hear. People think we're all crazy adrenaline junkies, but that's just nonsense. Most people who earn their shards don't even want to become Rifters. And even if they do, it's difficult. The terrain, the creatures, the lack of sleep . . . it's a bloody nightmare. Compare that to a comfortable bed, a warm meal, and a bottle of scotch . . . Simple choice, right?" he said with a smile before looking down at his left hand, as if gripping some invisible memory that he cherished. "But finding people in a Rift and helping them survive? Clearing a Rift and restoring hope to a city? That feeling of doing something good? Even just being present and on the scene calms people down. I'll always miss that feeling," Daniel explained as the smile widened.

"I think I understand. It makes sense," Lance said respectfully before nodding at the man. As he made his way out of the room, he caught a glimpse of Daniel still staring at his remaining hand and whispering something about purpose.

CHAPTER THREE

Break a Leg!

Ealing Hospital
London, England

LANCE

Lance glared at his phone, the unread message notification from his brother burning into his retinas. He could feel the pressure building inside him, urging him to open it and see what his sibling wanted. Before he could give in to the temptation, however, the locker room door burst open, and his co-workers barged in, effectively pulling him back to reality.

He placed his phone and earbuds in his backpack before flinging it over his shoulder. Lance strode into the hallway, but abruptly halted as a peculiar sensation coursed through his chest, leaving him with an uncomfortable itch. A fleeting discomfort, yet enough to unnerve him. *What in the hell was that?* Lance paused, waiting for the feeling to pass. He took a deep breath and shook it off, continuing his trek to the break room. Once he arrived, he grabbed a chair. He noticed Thomas wasn't there, leaving him to assume his friend was taking one of his illegal smoke breaks.

"Just five more minutes."

"Say, when is your holiday?"

As he sat there, Lance couldn't help but overhear a lively conversation going on between two nurses sitting nearby. The thought of taking a holiday himself was enough to bring a smile to his face, though he knew deep down that it was nothing more than a pipe dream. With his budget stretched to the limit since his mother's passing, there was little hope of it becoming a reality any time soon. He slumped further into his seat and glanced at the stack of magazines and newspapers on the table.

The newspaper next to him was all doom and gloom, detailing the latest military spending in France. He pushed it aside and glanced at the tabloid instead, hoping for a distraction. Unfortunately, splashed across the front page was a fluff piece about some actor who was playing a Rifter in an upcoming film, saving the world from an outbreak. *I've had enough of Rifts and Rifters for today. I'll settle for a warm meal and catching up on my reading,* he thought, closing his eyes. The worst part was that he knew Thomas would end up dragging him to see said film. *Please don't make me like it.*

"What about you, Lance? Any plans this—" the nurse asked but paused when a wave of nausea suddenly washed over her, making her falter. The other nurse also began to look unwell, and then Lance himself felt nauseous. He tightly gripped his chest with his hands.

"What the hell?" Lance muttered, lifting a trembling finger to point at the nearby coffeepot. The black liquid inside was moving against the laws of physics, rising in a mesmerizing swirl.

The others barely had time to register it when an ear-splitting screech pierced the air, disorienting everyone in the room. The ground buckled and tilted under their feet, and they careened to the side, unable to regain their balance. Chairs, tables, cups, and other items became deadly projectiles, slamming into the wall and the helpless nurses, leaving them bruised and battered.

"What the hell?"

"My leg! I think I broke my leg!"

"What happened?"

The room erupted into chaos as everyone began shouting at each other. Lance and one of the nurses scrambled to their feet and started clearing chairs out of the way. Rachel, the other nurse, remained on the ground with both hands clasped around her left leg, which was twisted at an unnatural angle.

Lance's colleague wasted no time taking charge. "Stay with her," he said. "I'll go find some help." His words were firm and authoritative. It reminded Lance that they were all trained medical professionals, allowing him to regain his composure.

"Alright, but watch yourself," Lance commented before the nurse left him alone with Rachel. Wanting to be useful, Lance quickly set to work, making the area more comfortable and safer for her. He cleared away debris and picked up a blanket that had fallen off a nearby shelf. "Here. Slowly now," he said reassuringly as he placed the blanket underneath her head. "Help will be here soon. We'll set the bones and have you in an ugly colored cast in no time."

"Yeah . . . It isn't that bad, right?" Rachel asked, her mind no doubt clinging to the prospect of normality.

Lance's voice faltered as he spoke to Rachel. "Yeah, it's just a minor fracture, don't worry," he lied. He continued to chat with her, to calm her nerves and his own, suppressing what he would otherwise be feeling. He suggested the accident must've been an earthquake or something similar. Lance knew it wasn't true. Earthquakes didn't make coffee defy the laws of gravity or suddenly give three people a feeling of nausea before it even started.

Occasionally, the two of them heard a groan, followed by a sickening cracking sound that signaled more of the building's collapse. Amidst the chaos, Lance picked up on the sound of people shouting and moaning. He couldn't help but wonder how many more injured there were, just like Rachel. Although he was a mess of bruises, he tried to focus on the fact that he hadn't broken anything. It was a minor comfort amid such madness.

Continuing to hear the anguished cries of others in need, Lance felt torn between the urge to rush to their aid and the knowledge that Rachel was in no condition to fend for herself with a broken leg in a room filled with unstable shelves and cabinets. *Stabilize the scene and the patient first,* he reminded himself, *then search for other survivors.*

Desperate to ease Rachel's pain, Lance scrambled for a solution. "I can crack open the window, let some air in. Would that be better?" he asked, hoping to offer her some relief. He studied Rachel's face as she gave a slight nod, her body tensing in discomfort.

No doubt the adrenaline is wearing off, he reasoned as he set a chair near the window. Normally, he'd be able to see out of the window from a seated position. The room was now tilted, forcing Lance to stand on his toes on a chair to open the window and look outside. He peered out, only to regret it immediately.

The sight outside left Lance speechless. He had braced himself for the aftermath of a natural disaster, but what he saw exceeded even his worst expectations. *What the hell is this?* he thought, his mind racing to find a logical explanation.

"Is everything all right? Why are you so quiet?" Rachel asked as she watched Lance staring outside as if seeing a ghost. "Is it bad? Lance?" But he simply kept staring outside, as if lost in his own thoughts. "Lance!" she finally screamed, forcing him to recover from his daze and face her again.

"It's not great, but we'll be fine," he lied, his mind unable to process the bizarre sight before him. He had expected to see broken buildings and roads, yet all he could see was a murky swamp and the shattered remains of the hospital slowly sinking inside. Towering trees also dotted the area, their imposing presence making Lance feel small and exposed. The sweltering, acrid heat penetrated the walls, an unwelcome intrusion in the air-conditioned comfort he was used to.

Lance's heart pounded loudly in his chest as he climbed off the chair. Everything was so incredibly wrong, but he couldn't let Rachel see that. "We'll be fine," he said, his voice calm despite the turmoil in his mind. With his back towards Rachel, he slid a hand underneath his shirt, touching the spot in the center of his chest. Instead of soft skin, he felt the rigid exterior of a Rift-shard there. *No,* Lance thought, suppressing his urge to hyperventilate and freak out. *A white-shard? When did it get there? Why didn't I notice it sooner?*

A Rift had just opened up around the hospital, swallowing him and everyone else inside of it. He now found himself in a strange world, a scenario like one Daniel and Dieter had talked about just hours before. Hearing Rachel call out to him again in a panicked tone, Lance did what he could at that moment. *Stabilize Rachel,* he thought, steeling himself against the panic. *Wait for medical help and keep her safe. And pray that Rifters will get here in time. Perhaps Daniel and Dieter are also here?*

He knelt next to her and placed a spare T-shirt under her neck from his bag. "We'll wait for the others. In the meantime, I'm going to have a look around for painkillers, all right?" Lance said, attempting to reassure her with a tight smile.

Lance stayed by her side, providing water and a dose of pain medication. He had resisted the urge to glance outside or venture into the hallway, mindful of Rachel's potential panic. The thought of looking out again sent a shiver down his spine, fearing it would cause him to freak out as well. As he offered her more water, the screams and moans outside suddenly grew louder, intensifying into a horrifying chorus.

Rachel and Lance were no strangers to hearing people suffering, having witnessed their fair share of pain, blood, and discomfort in their careers before, but nothing could have prepared them for the sounds that they heard outside of the room. It was a sound that was both visceral and haunting, resonating in their souls. Other noises accompanied the screams, similarly unfamiliar and bizarre. Some sounded like objects colliding with walls and other surfaces, others like roars and clicks echoing in the hallway.

Rachel's voice broke as she whimpered, "Lance, what's happening?" Her makeup was ruined, black streaks of smudged mascara streaking down her face, her cheeks wet with tears.

Lance's heart continued pounding, a part of him wanting to ignore the sounds and pretend everything was fine. But the shard lodged in his chest was a painful reminder that they were in deep trouble. "We have to stay quiet," he whispered to Rachel, his eyes scanning the room for any signs of danger. Suddenly, a new sound of something scurrying in the ceiling panels made them freeze, fear coursing through their veins.

Lance willed himself to stay still and silent, even as the seconds ticked by like an eternity. Rachel, too, seemed rooted to the spot, her eyes wide with terror. Suddenly, a panel crashed to the floor, followed by the appearance of a grotesque creature that left them gaping in disbelief.

With a loud crash, the monster was in the room with them. As it rose to its full height, it let out a low growl. Three claws on each of its paws were hitting one another, producing a menacing clicking sound. Blueish tinted scales covered its body in a tight pattern. Its full size reached that of a human teenager. The monster scanned the room with its yellow eyes, as if searching for something specific.

Lance found himself in the monster's crosshairs as its yellow eyes settled on him with an intensity that made his blood run cold. But Rachel's piercing screams drew the creature's attention away from him, its eyes flickering toward her instead. "Get it away, Lance! Get it away!" she screeched, her voice echoing off the walls.

Lance barely had time to react before the monster sprang at Rachel. It moved with the swift, feral grace of a predator, its claws and teeth tearing into her flesh with brutal force. The creature didn't seem interested in killing Rachel quickly, though—it savored each moment of her suffering, relishing the sound of her pained cries and the sight of her blood spilling onto the ground. Soon, Rachel's screams turned to choked gurgles as the monster mauled her beyond recognition.

"No!" Lance's voice was raw with fear and anger as he charged at the monster, slamming into it with all his might. But to his shock, the creature barely even flinched; it was like slamming into a stone wall. Lance gritted his teeth and tried to pull the monster away from Rachel, but its grip was like iron. With a savage snarl, the creature hurled Lance aside and turned back to its grisly meal.

Lance pushed himself to his feet, his body aching and his head swimming. He looked at Rachel's lifeless form, her eyes glassy and her body mangled beyond recognition. The creature had torn out her throat, her chest now reduced to a gruesome, bloody mess. Lance knew there was nothing he could do for her now; she was beyond saving. He looked around desperately. *If I stay here, I'll end up like her,* Lance thought as fear gripped his heart, overwhelming his shame and any hesitation at leaving her.

Lance's thoughts were a jumbled mess as he bolted past the monster and Rachel's mutilated remains. He knew he had to get out of there before the monster realized she was dead. *I'm sorry, Rachel. I'm so sorry!* he thought as he grabbed his backpack and slammed himself through the door. His feet tripped over the corpses of more dead colleagues as he sprinted away, the monster's angry snarls ringing in his ears.

As Lance darted through the ruined hospital, it seemed like hours had passed since he had entered, but in reality, only thirty minutes had gone by. Blood and carnage were everywhere, with monsters feasting on their victims without mercy. He stumbled upon several gruesome scenes of corpses scattered in pieces, and his mind could hardly process the sheer horror of it all. He had to fight to maintain his composure, stifling the urge to vomit or fall into a helpless daze.

Trudging through the aftermath of battle, Lance caught glimpses of slain monsters impaled by crude weapons. Their lifeless bodies were strewn among those of multiple human victims. He had spotted other survivors, holed up in rooms that they had barricaded, but they wouldn't let him inside and were barely registering his pleas for help. Most of them looked as broken as he felt.

Throughout all of this, he had already found himself on the brink of death three times. Twice he had run into monsters, forcing him to flee to a different floor in order to lose them. It was only his familiarity with the twists and turns of the hospital that had kept him alive.

His third close call with death happened when he barged into a room, thinking it would lead him to a secure office, only to come face-to-face with a precipitous drop. It was as if something had sliced off that section of the building and moved it elsewhere. Seeing the unnatural landscape on the other side, it again forced Lance to come to terms with the fact that he wasn't on Earth anymore.

For a brief moment, he allowed himself to silently cry, the weight of the situation almost crushing him. Then, he gritted his teeth and pressed forward. Staying in one place was a death sentence. It was dawning on him that he was in some kind of Hell. Death seemed inevitable.

Just as he was about to investigate the floor above, however, he stumbled upon a group of survivors, including some of his colleagues, with both sides shouting and nearly hitting one another.

Lance's breath came out in a ragged whisper as he addressed them. "I nearly had a heart attack," he hissed. Suddenly, he spotted Thomas among them. Relief flooding his veins, he latched onto him, seeking solace from his closest friend. Thomas didn't hesitate to embrace him back, both men offering each other a sense of comfort in the midst of all the chaos.

Thomas released Lance and gave him a once-over, scanning him for injuries. "Are you okay? Anybody else still alive?" he asked, his voice full of concern. He could see all the blood sticking to Lance, but he didn't know if it was his or from all the bodies he had been tripping over.

The word was barely more than a breath as Lance spoke. "No," he said, his voice cracking with emotion.

Thomas spoke slowly, choosing his words carefully. "Are you sure?" he asked, his eyes fixed on Lance's.

Lance's voice trembled with emotion as he snapped, "I said 'No!'" Lance could feel the weight of Rachel's death heavy on his conscience, the guilt threatening to overwhelm him. *I let her die! I let it rip into her! I just ran!*

Thomas read the distress in Lance's eyes and quickly switched gears. "Let's focus on the Rifters. The last time I checked, Mr. Kühn wasn't in the hospital anymore. Did Mr. Wells make it out?" Thomas asked Lance, steering the conversation to hopefully more optimistic prospects.

Lance gripped his backpack tightly, finding solace in its familiar weight. Some of the scavenged supplies nestled inside were a reminder that he wanted to survive. His unsteady mind had still realized food, water, and medical supplies would be vital. "I'm not sure," he replied to Thomas, still haunted by the horrors he'd witnessed. "Parts of the building are gone, including his room. But he might have made it out?"

"All right, we need to get you equipped and calm." Thomas suggested, his voice carrying an air of authority.

"Thomas, I'm fine. Honestly—" Lance started, before Thomas cut him off.

"No, you aren't! You're as pale as a ghost, covered in blood, and look as if you're a second away from a heart attack. Help yourself before you help others. Remember?" Thomas said, reminding Lance of medical emergency protocol.

Lance nodded slowly at that before properly joining the group. He felt hands pat his shoulders and heard encouraging words for surviving this long on his own. He wasn't sure if it was the human contact, or the shame he felt for being complimented while he had let Rachel die so brutally. In the end, it mattered little since his tears simply wouldn't stop flowing.

CHAPTER FOUR

Bloody Companions

August, 13 AR
Inside Rift 1

LANCE

Hold them back!" Thomas shouted as he instructed the group of survivors to keep pushing against the barricade. Seventeen souls, including Thomas, were now trapped in the pharmacy section of the hospital. They were using tables, cabinets, and other heavy objects to keep the monstrous horde at bay. The room was quite well protected, having a thick security door and reinforced glass on the sides to prevent thieves from breaking in. With monsters, it proved quite effective as well, although breaches had formed in some sections.

"Stakes on the west side! And where are those chemicals?" Thomas ordered, his voice carrying both urgency and the weight of command.

"On it . . ."

"Nearly done."

This section of the hospital had become a war zone, its survivors fighting tooth and nail to stay alive. IV poles, brooms, and crutches were stripped of their original purposes, turned instead into makeshift weapons to repel the monsters. Some of the survivors had fashioned spears for ranged attacks, while others wielded hooks to snare the creatures. Those without weapons grabbed whatever was at hand, be it sheets or thick metal rods, ready to join the fray.

At close range, the monsters would win with ease. But when the survivors used their numbers and tools to keep them at bay or trap them, they had a chance. They had already killed several of the monsters but now found themselves pinned down in this room. On the other side, monsters were frantically slamming into the door or attacking the window. The creatures were clearly desperate to get their claws on their prey. From what the survivors could see, there must've been more than a dozen of them out there.

"Ready with the next batch!" Thomas commanded, seeing the monsters slowly advance in one area. "Steve, Lance, get ready to throw it. Three . . . Two . . . One . . ."

"Lighten up on the door," Thomas barked, his voice ringing with authority. "Lance, Steve . . . now!" The two men leaped into action, pouring corrosive chemicals through the gap and onto the monsters' faces. The acid sizzled and burned, causing the beasts to thrash and howl. Though the acid wouldn't kill them, it was a cruel and effective way to blind or wound them.

Despite their best efforts, the survivors had been fighting the creatures for well over an hour. The beasts hammered at the door incessantly, their blows reverberating through the room. The survivors were showing the effects of the prolonged battle: exhaustion weighed them down, injuries slowed their movements, and their minds were buckling underneath the pressure of it all.

"Get the spray ready," Thomas said, pointing at a woman on his right. "Jack, you're bleeding. Treat those injuries." A second passed, but the man barely seemed to register Thomas's command. "Jack! Get the hell back and patch yourself up!" The man simply stared at the door, fixated on the monstrous wave on the other side.

"Grab Jack!" Thomas told Lance as he slammed a sharpened pole through another gap in the window, aiming it at the eyes or mouth of any monster. The makeshift spears might not be strong enough to pierce the scales, yet they could inflict damage on softer target areas.

"Jack, come on. Let's get those wounds checked out," Lance said, nudging the man away from the door and letting another survivor step in to maintain the defense. After checking him out, Lance realized that the man's wounds were shallow and not life-threatening. Some would require stitching later, but for now, a tight bandage to keep the pressure on it would be enough.

"I'm good . . . I can go on," Jack said, his eyes wide and unfocused.

Lance had a good idea of what the man was going through in that moment, having experienced it firsthand. Still, he himself was doing a bit better now, despite the obvious continued threat. There was something reassuring about facing these monsters together with his best friend. "I get it, Jack. But you have to eat and drink something, alright?" Lance said calmly, forcing his tone to be as reassuring as he could.

"But—"

"First things first. We need to get some food and water into you. We need you here for the long run, and we can't afford to lose you, Jack," Lance asserted, bringing the man's attention back to the task at hand. Jack blinked and then took the proffered water bottle and candy bar from Lance's outstretched hand.

"A—all right. I will be back soon," the man said as Lance walked away from him and took up his position near the door, pressing against it with his full weight, allowing Thomas to step back again and observe the scene.

Thomas is really good at this. Is it his background in sports, or something more instinctive? Lance wondered as he watched Thomas. The man was making his rounds again, boosting morale by motivating the others or just standing side by side to show support. Out of all the survivors, Thomas was the most athletic and was doing most of the heavy hitting. Lance knew his friend wouldn't be able to keep this up for long, nor could any of them. But for now, they at least had a fighting chance.

The worst part is the fear of the unknown. Are Rifters even coming from the outside to save us, and when will they arrive? Lance mused. From what he had read online, an Initial Rift, such as what they were in now, was still stable. It meant that Rifters could still enter it. Once they did, there would be a small window of time before the Rift became unstable and no further entry could happen until they were victorious or were all killed.

It could be hours, or it could be days, before someone can come and help us. I heard Thomas say that time may even pass differently inside a Rift. Who knows how long we'll have to wait for rescue? Lance thought, feeling a sliver of fear creep into his mind. He caught himself and shifted his focus back on his task: keeping the door closed!

"Keep that barricade up!" Thomas ordered, repeatedly slamming a steel pipe into the claws of a monster until it backed off. The beast had tried to climb past the large steel table that was pressed against the nearly destroyed window. The table showed dents in a dozen places, a sizable chunk of it torn out by the creatures' constant abuse.

"Hold!" Thomas shouted at the group of survivors, seeing the table slowly being pushed back until the monsters finally forced the defenders beyond the point of exhaustion. With a large clang, it fell, and several monsters rushed in.

With a flick of his lighter, Lance ignited the air freshener spray, creating a wall of fire that halted the monsters in their tracks. The acrid scent of the spray mixed with the stench of burning flesh, filling the air. Lance knew he had only a few precious seconds before the spray ran out, but it was enough to give the survivors a chance to regroup. However, three of the beasts had already broken through and were attacking with savage intensity.

"Sheets and spears!" Thomas ordered frantically.

A patient panicked when she caught sight of the monsters. "There are too many of them!"

"Where are those sheets?" Thomas commanded as he waited for the others to spring into action. Already several had gotten hurt in the frenzy. Eventually, the remaining survivors had pinned down two of the monsters while the third one ran rampant, slashing at exposed arms and legs.

"Thomas!" Lance yelled as he nodded towards the improvised flamethrower that he was wielding in order to signal that he had an idea. He tensed his muscles and waited for the rest to join in. Thomas seemed to understand what Lance was trying to do as he grabbed the table and called to another survivor to help him block the hole up again.

The moment they did so, Lance saw his chance. He redirected the flame towards the trapped creatures. The flames caught the sheets and raced up their bodies, turning them into monstrous torches. The heat was intense, and the acrid smell of burning flesh filled the air.

Lance felt a sick sense of triumph as he watched the monsters writhing and howling in agony as the flames consumed them, the hospital sheets acting as kindling. *Die . . . just die . . . just die,* Lance thought, hoping that the attack would be enough. Thick patches of smoke soon formed, while the scent of burning flesh persisted in the air.

Once these two monsters had been dispatched, it freed people up to either help strengthen the barricade that Thomas was trying to rebuild or hunt for the remaining enemy in the room.

The improvised flamethrower died out after a while. They had already used up all the other chemicals and corrosives. This meant that it was only a matter of time before the monsters truly overran them, with no chance of recovering and re-forming their defences. "That was the last one," Lance said, as he shared the bad news with his friend.

"I didn't want to hear that, Lance," Thomas remarked as the two of them fought desperately to keep the monsters outside.

Elsewhere, unbeknownst to Lance, Thomas, and the others, two Rifters advanced cautiously, their weapons gripped tightly in their hands as they motioned for various other survivors to remain silent and stay put. The mere presence of the Rifters had a reassuring effect, but with Daniel and Dieter now clad in steel and leather armor, that effect was even more potent. Daniel's equipment still bore the damage from his previous Rift, while Dieter's was in pristine condition, except for the red coating from all the monsters he had already stopped.

For the last few hours, the two Rifters had been tirelessly clearing the building floor by floor, striving to save as many lives as they could. Even for two Rifters, it was grueling work, battling monsters while keeping the survivors out of harm's way. With Daniel's lack of a right arm, he was unable to use his usual arsenal, meaning Dieter had to adapt to compensate for his partner's newfound limitations. As they approached the pharmacy, besieged by the monsters, the two of them evaluated the situation with caution.

"I think there are about seven in total?" Daniel asked.

"Eight," Dieter replied. He was focusing on his bond with Little Hans as he received the sensory information that the Rift-hound gave back. It was almost as if he could smell each individual monster and make out distinct differences between them. Dieter had worked with other animals before, but never as closely as he had done with Little Hans.

The two Rifters had plenty of Rift experience between them. Usually, they worked with at least a group of six to eight other people, if not more. For them to end up in an Initial Rift like this one was extremely rare and dangerous, but it also offered the survivors a better chance of making it out alive. With that said, the Rifters were on their own for now. A Rift response team could arrive within a few hours, or it could take weeks.

Daniel's medical condition also meant that there was a time limit on his effectiveness, with the infection in his arm getting worse the longer he was without proper medical treatment and based on how much he exerted himself. Depending on the Level of the Rift itself, two experienced Rifters could either make all the difference, or very little. They were all too aware of this.

"One," Daniel whispered, his gaze focused on the monsters.

Dieter gripped his mace firmly as he continued the count. "Zwei."

"Three," they murmured in tandem as they moved closer.

These survivors weren't sure what to make of the two Rifters. It was eerie to watch the two work so closely together. When Dieter spoke to them, he'd address them in English, albeit with a thick German accent. However, when the Rifters spoke amongst themselves, Daniel seemed to understand Dieter's German with ease. It was as if there was no language barrier between them.

Still, at the moment, the survivors didn't give a damn about the Rifters' peculiarities as Daniel and Dieter charged forward in a breathtaking display of speed. Both Rifters were holding their weapons out in an offensive stance while the first of several throwing daggers flew out of Daniel's hand towards the monsters. The moment they left his hands, those daggers glowed brightly, sparks of lightning forming on the blades.

In one quick charge the two Rifters changed the balance of power.

Both Lance and Thomas were a mess of minor cuts and bruises, and absolutely covered in blood and grime. The wounded and the fallen were all around them. The glass had shattered in more places, forcing the survivors to spread their forces. Each new breach resulted in fewer people to defend a contested spot.

"We can't hold it anymore!" those on the left flank shouted as they began to buckle. The steel cabinet was slowly being pushed backwards. Everyone in the room knew what that meant. Each one of them only had seconds remaining before a terrible fate awaited them.

With a loud clang the cabinet finally fell to the ground, and a monster quickly rushed in, attacking a doctor who tried to flee. Another monster was already half-way through the hole when suddenly something forced it backwards at an incredible speed. Soon, the sounds of fighting ensued, with large blood splatters covering most of the windows and thus their line of sight.

"What the hell is going on?" Thomas whispered, scared that even his voice might bring back the monsters. Something strange was going on, and the creatures that had once been hissing and screeching at them were now making unfamiliar sounds, as if they were in a great deal of pain and agony.

"I . . . I don't know," Lance whispered back, just as confused as Thomas was. Finally, he dared to peer over the edge of their makeshift barricade and through the hole. What he saw was two monsters laying on the floor, both bleeding out and fully torn to pieces. "Perhaps another monster? A bigger one?"

"You've got to be kidding me. Just what we needed, a bigger threat," Thomas replied. His voice carried a bit more venom because of his anxiety and overall fatigue that had worn him down to his core.

Thomas slowly slid the barricade to one side, peering through the opening to survey the macabre scene. It was identical to what Lance had witnessed earlier, save for another lifeless body, one of its eyes pierced by a dagger. The faint crackle of lightning still danced across its face, filling the air with the stench of charred flesh.

"A dagger?" Thomas commented. Seconds later, Thomas shoved the barricade to the side and stuck his head through the hole. The first thing he caught sight of was the large Rift-hound, Little Hans, biting into a monster, ripping it open as if it was as soft as a rabbit.

Dieter, in the meantime, was finishing a battle of his own. He stood over a fallen monster, holding it down with one foot as he repeatedly smashed its head with a massive mace. With each crushing blow, the creature's head caved in, showering the surrounding area in gory fragments. Even more remarkably, each hit left two deep gashes in the monster's flesh.

"The Rifters! They're here!" Lance and Thomas shouted as one.

Soon a rallying cry came from the survivors, newfound courage temporarily giving them the energy to stand up and attack the remaining monster within their room.

The remaining survivors converged on it, pummeling it relentlessly. Although each individual blow failed to penetrate the beast's sturdy scales, the continued blunt force trauma was quickly building up.

"Die . . . die . . . die!" the group began to chant in unison as they vented all of their fatigue, rage, and fear on the monster.

CHAPTER FIVE

Culinary Horrors

LANCE

Daniel withdrew his short sword from the monster's flesh, watching as the blade gradually left its scaly sheath. The hallway was now a brutal exhibition of blood and carnage, with the bodies of the dozen monsters they had slain scattered around. Sweat, blood, and dirt clung to his body, revealing the brutality of the fight. His left arm bore several fresh wounds, but none of them appeared life-threatening. He could feel sweat running down his body, which could have been the result of overexertion in the fight or simply the fact that he was still struggling with his infection.

"Are you both okay?" Daniel inquired as he caught his breath. The tall German responded with a nod before quickly assessing Little Hans. The Rift-hound had gone into a frenzied state, launching itself at the group of monsters, relentlessly biting and tearing anything it could get its teeth on.

Unlike a normal dog of his size, the Rift-hound was several times more powerful and durable, having experienced countless fights to further its growth. Whereas a normal human couldn't pierce those scales with a sharpened weapon, the Rift-hound could do so with relative ease, crushing and biting through them thanks to its immense jaw strength.

As he stroked the Rift-hound's powerful frame, Dieter murmured words of pride and gratitude. "I can make it through anything with this cute bundle of fur by my side," he said confidently. Standing up, he exchanged a knowing glance with Daniel. "Until the next dawn," they intoned before urging their ragged band of survivors to emerge from their hiding places. They did one more security sweep before they instructed the survivors to stay with the Rift-hound.

"Be a good boy and guard these people," Dieter instructed Little Hans, giving the dog a friendly scratch behind the ears before grabbing his bloodstained mace and heading toward the barricaded pharmacy. He leaned his weight into the door, forcing it open despite the clutter of cabinets and furniture blocking the way. "Friendly coming in. Anyone still alive?" he bellowed with his thick German accent, his voice carrying easily into the next room where the survivors huddled.

"Yes!"

"We're saved!" the survivors in the room cried out as one. As Dieter and Daniel walked in, they noticed the state of this group, seeing the many injured and the fallen. Some survivors had makeshift slings on their arms or bandages on their wounds. One guy even had used scotch tape to keep a wound closed.

After scanning the group, Daniel addressed them with a commanding yet reassuring tone. "I'm glad to see so many of you. You all did well in surviving for so long," he acknowledged. "We need to know how many of you there are. Can you move and carry the wounded?" His piercing gaze locked onto each person's eyes, and his air of cool confidence seemed to spread throughout the group like wildfire.

As Daniel's gaze finally landed on Lance and Thomas, his reassuring magnetism washed over them. Lance couldn't suppress a sense of hope rising within him as he looked upon the armored Rifters, standing before them like brave warriors from a storybook. *These men aren't mere survivors within a Rift, nor prey shivering in a corner. They're predators themselves,* Lance thought, admiring Daniel and Dieter as they took charge and led the group out of the room towards other survivors.

The disparity between Thomas's companions and the newcomers was striking. The Rifters had stumbled upon them early on, and they had since thrived under their protection. Lance remembered Daniel as a kind and damaged individual, recovering from his injuries in a hospital bed. But the man he faced now was an entirely different entity: a battle-hardened fighter who wielded his weapon with deadly accuracy. Dieter, too, had changed beyond recognition. No longer the amusing oaf, he exuded an air of ferocity and strength that was both frightening and reassuring.

Daniel's group welcomed the newcomers with open arms, administering first aid and sharing their limited supplies of food and water. "Small sips, small bites. You can eat all you want but try to take smaller portions. You don't want to vomit it all up," Daniel cautioned, as he passed out chocolate bars and apples that he had scrounged during their harrowing journey through the hospital. And as if he were wielding magic, he also conjured up rations, sharing them freely.

He stopped when Dieter returned from the room, holding a sack containing several items that suddenly—inexplicably—vanished from his hands. Both Rifters then discussed among themselves for a few minutes as Dieter pointed at Thomas first and then Lance. He handed Daniel an empty air freshener can that showed signs of being singed by flames recently.

"Lance . . . and Thomas, right?" Daniel asked, as he neared the two of them.

"Err . . . yes," Lance said, still shocked by the fact that the Rifters hadn't only survived but had turned the tide so drastically. Although the two of them had spoken at the end of his shift, that moment now felt like a lifetime ago.

Thomas, however, was quick to respond. "Yes," he said without hesitation, his eagerness spilling over.

"Thomas, I heard from the others that you're the one who led the survivors and bunkered down here. You took charge and showed leadership potential," Daniel said, eyeing the young redhead. "That isn't a minor feat to achieve in these circumstances. I want you to know that. All right?" He let the words hang there, waiting for them to sink in.

"We usually find far fewer people during a Rift," Dieter pitched in, stating the brutality of it all as mere facts.

"Indeed. You guys weren't just lucky. You remained focused and used tactics. Something we might need to continue to do as long as we're in this Rift. We'll be counting on you two to help lead the other survivors whenever Dieter and I are busy," Daniel said before glancing at Lance's hands as well as the burned spots on his uniform. "Did you come up with these tactics, or were you just the one wielding the weapon?"

"I . . . I mean—"

"It was Lance's idea," Thomas interjected excitedly. "We had a chemist with us earlier, but she's injured now. The two of them blended corrosive liquids to fend off the monsters. They even whipped up impromptu flamethrowers. It was the fire and chemicals that kept those things at bay." The excitement in Thomas voice hinted at the adrenaline still coursing through his veins.

"Well, the idea—" Lance said, but Thomas interrupted him once more.

"Pipes and hammers didn't do a damn thing to those monsters," Thomas burst out, as if he needed to relieve himself of a great burden. "But the fire? That worked like a charm." At that point, Lance was quick to point out the efforts of the other survivors in their group.

"Get some rest and grab some grub with the others. We're moving out soon. Damn fine work, you two," Daniel said before he checked on the new arrivals. The group now numbered over twenty souls, all safeguarded by two Rifters and one fiercely loyal Rift-hound.

Being rescued by the Rifters and their faithful dog was all it took for Thomas to cast aside any lingering resentment or fear he'd ever had towards Little Hans. The way he doted on the Rift-hound now made it seem like they had been the best of friends since childhood.

I can't blame him. I mean, look at it, Lance thought, seeing Little Hans playfully chomp on a severed monster arm it had brought with him either as a snack or to play around with.

Despite the terrifying strength of the Rift-hound's bite, its true advantage lay in its ability to detect monsters from afar. Little Hans's sharp senses could track monsters and even estimate their numbers, enabling the Rifters to avoid large groups and engage smaller ones.

The Rifters had arranged the survivors into defensive formations, clustering the wounded in the center while the able-bodied stood guard at the fringes. Each fighter held a spear or other crude weapon, poised to strike at any sign of danger. Meanwhile, the wounded who could walk on their own trudged on, their backpacks or slings heavy with provisions to keep them all alive for as long as possible.

Lance and Thomas spent their time nursing their injuries, applying bandages where they could. Meanwhile, a doctor from Daniel's original party had administered the last remaining antibiotics carefully through an IV drip for the ailing Rifter. While they waited, Dieter and Daniel had explained the situation to the rest of the survivors, painting a dire picture of their circumstances.

The reality of their situation was undeniable: they were stranded in a Rift, and it had transported much of the hospital with them. The white-shards embedded in their chests served as tangible evidence, a fact that even the most skeptical couldn't refute, if there were any left alive. These shards would lie dormant until their eventual return to Earth, at which point they would transform into bona fide Rifters, or at least in terms of their shards.

The monsters they had fought until now were smaller raiding parties considered by most Rifters to be less dangerous than the monsters further inland. From what they had seen, this Rift would be a difficult one, because even the weaker monsters were strong enough to wound a Rifter.

"Okay, like we explained before. Here are our three options for surviving this Rift. The first option, we take on every monster ourselves. Option two, we head straight for the Rift's center and take out the Rift-guardian in a quick strike. Option three, we sit tight and wait for other Rifters to come in to save us," Daniel explained to the survivors.

Dieter acknowledged Daniel's explanation with a nod, then chimed in, "The third option isn't likely, and the second option is something only a group of skilled Rifters can pull off."

"Days, weeks, or even months may pass before other Rifters arrive," Daniel stated, his tone laced with concern. "Time can flow differently inside the Rift compared to Earth, making waiting an unfeasible option."

A torrent of uncertain voices poured out towards the Rifters:

"But . . . there are too many!"

"We might die!"

"Perhaps the other Rifters will arrive in a few days?"

"Exactly! Shouldn't we wait at least a few more days?"

A single growl from the Rift-hound was enough to silence the group, allowing Daniel to continue with a calm tone as if there had been no interruption but rather he had simply paused for a moment. "I understand your fears, doubts, and confusion. Honestly, I do. I've been where you are now, perhaps even more confused and scared," he said, his voice gentle but firm.

"We have to face this head-on." He pointed towards their limited supplies. "We only have enough food and water to last us a week, maybe less. We can stretch it out, but it's not going to be pleasant." He let the words hang in the air for a moment before continuing. "We need to work together if we want to make it out of here alive."

"The monsters aren't the only threat here," Daniel cautioned, his gaze sweeping over the group gathered around him. "Dehydration, malnutrition, infections, and injuries are all lurking around the corner, waiting to take us down. We can't afford to wait for help. We have to take matters into our own hands and fight our way through, while we still have the strength to do so. Dieter and his loyal companion will take the brunt of the fighting, but we must all pitch in," Daniel said before Little Hans let out a joyful bark. It clearly enjoyed the term "companion" more than "pet" or "dog," once again demonstrating its unnatural intelligence and ability to understand human language.

"I'll be at the front line as well, but I'm running on fumes here, one-handed, and my infection will get worse. I will get slower and be less able to protect you. Soon, I'll be a liability, and it'll just be Dieter holding the line. It could mean that more of you will die if he isn't fast enough on his own or might increase the chance of getting ambushed when he needs to eat or sleep. So, like it or not, the three of us have already decided. We're taking the fight to them. You can either follow us or stay. It should be safer now that we've wiped out most of the monsters here," Daniel said as he dropped one harsh reality after another upon the unprepared group. The Rifters had shattered any resistance to the plan because of the straightforward explanation. Now the option was to remain here or fall in line.

"No, you can't leave us. I'll go."

"Yeah, me too."

"I can do it."

"I'll fight."

Slowly, one by one, the survivors all agreed to the terms of the Rifters. After all, what choice did they have? Thomas also agreed loudly, stating that it was their best chance of survival. *The way Daniel phrased it makes it seem like he had to make this call before. He might not like it, but he is thinking long-term here. I guess that means making brutal choices like this,* Lance thought, wondering what unmentioned things Daniel and Dieter had endured throughout their careers as Rifters.

Lance and Thomas shared a glance before nodding in unison. "You lead, we will follow," Lance said, nodding to Daniel and Dieter to show his commitment before he and Thomas joined the others and took up a position at the rear, protecting the injured as best they could. Still, Lance couldn't help but eavesdrop on the Rifters' hushed conversation.

"Wonderful speech," Dieter said with an amused expression.

Daniel grinned, watching as the Rift-hound gnawed on the last bits of the monster's arm. "I know," he said, a hint of amusement in his voice.

"Most of them won't make it," Dieter said grimly.

"I know."

Dieter merely shrugged his shoulders at that. "Decent chance we won't either."

"I know," Daniel said again.

"Little Hans, though," Dieter continued, a hint of wistfulness in his voice. "He's got luck on his side."

"That he does. And between the three of us is by far the prettiest," Daniel said before his friend exploded into laughter. Afterwards, Dieter went over to pet his companion, explaining in German what his role would be and what he was expecting of him. The Rift-hound simply listened, barked once and then went about his business, taking up the position that Dieter had suggested.

Afterwards, the group left the hospital after making one last sweep of the place, killing the last of the monsters that had still been roaming the halls. Ultimately, all of the survivors made the decision to align with the Rifters. Now armed as best as they could, while getting supported by the Rifters, the fights had gone a lot better. A dozen spears or poles could pin down a few monsters enabling the Rifters to finish them off.

It wasn't until they finally left the hospital that they truly came to accept that they weren't on Earth anymore. A marshy environment surrounded them as far as they could see in any direction. There were tall trees, strange and exotic plants, and weird noises made by unidentified wildlife unlike any they had ever seen before. The sky showed hints of nearby alien planets, casting a vastly different view from what they'd known back on Earth.

"How . . . just how is this possible?"

"What is up with those lines?"

As they gazed back upon the remnants of the hospital, the survivors noted that it was half-buried in the muddy ground at an unusual angle. A portion of the structure had crumbled and lay in ruins, while other parts remained mostly intact. However, some sections came to an abrupt halt, almost as if a perfect sphere had been excised from the building and deposited within this realm.

"Time to look on the bright side," Thomas said with a grin, clapping Lance's shoulder as he spoke.

"What bright side?" Lance asked incredulously, his brow furrowed in bewilderment.

"Well, the Rift swallowed up a chunk of the cafeteria too," Thomas responded with a smirk. "Even if we don't survive, at least humanity's spared from the culinary atrocities we had to suffer through on every shift."

In front of the ruins of the hospital, surrounded by hostile monsters and foreign lands, the two friends began to chuckle. The chuckles rapidly grew into side-splitting laughter. At that point, in that moment, not even the dangers of the Rift could scare the men into keeping quiet.

At least until a bulky Rifter shouted at them in German.

CHAPTER SIX

Leap of Faith

LANCE

The exodus began at a sluggish pace as survivors navigated through the boggy terrain, carefully avoiding thorny vines and corrosive puddles. The Rifters, on the other hand, moved with a natural grace, adapting quickly to their new surroundings. As they left the hospital behind, morale steadily declined. Doubt crept back into the survivors' minds as exhaustion, fear, and the daunting task of eradicating the monsters weighed on them.

"They know what they're doing, right?"

"It will be all right . . . It has to be!"

"Perhaps we left too hastily. A few more days wouldn't have hurt."

The survivors whispered amongst themselves, not daring to speak their minds openly. The Rifters themselves were aware of these growing concerns. They didn't need to rely on their improved Perception to read the concern on frightened faces.

Lance also couldn't ignore the nagging doubts that gnawed at him, but he understood why they couldn't linger. Their food and water supplies were rapidly depleting, so staying put just wasn't sustainable. A few of the others were quick to dismiss his concerns, insisting they could find more food and learn how to purify the water.

If survival were that easy, then why did Rifters usually bring provisions for several weeks with them? Beyond that, our Rifters were ill prepared for this Rift as well. Dieter hadn't restocked his supplies since his last Rift, while Daniel lost much of his gear when he got injured and is now using daggers and a sword instead of a ranged weapon. What little they have left they're already sharing with us, Lance thought as he followed the group. In his left hand, he held an improvised shield made from a steel cafeteria tray, and in his other, he carried an IV pole that he had sharpened to a deadly point.

Throughout the day, he'd become more confident in his weapon, having seen Dieter use a similar steel tool as a javelin to impale a monster at a distance. The sheer force of Dieter's throw had embedded it inside the monster *and* the tree behind it. None of the survivors could pull it out afterwards, while Dieter had done so with ease. *The problem lies not with the tool, but us. We're simply too weak to combat these monsters unless we outnumber them.*

"You're doing that thing again," Thomas commented, as he nudged his friend in the ribs.

"What thing?"

"You know . . . when you zone out for a few minutes and stare off into nothing. It looks creepy," Thomas explained, as he knew his friend was prone to overthinking. It was a handy trait to have since Lance was quite creative. The downside was it also sometimes made him slower to react or less aware of his surroundings.

The group of survivors slowly moved forward, stepping on dry marshland to avoid the soggy soil that would otherwise steal a shoe or sock if they were to sink in too deep. The further they traveled onwards, the more their experience in this strange land increased. Now and again, a Rifter pointed out some tips to make life easier for the group or assist them with carrying heavier bags or the wounded. But the deeper they found themselves within the swamp, the harder it became to breathe because of the stench of rotting wood and carcasses.

"I can hardly breathe here," Thomas commented as he wiped his brow, which was slick with sweat. He forced himself to labor onwards, but even his athletic build struggled with the oppressive heat and the dense, muggy air that felt like it was suffocating him.

"Try to breathe less through that big container you call a nose. It helps. The air is clean enough to breathe. It just smells horrible," Lance quipped, trying to lighten the mood.

"I'll try. And for the record, you're a real ass," Thomas muttered, his nostrils flaring with disgust.

Lance simply laughed at the remark before the two of them helped one of the wounded over and down a fallen tree. Afterwards, Lance offered to carry her backpack for a little while as he nodded to her. It was during this time that Lance became convinced that what Daniel had told them in the beginning was true. *The environment is just as dangerous as the monsters are.* Already he could see people sweating profusely, as well as reopening their wounds or ending up with new ones after having cut themselves on thorns and prickly vines. Several of the survivors were former patients, or people who were quite a few years older than Lance. *A few days of this will break most of them if we aren't careful.*

A few moments after they began walking, the Rifters motioned for them to stop, and they all sighed in relief. Dieter reached into his pack and brought out a small canister that held a dark, oily substance. He passed it around, explaining that it would help block the smell of the putrid air that surrounded them. The group exchanged skeptical glances as they smeared the substance inside their noses. The feeling was far from pleasant, but it was better than the smell they had been struggling with.

As with the previous item, the Rifter made it disappear when he was done with it. It was as though it had never been there. "We'll take a quick break," Daniel said, looking around at the weary survivors. "Five minutes. We must find a safe place to camp for the night," Daniel explained as the survivors grabbed what little rest they could.

"Maintain ranks!" Thomas shouted to the other survivors. His voice was barely audible above the din of battle. Only an hour had passed since their last pause, but everyone looked close to breaking already. The sounds of metal hitting flesh, people groaning, and of monsters and people dying hung thick in the air.

"Hold the line! Keep them at bay!" Thomas screamed, his face red from the exertion. Sweat dripped down his face as he shoved his crude spear at the monsters, aiming for their vulnerable joints or even their faces. The Rifters had dubbed these monsters as Lizardlings.

Although Daniel and Dieter had never encountered Lizardlings, they had heard about them from fellow Rifters. Still, the familiarity of a monster didn't mean all that much since the Level of a Rift determined the monsters' strength. A Lizardling fought at a lower-Level Rift would be a different experience compared to fighting one in a higher-Level Rift.

The survivors presented a fierce wall of spears and shields to the beasts, desperate to keep them at a distance. The Rifters had instructed the most fit, healthiest survivors to act as the defensive screen. The injured were behind them, throwing rocks, clumps of mud, dirt, or even improvised wooden javelins at them. They aimed each throw at the eyes or other unprotected areas, hoping to blind or confuse the enemy.

The survivors barely held back the seven Lizardlings they were fighting. In terms of raw strength, they were clearly outclassed. Still, they had one major advantage: their Rift-hound.

Each time the wall of shields appeared to falter, they would suddenly find it strengthened by the enraged Rift-hound that would attack the enemy from behind. Thomas screamed at the top of his lungs, hoping to squeeze out what little strength the survivors had left. "Just a little longer!"

The right side of their defensive line hugged a steep ridge that led to a bog, an impossible obstacle to cross for most. On their left, a menacing mountain range stood as a natural barrier, with sharp, jagged rock pillars poking upwards. This treacherous terrain had served as a chokepoint, and it was the reason the survivors had been fighting in a straight line for so long and why maneuvering was impractical.

"There are too many!"

"It hurts!"

"Just a few more minutes! The Rifters will return any minute!" Thomas bellowed, urging them to hold out just a bit longer, his spear thrusting forward to keep the monstrous Lizardlings at bay. Injuries were multiplying with every passing second, and the fight that had once seemed simple was now proving to be a grueling test of willpower and strength now that his troops were without their Rifters.

How long has it been since we last saw the Rifters? Lance pondered, feinting with his spear before abruptly thrusting it down. The tip of the weapon hit a Lizardling's knee, causing some harm but not enough to break the tough scales. *They should've taken care of them by now. Are they even still alive?*

The combat had started out with the survivors and the Rifters fighting against a group of monsters. Lance recalled how chaotic it all had become when the Lizardlings suddenly got reinforcement. Even more Lizardlings would've been bad, but what came crashing into their ranks were monsters of a different and higher caliber. Three large Lizardmen had joined the fray alongside several Lizardlings. Within seconds, these bulkier Lizardmen had torn apart two survivors, simply pulling off limbs as if their bodies were made of paper.

With lightning-fast reflexes, Dieter had launched himself at the monstrous reinforcements, unleashing an unbelievable display of strength as he tackled both beasts and several Lizardlings down the steep ridge. Meanwhile, Daniel had flung a barrage of daggers at the remaining Lizardman, wounding one of its eyes and drawing its aggression as he lured it away from the group of survivors.

We need to change the balance of power drastically. If we don't, then the Rifters will find only corpses, he thought, racking his brain as he glanced at Thomas, who was shield-bashing a monster while desperately trying to strengthen the defensive line. Lance shouted as loudly as he could, hoping his voice would reach his friend. "Thomas! I need three minutes."

"Are you injured?"

"No, but I will be soon. I've an idea!" Lance called.

"I . . . Argh! Dammit. You've got two minutes," Thomas said as he rushed to Lance's side and slapped him on the shoulder, signaling that he'd take over his spot. The second they switched places, Thomas slammed his steel pipe against the shoulder of one of the Lizardlings three times in a row. Each hit shattered more bits of the monster's scale because of Thomas's sheer stubbornness and resolve.

Backpedaling frantically, Lance almost collided with one of the wounded survivors, who was about to throw another rock at a monster. "Quick, hand me the rest of our spare clothes. Now!" Lance yelled, his voice raw with desperation.

"What? Why?"

"Hand them over to me or we all die! Clothes, now!" He could see the fear in the survivor's eyes, and it made him feel sick to his stomach. But there was no choice—they were all in danger, and he needed every advantage he could get. With a shaky hand, the man passed over the clothes he could find. Lance hastily donned them, wrapping some of the fabric around his chest and stomach for extra protection. It wasn't perfect, but it was better than nothing.

I hope this works, Lance thought as he left the wounded man. Lance rushed back a few paces as he searched for a way up the mountainous terrain at their flank that was covered in large, sharp rocks. He eventually found a small path that offered him what he was looking for as he began climbing towards the top. Lance forced himself to go as fast as he could while he prayed that his absence from the frontline wouldn't result in even more injuries or deaths.

This is it . . . Please work, Lance muttered under his breath as he hurtled past the rocks, his layers of spare clothing offering some measure of protection from the worst of the cuts and scrapes. Finally, he reached the top of the hill and saw the thin, twisting rocks stretching upwards. He quickly selected the one that looked the weakest and positioned himself for the next stage of his plan. With a grunt of effort, he pushed against the jagged edges, using his makeshift armor to cushion the worst of the pain.

"Move, dammit!" he shouted and cursed as he applied more force to it with his spear, wedging it at the bottom to transfer more energy. It wasn't until he was using his feet against a nearby rock and pressing with his back into it that he finally felt it move.

"Thomas!" Lance's voice rang out across the rocky slope as he felt a shift in the rock he was pushing against. A second later, he experienced a feeling of weightlessness before falling on his back. He realized he was tumbling down the slope towards the monsters, albeit behind a rock that was now hurling itself at them.

Please let this work! he thought as he felt his body scrape against smaller rocks and ram into the dirt before he finally slid across the ground with enough force to knock the breath out of him.

Thomas was the first to spot the danger, and he sprang into action, yelling at his men to get back. "Back! Move back!" The survivors scrambled out of the way just in time as the large slab of rock slammed into the monsters. A few of the creatures had spotted the danger and avoided the attack, but the surprise of the onslaught, combined with a quick feint attack from Little Hans, caught the remaining Lizardlings off guard.

The survivors and the monsters alike were left dumbfounded as the thunderous crash of the rock echoed across the terrain, shattering bone, tearing scales, and splattering Lizardling blood across the rocky ground. The former savage stalemate had now become a brutal advantage for the survivors, as the Lizardling numbers were now down to three.

"Attack them in groups! Protect Lance!" Thomas shouted as he rushed forwards, leading several survivors forward in a charge of anger and haste. They all knew that each second that passed was another second that Lance remained exposed amongst the surviving monsters.

Lance, already battered and bruised, felt claws and teeth digging into his chest and arms. Despite his efforts to protect his vital areas, such as his face and neck, the claws dug deeper and drew blood across his shoulder and chest. With a last surge of strength, Lance kicked one of them away, but he was too weak to defend against the other. A claw slammed into his chest with tremendous force. He gasped and his vision began to fade. He knew he was about to lose consciousness.

Is this how I die? Lance thought, as his mind grew sluggish. His body barely registered the monsters slashing at his body and pulling on his limbs. In the distance he heard Thomas roar as the survivors pushed forwards, unleashing a hail of spears upon the monsters. When the first beast finally fell, the survivors rushed forward like a tidal wave, kicking, stabbing, and pinning down the remaining two until they stopped moving.

"Hold on, don't touch him yet! We need to support his neck," a nurse warned as Thomas lifted the last slain monster from Lance's body, taking in the bloody mess of cuts and scrapes that covered his torso and limbs.

"Are you alive, you idiot? Lance? Lance! Say something!" Thomas shouted, moving closer to his battered friend. He approached Lance cautiously, afraid of aggravating any potential injuries. As he placed his fingers on Lance's wrist to check for a pulse, Thomas's eyes widened when he noticed his lips move.

"Thomas," Lance rasped, gritting his teeth against the agony that seared through his body. His breath came in shallow pants as he struggled to move, but his limbs refused to obey. He wanted to reassure his friend that he was still alive, but the pain proved too much, and he blacked out.

The last thing he heard was a doctor screaming for a knife or scissors while Thomas kept calling his name.

Some time later, Lance woke up with a start, yelling and flinging his hands before he felt two survivors pressing him backwards again, each one telling him it was all right and that he was safe in a camp.

It took several minutes for him to come to terms with his situation and stop struggling. His mind was still processing the fact that he was no longer in danger. After he had some water and food, he asked for Thomas, who arrived with Daniel a few moments later.

Despite their fatigue, Lance couldn't help but notice the Rifter's battered appearance. Bruises littered his face, and a recently sewn-up wound on his left arm was still red and raw. *Just how long was I out?* Lance thought as he took in the state of them.

"You had us scared there for a few hours," Daniel replied as he placed his hand on Lance's knee and calmly explained what had happened after Lance had made his suicidal jump.

Despite the success of his plan in tipping the balance in their favor, Lance had suffered significant injuries. He had dislocated his left arm, broken two of his ribs, and dozens of cuts and scratches covered his body—some superficial, others deep enough to leave scars in the future.

"If you wanted to die so badly, you could've told me! You're lucky to be alive," Thomas said through gritted teeth, his face twisted with anger and guilt. Lance could see the pain etched in his friend's features, and he knew that Thomas was probably blaming himself for what had happened.

Sensing the palpable tension in the room, Daniel tried to ease the mood. "We did all we could to patch you up, but it looks like you won't be dancing a jig for a while," he said, attempting to inject a bit of humor into the situation.

"Not that he could before all this," Thomas said bitterly as he got up and excused himself, telling Daniel that he was going to check in on Dieter again.

Daniel nodded and waited until Thomas left the crude hut before he continued. "You do realize how close you were to death, don't you? The fall, the monsters, even just climbing the slope on your own," Daniel said calmly, but with a hint of reprimand. Still, Lance couldn't shake off the feeling that Daniel was studying him, as if a reevaluation was happening at that very moment.

Daniel then filled in what Lance had missed. He recounted how Lance's unwise, yet creative, maneuver had shifted the odds in their favor, leading to Thomas rallying the survivors to take down the remaining monsters. Once the dust had settled, Thomas had set up a makeshift triage to tend to the wounded and had assigned guards and sentries to keep watch. After that, he had taken a third of their fighting force to search for the Rifters.

Thomas and the others had found Dieter already done with his fight, having killed the two Lizardmen and the smaller Lizardlings. Dieter had suffered a nasty head injury during his fall and wasn't in any condition to fight for a while. By the time they had reached Daniel, they had seen the Rifter finishing off the Lizardman he had been fighting.

"The two of you keep impressing me and Dieter. You saved a lot of lives today," Daniel said as he gave Lance a reassuring smile. Lance was surprised how much that compliment mattered to him in that moment.

"We'll be setting up a temporary camp here for a few days until Dieter and the rest of the injured have healed up a bit. You won't live to see thirty at the rate you're going, but you really did great." Daniel then patted Lance's knee one last time before he got up and let the young man rest for a while.

CHAPTER SEVEN

Camping Supplies

THOMAS

At least the weather is decent today, Thomas thought to himself as he and Lance strolled around the edge of their makeshift camp. Despite several days having passed, Lance's injuries still clearly bothered him, but he had healed enough to take longer walks without passing out. The walks had also given Thomas a chance to reveal to Lance all the things he had seen in this world or learned from Dieter and Daniel.

The survivors' camp was a collection of humble shelters made from wood and dirt, clustered around flickering campfires. A crude wall fashioned from mud and rocks encircled the encampment, with sharpened spikes protruding from its perimeter to deter weaker monsters. The survivors had even set up traps and snares to capture the occasional wildlife that wandered into their camp.

Thomas glanced over at Lance, who was struggling to keep up. "Are you doing okay?" he asked casually while running a hand through his red hair.

Lance managed a half-hearted smile while nodding. "It's a lot better than yesterday."

Thomas knew better. Lance was still hurting, and it showed on his face. He understood why Lance was lying—there was no point in dwelling on the pain when there was no way to fix it. But he also knew Lance had a habit of keeping things bottled up, which concerned him. *Stubborn old goat. He should stop overthinking so much.*

The encounter with the Lizardmen had taken a heavy toll on the group. Four people had died, and many of the other survivors were still reeling from the experience, both physically and mentally. It was a stark reminder of just how dangerous their world had become. When they'd left the hospital, they'd been more than twenty strong. Now, that number was dwindling rapidly, and everyone was aware of it.

Lance's cracked ribs would need more time to heal before he would be in fighting shape. *No doubt even coughing twice in a row is taxing for him. Still, seems to be doing a lot better,* Thomas thought with a smile. It helped that most of the survivors had a medical degree, so everyone got decent treatment and care, considering the circumstances. Daniel had even been pitching in, sharing some ointments that temporarily eased the pain of injuries. It wasn't a perfect solution, but it made all the difference within the Rift.

"Looks like Dieter's back in fighting shape," Lance remarked as they watched him hammer wooden stakes into the dirt with his bare hands. Despite his recent injury, the imposing German had fully recovered after two days. "The man's a bloody machine," Lance muttered, impressed.

"I still say that they're mocking us by rubbing it in our faces," Thomas brooded. He couldn't deny the Rifters' resilience and ability to recover from even the most devastating injuries, but it only made their mere human counterparts feel even more vulnerable. *Well, at least I don't have to deal with cracked ribs,* he thought, knowing that Lance was just as impressed and frustrated by the Rifter's speedy recovery.

Thomas glimpsed Lance rubbing his chest for a moment. "Hey, man," he said, his usual teasing nature giving way to a rare moment of concern when the nurse in him was stronger than the witty best friend, "are you sure you're not pushing yourself too hard?" His brow creased into the hint of a worried frown.

"*You* are asking *me* if I'm pushing myself too hard? Really?" Lance's voice suddenly dripped with bitterness as he turned to Thomas. "I'm not the one who went on six consecutive trips with Dieter to hunt monsters these last few days. Six!" He even jabbed a finger into Thomas's chest, driving the message home. "That's just stupid, even for you."

"Well, it makes sense, doesn't it? I've got fewer injuries than most," Thomas countered, sensing the turmoil in Lance's emotions. *He's probably wondering if it's worth breaking his own ribs to punch me.* Although he could empathize with Lance's anger, he also knew that his friend would see reason. As a large group, they were vulnerable to ambushes, as they had experienced a few days ago. But when a small group went out with just Dieter and the Rift-hound, they were the ones doing the ambushing and clearing the route that the main group would later take.

Thomas leaned in close to Lance, his voice calm but firm. "Listen, mate. We've got to take these monsters out in smaller groups. Use the element of surprise to thin them out. Dieter and the Rift-hound are doing the heavy lifting, and me and a few survivors support where we can. It's the only way to clear the path to the Rift-guardian and get us the hell out of here." He smiled when he watched

Lance back off, his anger deflating a bit. "I know, I know," Thomas continued now that he had him on the ropes, "it's dangerous. But what's more dangerous? Taking on a few monsters or riding a large rock down a mountain like you're in a rodeo?"

As he gave his best friend a reassuring smile, Thomas couldn't shake the feeling that he had failed his colleagues and patients back in the hospital. A part of him blamed himself for not having done more to save the others. This feeling of guilt and loss had instilled a sense of duty that he was now trying to uphold. Thomas's dreams were still haunted by the memory of mutilated bodies, a never-ending cycle of pain and regret. But it wasn't just the dead patients and colleagues that weighed on his mind.

The terror in Lance's eyes when they had reunited in the hospital had been burned into his memory, a silent reminder of the horrors that lurked within this Rift. *What sort of hell did you experience back then on your own?* Thomas thought, his mind heavy with the weight of the unspoken question.

"How long do you think it will take before we finally leave this place?" Lance asked finally, clearly having suppressed his anger and concerns for his friend, at least for now.

Thomas hesitated for a moment before replying, "I'm not sure. It depends on the energy density or Level of the Rift," he explained, eager to demonstrate his vast knowledge of the Rifts and their mysteries. Countless hours spent watching documentaries and a proper crash course from Dieter had equipped him well. "Dieter said that each Rift is unique. So, it's hard to say." Thomas and the German Rifter had connected over their shared approach to problems, which usually involved punching things.

The redhead continued after that, taking full advantage of the moment to lecture his friend. "Last time we went out, Dieter said that we're slowly thinning out the roaming parties. He figured another week of hunting will take care of most of them, leaving only the remnants that linger around the center of the Rift. That way, when we attack the Rift-guardian, we'll have less chance of getting shanked from behind by roaming monsters." Thomas smiled when he was done with his speech, clearly having enjoyed lording his vast amount of knowledge over his friend.

One point had clearly confused Lance. "The Rift has a center?"

Thomas paused at that for a moment. "Not quite . . . I mean . . . Look, I'm just regurgitating what Dieter told me. It is a place where the energy of the Rift originates from. It is the anchor point that ties this Rift to our world. Some Rifters refer to it as the Rift-center or the Rift-event," Thomas explained as the two men finished their walk and slowly made their way over to the others.

"Dieter said that the Rift we're in now is an Initial Rift, meaning it's still new. These types of Rifts pose an enormous threat when they first appear, but only initially. He said that the energy within an Initial Rift is also more unstable. So, in these types of Rifts, the monsters are often weaker when compared to a Rift that has had more time to establish itself," Thomas said, trying his best to make it all sound logical.

"Are they calling the Lizardlings weak?" Lance asked Thomas. No doubt his mind did its best to grasp what type of threat an established or more complex Rift might hold. "Just how strong are the monsters they're used to fighting?"

"I don't want to find out. I mean, even Daniel could kill several of these Lizardlings with one hand and not using his preferred weapon of choice. A prepared squad of Rifters would manage a Rift such as this with far more ease." As he said so, he imagined himself being in one of those squads in the future. He knew it was silly to fantasize about it, but the nurse in him knew that anything that added to his mental stability would be a boon.

"Yeah, that makes sense," Lance said, before pausing for a moment, as if he was wondering how Daniel or Dieter would handle a Rift like this if they had better tools, provisions, and all their arms still intact.

"Come on, Lance. You got to look at this strategically. Each time we go out, we lessen the chance of an ambush. Each enemy killed is a step closer to us going home and eating something beyond chocolate bars, dried jerky, and sour fruit."

At that, Lance had no choice but to nod and reluctantly agree with his friend.

A while later, Thomas was gripping his makeshift spear hard enough to drain the color from his hands. "Hold," he whispered, as he watched the tall German blend in with the environment with skill that seemed almost unnatural. The Rift-hound could do this even better since it could approach and sit next to a person without having been spotted or heard. Although this was Thomas's seventh hunting raid, it never ceased to amaze him how different a Rifter was to an average person.

Peering across the ridge, Thomas and the others spotted five monsters feasting on a six-legged animal that looked like it was native to this world. Unlike the beasts that were eating it, the creature had a white-shard embedded in its chest. This alone raised a lot of questions in Thomas's mind about the nature of these creatures.

The corpse looked bloated and rotten, but four Lizardlings and a Lizardman were tearing it apart without hesitation. The Lizardman ripped off larger chunks and hissed and clawed at its smaller brethren to assert its dominance. It was a frightening display of power, but Thomas felt reassured by the six other survivors at his side. He knew full well that any one of them alone wouldn't stand a chance, but there was something about being in a group that gave him strength.

Wait for the signal, he told himself repeatedly, like a mantra. He needed to keep calm and focused. The entire plan revolved around them being precise and in control of the fight.

Then, without so much as a sound, Dieter made his move. Holding his position, he threw a burning spear that landed directly in the stomach of a Lizardling. The force was enough to propel the monster back before it slammed into the dirt. Thomas wasn't sure, but he thought the spear had impacted the monster twice at the same time. *Had Dieter just used a Skill?*

The impaled monster was still alive, flailing in agony at the large wound in its torso while flames licked up and down his body. Dieter had tied bits of oiled cloth on the handle of the spear before he had lit it and thrown it, making it quite an effective tool for shock and awe. The fire slowly began to eat away at the monster as it screamed, demoralizing the others of its kind as they watched one of their own become an amalgam of flame and pain.

At the sudden attack, the other monsters had sprung into action, hissing, and clicking their claws angrily as they tried to locate their enemy.

"Three . . . Two . . . One," Thomas counted aloud. Like they had practiced, the group of survivors quickly stood up and hurled six makeshift spears toward the monsters. The downwards angle added a bit more punch to their projectiles, although the attack was a distraction rather than a genuine assault. All of them rushed back into cover the moment they had thrown their spears, quickly crawling to the side to find a new spot to hide themselves.

The second the monsters shifted their gaze toward where the spears had come from was the moment the Rift-hound shot out of the bushes. In a burst of speed and feral aggression, Little Hans snatched a Lizardling by the leg, before dragging the screeching monster away from its brethren.

The monsters shifted their sights towards where Little Hans had run off to, which was what Thomas was waiting for. "Now!" As one, the survivors came rushing out of cover again, carrying several rocks and showering the remaining two Lizardlings and the Lizardman with stones. Once more, they aimed for the monsters' faces to distract and inflict damage, yes, but mostly to draw their aggression. The enraged Lizardman roared as it prepared to charge the survivors, only to stop in its tracks when it heard something large hitting something squishy behind him. As it turned around, it also heard a destressed squeal from a Lizardling.

"Form a barrier!" Dieter yelled as he lifted a blood-stained mace upwards. The man's left foot was pressing down at the back of the Lizardling's neck with enough force to fracture several of its scales. The trapped and wounded Lizardling hissed desperately as it struggled to free itself.

"This isn't going to end well for you," Dieter delivered with a grin as he forced his foot down hard on the struggling Lizardling, snapping its neck. The Rifter stepped over the broken monster, making his way over towards the Lizardman. The blood on Dieter's mace hinted at what he had done with the other Lizardling lying a few paces behind him, its head caved in.

Within moments, the party had taken down four Lizardlings and had surrounded the large Lizardman. In terms of strength, the Lizardman could beat the survivors with ease, but that meant that it would have to ignore the Rifter. If it tried to do so, Dieter wouldn't hesitate to kill it.

Beyond the humans, there also was the threat of Little Hans who had returned to Dieter, its face covered in blood and crunched-up bits of scale, a playful expression on its face. It was clear to anyone what had happened to the monster that had been dragged away from its kin earlier.

"Hold the spears outwards, and be ready to assist one another," Thomas instructed the other survivors as they slowly inched forwards. They occasionally poked and prodded the Lizardman with their spears. Dieter attacked the monster each time it lost its concentration or gave into its rage. The Rifter's heavy mace would break scale, ruin muscle, and fracture bones with each hit. Each skirmish chipped away at the Lizardman's body, bruising it, or even shattering a claw that had tried to go for Dieter's neck.

By now, anyone could see how this was going to play out. The monster was already depleted, having had to defend itself constantly from several angles. Dieter himself looked energetic and fresh thanks to resting for a few seconds between each attack.

Finally, at a nod from Dieter, the Rift-hound rushed forwards. It bit and clawed at the Lizardman's left arm while Dieter grabbed the monster's right arm, simultaneously slamming his mace down on its shoulders several times in a row. Seconds later, the Lizardman was on its knees, exhausted and broken. The survivors watched the defeated monster from a safe distance, fixated by the Rifter's sheer strength. Then Dieter simply paused.

What is he waiting for? Thomas wondered. The man held the monster's mangled wrist and applied continuous pressure until everyone could hear bones breaking and shattering. Dieter kept watching the monster with a calm expression as if he was studying the Lizardman.

Eventually, Dieter ended it, either having learned enough or because he had grown bored. He smashed the mace down on the Lizardman's skull three times until it was no longer twitching. Then, as if this were all perfectly normal, he turned to the survivors with a warm smile. "Good job on the timing. It was better than last time, no?" Dieter asked cheerfully.

"Ah . . . yes! It was."

"We did a lot better! No one got hurt and there were even more monsters this time," one of the survivors said.

Thomas agreed with him. Sure, it was scary and there was the chance of injury and death, but Dieter knew what he was doing.

"Now, we'll harvest their black-shards," he told them as he stepped backwards, allowing the survivors space to work. The survivors then cut out the blackish crystal-like objects that were inside the chest of the dead Lizardman and Lizardlings. They were comparable to the white shards that Rifters and survivors had in their own chests.

It took a bit of cutting and prying before they had harvested the black-shards and handed them over to Dieter, who would hold them for a moment before they disappeared into his Inventory.

"Is this the fastest way to retrieve their shards?" Thomas asked innocently before Dieter leaned in close and shared a horrible and bloody story that would forever stay burned in Thomas's memory.

CHAPTER EIGHT

Clearing Out

LANCE

"All clear here!" Lance shouted, letting the others know that they were done with their task. Three other survivors were with him, each of them armed with an improvised shield and spear. They had all grown in skill and determination these past two weeks. Most of their injuries had recovered, including Lance's ribs. Proper care and Daniel's mystery salves and ointments had helped a lot.

All around them were dead Hatchlings. They were a smaller breed of reptilian monsters. They were smaller than the Lizardlings, and their scales were softer, almost leather-like, making it easier for the survivors to cut or stab through them. Although weaker, these Hatchlings could still put up a fight and rip out an eye if you weren't careful.

Lance took another look at these slain Hatchlings. They reminded him of children. *I hate doing this,* he thought, tearing his gaze away from their small frames. He knew he had to kill them to maximize his own people's chances of surviving, but it didn't mean that he took pleasure in the act.

"All right, retrieve the shards and let's head back," Lance said as he patted Little Hans, who was sitting down next to him, its mouth covered in blood and gore. *At least someone enjoyed himself.* He patted the Rift-hound's head and rubbed his ears, appreciating all that the loyal dog had done for them. While Thomas had been accompanying the Rifters on hunting raids, they had tasked Lance and a few others to take out the smaller nest. Daniel joined them on two of the trips, their group having earned the Rifter's trust.

These nests were usually located underground in either natural caves or tunnels that the monsters had dug. Lance's group was getting better at finding them, but it was easier for Little Hans. On the surface, spears and shields were splendid weapons, but in cramped tunnels the survivors frequently had to shift to just using their shields and a heavy rock, which is they rarely fought them directly underground. With larger nests, they would block most of the entrances, using fire and smoke to kill the Hatchlings inside of the tunnels. In smaller tunnels, it was enough to send in Little Hans and simply wait until the hissing and screaming stopped.

It wasn't as impressive compared to what Thomas and the others were doing, but Lance didn't mind. He just wanted to get home in one piece. The five of them made their way back to the entrance of the tunnel, stepping over burned Hatchlings and destroyed pieces of nesting material. His companions were speaking among themselves as they reached the entrance.

"How many more nests do you think we need to clear out?"

"I reckon at least five more. Didn't Dieter say that there were about a dozen of these things?"

"Nice!"

Although the Rift-hound had done most of the arduous work, the survivors still had performed well. Nearly every one of them now knew advanced survival skills and tactics. The Rifters had trained them quickly on how to avoid detection, track monsters, and the value of a proper ambush.

"Can't wait!"

Lance heard the other survivors talking. He could understand their eagerness to get out of here. A part of him wanted to join them, but it also annoyed him that they were so relaxed. It was not that long ago that they had been the ones being hunted.

When I started my shift in the hospital, there were hundreds of people inside. Less than twenty are still with us now. Even if we manage to get home, is that truly a win? Lance stopped his train of thought, knowing full well it would only make him feel worse. Just remembering those days was nearly enough to start him trembling again. Most of all, he remembered Rachel screaming.

Pushing those thoughts away, he took control of his squad, addressing them firmly, like Thomas would do. "Let's try to keep quiet until we get back, all right?" He looked at his companions, seeing their expressions change as they nodded. *No one likes to be criticized, but they know what is at stake here,* Lance thought as they left the nest, climbing out using their makeshift rope ladder while the Rift-hound just jumped and clawed his way upwards with ease. *Finally, out,* he thought as he wiped off all the grime and gore that had stuck to him during the battle and the climb.

All of them looked nothing like the people they had been before the Rift. Many of the men were unshaven, and everyone was wearing worn-out clothing that was either hastily stitched with thread or held together by duct tape. Most of them probably wouldn't even have recognized themselves until they managed to take a long bath, or several for that matter. Lance still remembered the films about Rifters that he and Thomas used to watch. The main character always emerged from those horrible Rifts clean, well-fed, and with a clean shave. How wrong they were was almost funny to him now.

Half an hour later, Lance spotted the camp in the distance. The Rift-hound barked three times before it dashed off towards the camp, obviously eager to return to its handler, Dieter. As soon as they reached the defensive layer of rock, mud, and wood that protected the camp, they spotted the sentries who were on guard duty.

"Lance, do you think what the others said about Dieter is true? About him killing a dozen Lizardmen in a single fight?" one of Lance's companions asked.

Lance sighed as he led his group past the walls, deliberately ignoring the question. Lately more stories had popped up, making the Rifters seem even larger than life. At first it had been a retelling of Dieter breaking a Lizardman's wrist, then it had been him holding off five Lizardmen at once. Every day the grandeur grew, and Lance was fairly sure that Thomas was directly responsible for half of the rumors on his own. *He could have at least kept it slightly realistic,* Lance thought as he led his men towards Dieter while he explained he wasn't sure if Dieter had faced a dozen at once or over the course of several engagements. *Who am I to ruin their morale? We all need a bit of hope now.*

The party made their way over towards Dieter and reported that they had successfully cleared the nest and collected fifteen black-shards. At first, Lance had found the Rifters tasking them with collecting the shards silly, since there was no actual use for them now. Each shard would sell for a lot of money back on Earth because of their value in crafting or when used with certain Skills. He had considered it might've been greed that the Rifters wanted to at least get paid for all that they were doing. But the more time he had spent in the Rift and with the Rifters, the more Lance figured that there was more to it.

"Glad to have you all back. Lance, how did it go?" the tall German asked as he inspected Lance's party, checking them for wounds.

"It was all right. Mostly hatchlings and two Lizardlings that guarded them. Our hero here took care of the latter," Lance said as the Rift-hound seemed to stand up straighter at the comment, clearly enjoying the praise he had gotten. Beyond that, Little Hans appeared unbothered by anything else Lance and Dieter discussed.

"Good job. Get some food and some rest. Were any of you injured?" Dieter asked as he stored the Rift-shards in his Inventory without even counting them.

They're making us do all this to desensitize us, to see the monsters as more than just hellish creatures. It is harder to see them as a threat if we're constantly being reminded that, for some Rifters, these monsters are just a source of income. Each time we cut out a shard, we force ourselves to see their innards and the fragility of their bodies. They're conditioning us to be less afraid. Laying the groundwork for us to become proper Rifters. If we survive, Lance thought as he watched Dieter for a moment. He knew he was probably overthinking things, but it made sense to him.

"Just some bruises, nothing more," Lance said finally, with the rest of his team agreeing with him. He didn't bother to share his feelings with Dieter about how strange it felt slaughtering the Hatchlings. Still, Dieter seemed to sense the mood somewhat as his large hand found Lance's shoulder, patting it gently as if the young man were a hound himself. Lance smiled afterwards as he walked away from the man. He remembered what Daniel had said to him back before the Rift, about how Dieter had the tendency to treat people like his hound.

Lance and his party then went their separate ways after grabbing something to eat. He found a quiet spot to sit by himself as he ate a small circular bit of fruit that they had been harvesting here inside the Rift. It tasted horrible, but it was edible, and the human body could digest it without problems.

God, this makes me miss the old hospital soup days, Lance thought as he leaned backwards and glanced at the large construct far in the distance. It was only a small spot on the horizon, but from what he had heard from Daniel and Dieter, it was several stories high and chiseled into several plateaus. It wasn't too different from one of those ancient Mayan temples back on Earth.

Just looking at it, I can sense that there is something wrong with that place, Lance thought, as if he could almost feel the Rift-energy coming off from that place. One didn't need to be a Rifter to realize that something wasn't right there. According to the Rifters, that spot was where the Rift was at its strongest. It was the Rift-event, and it marked the location where they would need to be to return to Earth. The closer they were to it, the less momentum their bodies would have when they exited the Rift.

"Just two more days until we launch our attack," he said aloud as he tried to imagine how high it would be at the top. The remaining monsters would be there, close to where the Rift-energy was at its strongest. The Rift-event was the spot where the energy of the Rift was most densely concentrated and was thus usually watched over by the Rift-guardian.

A part of him was curious about the nature of the Rift and these monsters. He had learned a lot from Thomas and the Rifters, including how a Rifter's white-shard activated when they survived their first Rift. In order to do so, they had to kill the Rift-guardian.

Every monster had a black-shard, but the Rift-guardian had a red one, hinting that it contained more energy. Dieter had even told Thomas about the rare chance that one of those Guardian-shards had a Skill-shard embedded into it. *No doubt there must be a connection between their shards and ours. What is the purpose of it all?* He sighed as he shifted his gaze towards the entrance of the camp and noticed Daniel, Thomas, and several other survivors return. All of them were bloody and looked disheartened.

Don't tell me we lost another person, Lance thought as he began making his way over to Thomas to hear about what had happened and help his friend out.

A few days later, Lance rubbed his hands as he looked at the stone structure before him, knowing that today was the day that they would clear it. That or die trying. In a strange way, he could feel the pull of that place through the white-shard in his chest, which was acting like a compass. He gazed upwards, seeing the star-filled night sky that was so different to Earth's. There wasn't a moon or planet that Lance recognized or a constellation that he was vaguely familiar with. All this only increased his yearning to go home.

He grabbed his smartphone and slid his fingers over the small cracks on the screen. It might've seemed silly but, even though the battery had long since run out, touching it calmed his nerves. It reminded him of music, laughter, familiarity, and that there were people he cared about back on Earth. *Soon,* he thought as he placed it back in his backpack. Just then, Thomas walked over to him, looking just as grim as Lance was feeling.

"Are you ready?" Thomas asked, although he was probably not expecting a positive answer.

Lance shrugged his shoulders as he replied, "No. But what sane person would be, right?"

"Got to love that optimism of yours," Thomas said as he patted his friend on the shoulder. "You should write inspirational books."

"Sod off. Just try not to fall on your own spear, all right?" Lance countered with a grin as they checked their clothes, weapons, and shields one last time before joining up with the others.

There were sixteen survivors in the group, three of them too injured to fight. Those three had suggested that they stay behind while the others cleared out the top, but the Rifters had refused. They had explained that anyone doing so would end up dead the moment they cleared the Rift and returned to Earth. Not because of any monsters, but because of how a Rift-event closed.

I'm still unsure what they meant by that, but we need to trust them, Lance thought as he gripped his battered, worn-out steel spear. It had seen quite some damage and wouldn't last for much longer. If luck were on their side, it would only be one more fight until they all went home.

"All right, listen up," Daniel said as he joined up with the survivors. He looked at everyone and gave them an encouraging nod. They all knew what was at stake here. At dawn, they would assault the structure and kill the Rift-guardian or die trying.

"Today we take the fight to these bastards and use their blood to paint that ugly piece of rock they're guarding. We will not rush in, nor lose our heads. We didn't clear out all the nests and their roaming parties for weeks only to mess up now, right?" he asked his brothers- and sisters- in-arms as he walked sideways, clenching his fist to emphasize his determination.

"Hell no!"

"Let's see how they like it!" the survivors said proudly, with even Thomas shouting along to vent off some of his adrenaline.

Daniel nodded proudly before he pointed at the stone structure in the distance. "Just focus on what we've been doing until now. Keep them at bay and let us Rifters do the damage-dealing."

Lance felt his nerves settle somewhat. No doubt it was because of the pull of Daniel's leadership. Looking around, he could see the others react similarly.

"If the formation breaks, you split up into smaller groups. Keep holding the smaller monsters back. Pepper them with rocks, dirt, or the very anger in your lungs. Make them bleed and hurt for every step they take while we stay calm and collected," Daniel said finally. The speech ended after that, with people given the chance to express their feelings before they all steeled themselves for what was to come.

Lance mostly kept to himself. Both excitement and fear swirled around in his heart and stained his thoughts. *We don't know what we might face there. Even Dieter and the Rift-hound couldn't scout out the exact numbers of enemies,* Lance thought as he looked around, seeing all the other survivors. Many of them bore fresh or older wounds. The scars and the fatigue had marked their bodies in a way that would forever linger.

Even Daniel looked exhausted, with his fever eating up his remaining strength. *He is no doubt in pain and discomfort. Still, we need to cling to him. Please, just hold on a while longer,* Lance thought as Daniel and Dieter began leading the way towards the stone construct. It wasn't long before they'd find out what fate had in store for them.

CHAPTER NINE

A Red Shower

LANCE

"Hold . . . Hold . . . Now!" Thomas commanded. As they had practiced, the shield-wall suddenly split into two, letting the monsters pour forwards. This allowed the survivors to funnel them to near the edge of the plateau.

"Re-form!" Thomas instructed as the shield wall turned into a half-moon formation, preventing the monsters from escaping. Spears and javelins started poking and prodding the enemy, pushing them each off one by one. The Lizardlings fell down the steep drop, splattering on the stone plateau below.

"All right, two minutes. Catch your breath before we go up again," Thomas said, panting. So far, they had cleared several levels of the rocky construct during the last few hours, each plateau another step closer to home. They still had a long way to go, and even Thomas was feeling it. "It's like there is no end to them."

"I thought I was the pessimistic one between the two of us. We just need to hold on for a while longer," Lance responded as he turned his gaze upwards. He could see Dieter and Daniel fighting back to back, hacking and slashing at the monsters that assaulted them from every angle.

Each time Dieter moved, it was like a bull charging and slamming into the monsters with its massive figure. The man was caving in skull after skull like it was his passion. Each time a monster tried to sneak up on him, it would find Little Hans suddenly there, ready to tear them to shreds.

Whereas Dieter was raw strength and violence, Daniel was pure speed and elegance. The man used his short-sword to make quick thrusts, hitting weak points, and piercing between the scales of the Lizardmen. The Rifters' proficiency at killing these types of monsters had improved dramatically, as if they intrinsically knew how best to counter their foes and aim for weak spots. Lance was in awe at the orchestra of brutality and synergy between them.

Luckily, Thomas kept his mind focused on the task at hand. "Two minutes are up!" He helped re-form the group. As one, they walked upwards again, slowly climbing the stone staircase. Nearing the enemies, the group started bashing their shields and spears into one another, creating a loud drumming sound.

Dhum

Dhum

Dhum

The wall of spears and shields moved forwards as one. Unified, the survivors in the front held their spears at the ready as the row behind them peppered the monsters with sharp rocks. "Like we practiced. Rage!" Thomas commanded the survivors.

The survivors shouted, roaring at the top of their lungs as they increased their marching speed, startling some Lizardlings. Daniel noticed the sudden change in strategy from the corner of his eye.

"Have they gone mad? Did you tell them to do that?" Daniel asked, spinning on his heels and severing two Lizardling heads in one movement before ramming his back into Dieter's.

"Yes, I did. It looks impressive, no?"

"Correction, you're the mad one," Daniel said with a grin as they rushed forward again, sword and mace killing monster after monster. When the survivors arrived to help pin down the rest of the creatures, the speed of the slaughter immediately increased.

The survivors could only handle a few Lizardlings by themselves. But the intimidation effect of a shield-wall roaring as it charged the monsters was quite effective. The slight pause, the lingering fear, all of it made it easier for the Rifters to do what they did best: slaughtering monsters by the dozen.

A few minutes later, they had killed all but one, staining the plateau they were standing on crimson. The remaining Lizardling was missing its legs and rapidly bleeding out. One survivor grinned as he followed the Lizardling up the large stairs in its desperate attempt to crawl to the next plateau to escape.

Thomas observed the man following the wounded monster. "Seriously, Jacob. Get back in formation," Thomas said, shaking his head. He no doubt understood why Jacob wanted to vent his pent-up frustration, but it still wasn't safe on the higher levels. Lance joined Thomas as he watched Jacob use a spear to poke at the wounded monster.

"One victory and we all turn into idiots, right?" Lance asked Thomas as he checked his gear one last time.

"Who said anything about turning into idiots? I knew you were one from the start. Why did you think we get along so well?" Thomas countered as he leaned on his steel pipe to steady himself.

Lance could see how tired Thomas was, his state reflecting what every survivor was also feeling. Thomas then led Lance back to Dieter and Daniel to go over the strategy for clearing out the next rock plateau. In the background, they could hear an injured Lizardling hissing as Jacob continued to bully it. Daniel ignored it for now as he wiped away the blood from his sword and greeted Thomas and Lance.

"How many people did we lose?" Daniel asked Thomas, his voice strained from the constant fighting.

"Two more. Finley fell, and a Lizardling hit Lucy in the neck. We tried to help, but it was too late," Thomas said. His face was devoid of emotions, but anyone could see he was struggling with the reality of the situation. No one mentioned it since they needed to focus on the task ahead.

"Dammit. Still, this could've gone worse. For now—" Daniel stopped talking when a soul-wrenching scream came from the plateau above them.

Both survivors and the Rifters watched as a large red-scaled monster appeared at the top of the stairs connecting to the next plateau. The creature dwarfed even the Lizardmen as it stepped downwards. The black-shard inside its chest flared red, confirming that it was the Rift-guardian. It clasped Jacob its claws. Several Lizardmen and a dozen Lizardlings accompanied the large red behemoth.

It hissed as if amused as it slowly lifted Jacob above its head, Jacob's upper body clenched in one arm and his lower body in the other. The monster savagely pulled in opposite directions, Jacob splitting into a veritable fountain of blood and gore. A red tide flowed freely into the monster's gaping mouth. Afterwards, it threw Jacob's remains to the side, letting the smaller monster feast upon the scraps.

"What the hell is that?!"

"Is that the Rift-guardian?"

"We can't fight that!"

The survivors screamed, as panic spread like wildfire.

Daniel and Dieter barely had time to give instructions before the monsters suddenly descended upon them in a torrent of glittering scales and shocking violence.

"Hold or we die!" Thomas screamed at the top of his lungs while he held onto his shield and braced for impact. Most of the survivors huddled together, bearing their own shields, and holding their spears tight. The wave of Lizardlings and Lizardmen rushed downwards, hissing and roaring as they came closer and closer. The shield-wall would have broken immediately had the Rifters not taken up a position just in front of the survivors.

Dieter raised his voice to warn them. "Hold on tight!" He held out his mace above his head and held still for a few seconds.

What is he waiting for? Lance thought anxiously. It looked as if the Rifter was simply pausing, yet the longer he stared the more he noticed things that were off. Small pebbles and dirt were being shaken around Dieter by some unknown force. The man's arms trembled as if he was holding onto something heavy.

It dawned on Lance that Dieter was about to do something dangerous to potentially change the flow of combat. *A Skill! He is going to use a Skill.* He quickly shifted his gaze towards Thomas. "We need to take cover!" Lance shouted as he pointed at Dieter a moment before the German slammed his hammer down hard. In mere seconds, Dieter had transformed the landscape as dust, stone, and torn monster limbs flew everywhere. From what Lance could see, his attack had completely shattered the stairs leading upwards.

Thomas slowly got back to his feet and quickly realized they needed to regroup, fast. "Re-form!" He shouted as he observed his surroundings. Dust was still obstructing much of his vision. From what he could see, several monsters lay buried underneath the rubble. Some had even fallen off the plateau and had plummeted down to a lower level, transformed into a red smear. Even after the attack from Dieter, there still were dozens of monsters left alive. One by one, these Lizardlings and Lizardmen got up and continued their attack as they slid down the ruined stairs. Thomas spotted them and yelled for the rest of the survivors to prepare. "Brace!"

The Rifters tried to stop the flow of monsters, but with several Lizardmen on their hands, they could only do so much. A few Lizardmen and Lizardlings slipped past them and charged into the shield and spear wall. The force of the monsters as they hammered into the survivors was beyond anything that they had encountered before. Many of the survivors screamed and shouted in fear and confusion.

"My arm!"

"We need to run!"

"They killed Holly!"

The shield-wall crumbled. These hulking beasts appeared indifferent to the survivors' spears. Compared to Lizardlings, a Lizardman could ram into shields with enough force to break arms or even throw a person down several flights of stairs.

Even the Rift-hound proved ineffective, with the Lizardmen shrugging the beast off as if it was a mere insect. It didn't stop Little Hans from fighting desperately to protect his humans. Thomas noticed the imminent collapse of their formation and shouted at them before their morale shattered completely. "We need to hold, or we die!" His eyes widened as he noticed more survivors screaming and moving backwards. One of them even ran away in panic.

This is bad, Lance thought. After the wall collapsed, more monsters flanked the remaining survivors, with the humans no longer having enough numbers to cover the width of the stairs they were retreating to. They had to do something.

Lance gritted his teeth as he felt another hit his shield, denting the metal. He shifted his gaze towards his friend as he shouted for him: "Thomas, I—"

A Lizardman silenced Lance in one quick movement. It grabbed his shield and threw it down the stairs leading to the lower plateau with Lance still attached to it, forcing the young man to hold on to his own shield desperately as his world turned into a whirlwind of movement and bruises.

Everywhere around him, he could hear people either fleeing or dying.

Several minutes later, Thomas and Lance were running with all their might. "Just keep running!" Thomas screamed at his friend. Both men were exhausted from the constant skirmishes and dashing to safety. Every part of their body felt bruised, and they had several new lacerations that were visible across their chests and arms. They weren't sure if they had been running for a few minutes or hours at this point. The only thing they knew was that their formation had shattered, and that everyone was simply trying to survive.

"What the hell do you think I'm doing?" Lance snapped at Thomas as he ducked down in time to dodge a wide swing from a Lizardman.

Lucky for them, the monster didn't seem to treat them as a genuine threat. It was like it was toying with them at this point. The creature had painted himself crimson from the blood of another of their party it had killed. It hissed and growled every time it swung at the two survivors.

Thomas rolled to the side, nearly falling from the stony plateau, but dodging another swipe from the monster. The Lizardman was about to swing again when it felt the impact of a spear hitting the underside of its tail.

Hissing, it turned around and faced Lance, who was holding onto the spear. Noticing the anger, Lance backed off before quickly running away in the opposite direction. Sounds of claws digging into stone and a feral growl filled the air behind him.

I can't jump for safety, and I'm near a corner, so the stairs are too far, Lance thought as he felt his lungs burn from all the effort. He wouldn't be able to keep this up for long. Despite weeks of constant physically demanding work that had strengthened his body, he was still only human and was running on fumes at this point.

The edge of the plateau came closer as he hastened forwards. For a split second, a thought tempted him to jump. *Wouldn't a fall to my death be a better alternative to getting eaten alive?* The monster was faster than Lance and was clearly gaining ground. Desperation fueled his thoughts as he produced a last-ditch plan.

No matter how strong something is, it's still a slave to the laws of physics. No way is that thing able to come to a halt as quickly as me, right? He recalled how some of these monsters occasionally slid across the plateau, having to dig their claws into the stone to seek purchase. Their feet wouldn't work the same way as Lance's shoes, which had a far better grip on the floor. As he neared the ledge, he yelled one last defiant cry. "This is stupid!"

He dropped the spear and grabbed his worn backpack in one hand, holding it to his side. As soon as he reached the end of the ledge, he stopped. He came to a halt before he spun on his heels, throwing the bag towards the monster's face, hoping to blind it. *Now!* Lance thought as he jumped to the side.

The Lizardman simply blocked the bag and slammed it to the side. It realized the danger it was in as it dug its claws into the stone and slid to a stop, just barely managing to not tip over the edge of the plateau. Hissing, it got up, slowly. It towered over Lance and almost looked amused in that moment before Thomas's sudden impact forced the Lizardman to the side.

Thomas had body slammed the monster in the back and forced it over the ledge in one violent push. "No . . . no!" Thomas yelped as he felt himself go over the edge as well. Lance just barely grabbed Thomas's arm in time and yanked him back up. Thomas nearly soiled himself out of fear. "Bloody hell! Thank you. Thank you!"

"Let's not do this again," Lance replied as he hoisted Thomas up, having heard the Lizardman splatter on the plateau below them. "I hope the others are still alive." The last Lance had seen of the other survivors was them scattering in all directions, while a large group of them fled down the stairs.

On their plateau, they could see corpses littered left and right, both human and monster alike. Even the Rift-hound lay unconscious on its side, its breathing slow and painful. Lance and Thomas could see half a dozen slaughtered Lizardlings next to Little Hans. The Rift-hound had clearly put up one hell of a last stand. Grabbing his equipment, Lance turned to Thomas. "What about the Rifters?"

Before Thomas could reply, the two men heard another loud impact coming from above them, showering them in copious amounts of stone. Thomas was the first to reply. "We need to help. Don't think, just do."

"Are you insane?" Lance hissed, but Thomas was already rushing towards the sounds, speeding up the stairs, determined to get to a higher level of this rocky construct. With a sigh, Lance followed Thomas, knowing full well that they were rushing into certain death.

CHAPTER TEN

Gravity and Lightning

DANIEL

Daniel and Dieter had fought like lions when the shield wall had collapsed. They had franticly tried to pull the aggression of the monsters towards them while saving as many lives as possible. In doing so, the two Rifters had lost sight of one another. The last thing Daniel had seen of Dieter was the man charging into the Rift-guardian at full speed.

How long has it been? Daniel wondered as tried to ignore the ache in what remained of his right arm. He felt hot and sickly as the infection sunk its talons in deeper. The battlefield had broken apart and spread out over the many plateaus, resulting in smaller pitched battles and skirmishes. These skirmishes were helpful for him, since he could pick off smaller groups of monsters, but it came at the cost of human lives.

Daniel backed off quickly from the monsters he was facing now. He retrieved one of his throwing daggers from a nearby corpse and placed it between his teeth before he grabbed his sword again. His thoughts came fast and focused. *This is bad. I need to help the others.*

He forced himself to draw his attention to the fight in front of him: two Lizardmen and one annoying Lizardling standing in the middle, surrounded by the corpses of its kin. The Lizardling had simply refused to die like its brethren, despite many attacks from Daniel. *These critters are resilient. I barely have enough time to react, let alone check on how the others are doing. I need to finish this quickly,* he thought as he glanced to the side, seeing signs of slaughtered survivors wherever he looked. The carnage enraged and threatened to consume him, but he kept his attention on what lay in front of him.

I was already low on stamina from the earlier fight. I need to make this count, Daniel thought as he gripped his sword tightly. He settled into a crouched position from which he could speed up quickly. His body hungrily drained Stamina as his muscles contracted. Every fiber of his body was preparing itself for the Dash Skill that Daniel had honed throughout his life. At lower Levels, the Skill allowed a Rifter to rush away quickly in a burst of speed. But, after years of using it and Leveling it up, it could settle a fight in one violent move.

Dash.

The first Lizardman screamed and hissed as it charged Daniel. It swung its scale-covered arm towards the Rifter's neck only to miss as Daniel suddenly shot forwards with enough force to create a cloud of dust behind him. When the Lizardman turned around to locate the Rifter again, it found him standing over the decapitated corpse of the other Lizardman, the head rolling off to the side.

At that point, Daniel was breathing fast, as if he had just run a marathon. His face was pale from exhaustion and the infection. Without it, he'd recover his Stamina far quicker. His mind wondered if they hadn't spent too many days clearing out the Rift before they went for the Rift-event. Each day had chipped away at his agility and strength.

The smaller Lizardling in the middle took several steps towards Daniel, clearly intent on charging at him. After another step, it collapsed onto the floor, a throwing dagger lodged in its throat. This left just Daniel and the Lizardman.

His voice came out rough and forced. "You bastards are tough. I'll give you that," he said as he took a step forward, swinging his sword to the side to clean it of blood. His eyes met the remaining Lizardman as he continued talking to it with an intimidating calmness. "Still, this close to the finish, I can smell the bottle of scotch that is waiting for me at home."

He stepped over the bodies of the dead monsters as he pointed his sword at the remaining one. "And I'll be dammed if I let you ruin that for me." He flexed his arm before rushing forwards, pressing the advantage now that it was just the two of them.

Double strike.

The force of his strike reverberated as his blade carved through the monster's arm, gouging twin gashes that shattered the protective scales. His high Perception stat allowed him to detect a subtle twitch in the creature's stance—a tell-tale sign to a charging attack. Reacting swiftly, he shifted his weight, narrowly evading the oncoming assault as the beast raced past him. *Now!* his thoughts ignited, propelling him forward as he dove low, springing a surprise at the creature. The monster whirled around, suddenly confronted by the Rifter.

Before the Lizardman could even react, Daniel had already buried his sword into its mouth, forcing it in as deep as he could. The monster was still struggling to come to terms with the fact that it was fatally wounded as it tried to claw at Daniel, only to find its body no longer working. Sinking to its knees, its once formidable body paralyzed and impotent, it watched helplessly as the Rifter nonchalantly withdrew the sword, dismissing the creature as an obsolete threat that would bleed out soon.

Daniel wanted to sink down to his knees and give in to the fatigue he was feeling. He was bruised, battered, and exhausted. His Stamina was nearly depleted, and his Mana held enough charge for one or two more Imbue lighting Skills; after that, he could only rely on his wits and his speed.

I miss using my bow, Daniel thought as he collected his throwing daggers again and stored them in his Inventory before he moved upwards, intent on backing up Dieter. Had he still been able to use his bow, he would've had several more Skills at his disposal. He would have had an easier time thinning out the enemy numbers, not to mention being better at supporting Dieter.

He suppressed his groans as he felt the entire structure shake once more. *At least I know that oaf is still alive,* Daniel thought as he moved faster. He knew firsthand just how strong his fellow guild member was. The Skills the man used were nothing short of pure power output and zero intelligence. *Who else could produce a tremor as potent as that?*

Gritting his teeth, Daniel shot upwards, hoping to make it in time to help his friend.

Just die, Daniel thought as he just barely evaded the Rift-guardian's attack. He slid to the side and picked up his dagger again, holding his sword between his torso and his right upper arm. Ten minutes had passed since Daniel had found Dieter and the Rift-guardian, but already it felt like a lifetime to him.

He threw the dagger towards the monster's eye, intent on blinding it. The monster dodged the weapon just in time, hissing angrily before it spat out a brown ooze towards Daniel. The Rifter jumped away, hearing the substance hiss as it started to melt the stone surface it had hit instead.

"Dieter, I need you to get up!" Daniel shouted to his unconscious friend as he circled the enormous monster again. He knew full well that he wouldn't be able to solo it. The beast was twice as massive as a Lizardman. His sword couldn't easily penetrate its gray and red scales.

Dieter's mace had done some damage, having crushed one of the monster's knees. Doing so had cost Dieter dearly, however. He was riddled with wounds and no doubt missing much of his Health and Stamina. But the sacrifice had reduced the monster's speed, meaning Daniel was now quicker. He darted forwards, feinting an attack with his sword to keep the aggression focused on himself, lest the monster go for Dieter's unconscious form.

It was hard for him to see his friend bleeding out onto the stone surface, surrounded by slaughtered Lizardmen. Daniel knew the large German had given one hell of a show, ripping, and tearing into their ranks, but in the end, he was just one man. Normally they'd have a team of several strong Rifters to take down a

Rift-guardian or would have done more prep work. He hated the fact that his friend had charged in alone and lured as many monsters as he could. Daniel didn't doubt the man had done so to give the survivors a fighting chance, but also to protect him.

I would've preferred to die in a comfortable bed. But perhaps this is my fate, Daniel reasoned. He took another look at the shard within the monster's chest, seeing the red glow within the black material, marking it as something to fear. These Rift-guardians were usually the strongest or the most intelligent of the monsters within a Rift. Beyond that, they could occasionally also use Skills. It was their presence that maintained the Rift-event. Kill the guardian and the Rifters would stop the current Rift-event.

Feinting won't work. Perhaps another Dash? I've enough for one more, but then I'm out, Daniel thought as he felt the burden of choice. There wasn't any way he'd get past the monster's thick protective scales. He was contemplating simply throwing the monster and himself over the edge to at least stop this Rift-event but stopped when he suddenly heard shouting.

"Look here, you big mongrel."

"Are you as daft as you look?"

"Oy, Scales-For-Brains! Are you too dumb to figure out what is going to happen?"

Daniel spotted the survivors near the edge as he heard them shouting to distract the monster to the best of their ability. Not long after that, some other survivors appeared on the other side, all of them heavily wounded.

It surprised Daniel at first, but he soon figured out their plan when he noticed Dieter was no longer unconscious on the ground. Instead, he caught sight of Lance and Thomas standing next to the wounded German with an empty plastic bottle. He realized that they had used the last of their water to help wake up Dieter. *Clever lads,* Daniel thought, grinning as he processed it all.

Muscles coiled, Daniel prepared for one last burst of energy, clutching his sword like a spear. He poured every bit of Stamina he had left into one last attack while forcing what little Mana he had into the sword. Arcs of lightning crackled along the blade's edges, illuminating his eyes in a brilliant blue hue. Fueled by sheer determination, he burned through the rest of his Mana, his mind fixated on a single thing. Raising his voice, he bellowed to his companion, "Dieter, just give me one opening!"

It wasn't the first time Daniel faced death with only one shot at surviving. This is what it was to be a Rifter in his mind: putting everything on the line to save others.

The opening materialized when Dieter's mace collided with the monster's back, eliciting a guttural cry of agony from the Rift-guardian. Harnessing the last vestiges of his strength, Dieter forced the creature to kneel. "Now!" he roared, dropping his mace and grasping the beast with both hands. The monster retaliated with savage slashes and vicious claws, ruthlessly rending Dieter's flesh, leaving a gruesome trail of blood.

The atmosphere crackled, electrified with an impending storm, as if lightning itself were poised to strike. The monster, too, sensed the disturbance, its enraged gaze shifting from Dieter to Daniel. In a sudden instant, the one-armed Rifter vanished, leaving behind only the echoes of his battle cry that lingered in the air.

"Die!"

Daniel surged forward, pouring every ounce of his being into the momentum. Muscles strained and screamed in protest, threatening to tear apart as his body pushed beyond its limits. The searing agony that engulfed him became a distant whisper as he focused solely on his target. He leveled his sword at the monstrous creature before pushing it forwards with reckless abandon. The blade plunged into the left eye of the beast, penetrating deep into its skull with a single, devastating, and twisting thrust.

As the impact reverberated through his body, Dieter issued a dire warning to his comrades, urging them to brace for the impending onslaught. He let go of the monster and rolled away from it. "Get back!" he bellowed. Responding with instinctual survival, many of the survivors hurled themselves backward or assumed prone positions. Within moments, the air became dense with the cacophony of the Rift-guardian's demise, its flesh boiling from an internal, electrified inferno. The storm of lightning unleashed by Daniel's sword had mercilessly ravaged the monster from the inside out. The excruciating ordeal persisted for two agonizing minutes until, at last, the Rift-guardian's howls ceased, its lifeless body slumping to the ground, still shrouded in steam. In the aftermath, amidst the lingering pain, only Daniel stood, a solitary figure defying the odds.

The survivors wanted to cry out in delight but stopped when the very world rumbled. They quickly realized that the Rift-event was ending, and that they were in a different type of danger now.

Daniel took control of the situation. "Grab anyone you can and get to the center!"

From there it was a frantic dash to the top, with survivors dragging the wounded and even the dead before they realized it was useless. Dieter had rushed away from the group only to return later with his unconscious dog slung over his shoulder despite the numerous injuries the man himself had sustained.

Daniel grabbed people, forcing them closer to the center. Compared to how composed Daniel normally was, he was now on edge. He was being as rough with them as he needed to keep the survivors alive. This close to the center, anyone could see the pulsating black energy that reached upwards in a beam. It was impossible to pass through it, but Daniel wanted everyone to hug it as tightly as possible despite the way it was making everyone feel.

A second later, that black pulsating beam imploded before a massive black wave of energy engulfed everything in its path. None of the survivors had time to even process it before the Rift ravaged their bodies and forced them out in a violent display of unfathomably powerful energy. After that, none of them would ever be the same. In mind, body, and in their white-shards.

[You have cleared this Rift]
[You have been awarded a Level Up]

CHAPTER ELEVEN

Blissful Retirement

Outside Ealing Hospital
London, England

JEFFREY

The gray-haired man shivered as he walked back into the trailer, shaking off the rain from his raincoat before taking it off. He still felt miserable despite having worn it. It was hard not to when enduring a typical British downpour. From what he had heard, the weather would stay like this for the next few days.

"Ten more years until I can retire," Jeffrey Oakfield mumbled as he walked towards the kitchen and poured himself a cup of coffee. After that, he took a seat behind his computer. He entered his credentials as site overseer and recorded his daily report as well as uploaded the footage he had recorded of the Rift.

"The time is 2200, August 23rd. Rift 97-B is giving off the same readings as before. Conditions are within acceptable parameters, and I can find no signs of any growth or expansion of the Rift itself," he said, recording the measurements before pausing and double-checking his findings. Every Rift was different, so constant measurements were required to better understand them and gauge their strength.

He stopped midway when he heard the trailer door open as two vocal young men dashed inside. They were talking with one another as they took off their GRRO-issued raincoats. Like him, they were all employees of the Global Rift Response Organization, temporary or not. Calling it global might have been a bit of a stretch, since each country had its own interpretations of the initiative, and some outright refused it. Nations like China, Russia, and the US had opted for something of their own creation, tailoring it to serve their nation without having to deal with the red tape of other countries.

Jeffrey eyed the younger men as he took another sip of his coffee before he interrogated them. "Did you check the lines?"

"Yeah . . . yeah. We did," the man on the left said as he ran a hand through his soggy hair.

"Good. What about the safety nets?" Jeffrey asked, switching his gaze to the other man.

The man on the right was more curious, since he was a recent addition to the roster. "Yes."

"And you did your rounds?" Jeffrey continued with his barrage of questions. Eventually, they only rewarded Jeffrey with nods.

The man on his left was Dillan, a former firefighter. The GRRO had scouted him a few months ago and had offered him a permanent position. He showed a lot of promise, but the man had never experienced a bad Rift-scene before, and it showed. He joked around a lot and was developing a lazy streak.

On the right was Ali, a medical student who was doing his internship within the organization and was a recent addition to the GRRO. Because of the impact Rifts had and the scarcity of Rifters, there was a need to always have a trained medical professional on site or nearby. With most Rifts, that meant sitting for hours on end until a shift ended.

Dillan finally had enough of the constant questioning. "Relax, we checked it, twice, as you asked. Besides, it isn't like something will happen soon," he said as he poured himself a cup of coffee, adding a few lumps of sugar to help with staying awake.

Ali was standing in front of the window and looking outside, seeing the massive Rift in front of them instead of a hospital. Ali had never worked in Ealing Hospital, but he had heard of it before the Rift had spawned there and destroyed a substantial portion of it. The unnatural black energy made it impossible to look inside the Rift or even pass through it. The closer someone got to it, the more they could feel the energy in the air itself.

The GRRO had installed large nets around the site with several flexible cables. There were layers upon layers of these. The nets would catch anything that might exit the Rift with momentum. Behind that were concrete and steel walls, acting as a last line of defense before something reached the city itself.

All of this formed a ring around the Rift and the partially collapsed Ealing Hospital. Beyond the concrete and steel walls, there were security posts as well. Either the military or GRRO security personnel would staff those posts, adding another line of security. When a Rift threatened to turn into an outbreak, the military would take full control of the site and quickly scale up the defences.

Ali then broke the silence in the room as he continued to stare at the large pulsating Rift, mesmerized. "I still can't wrap my head around the whole time thing".

Sighing, Jeffrey shifted his gaze to the young man. "Time thing?" he asked, sipping his coffee while wishing they assigned him fewer vocal underlings this evening. He just wanted a quiet shift and catch up on sports.

"I've been reading up on the time difference between Earth and these Rifts. The GRRO manual goes into some detail, but is it as bad as the manual makes it out to be?" Ali asked as he watched the Rift outside fluctuate now and again but otherwise remain dormant. The Rift at Ealing Hospital was newly formed and still stable. That stability meant that a Rift team could still enter it. Afterwards, it would turn unstable and more hazardous, preventing further entry.

"Time flows differently, lad. It isn't uncommon for Rifters to report having spent weeks inside a Rift, while only a few days had passed back on Earth. It can be quite taxing for them after a while because of the difference in experience and age," Jeffrey answered, his eyes glancing at the Rift outside and the spikes of black energy. "But the time difference isn't the hard part."

"Hard part?" Like most people, most of what Ali knew about Rifts was from the news, movies, and articles. A lot of the information was credible, but so much more was mere speculation or internet rumors. Ali had gotten a crash course from the GRRO, but even then, there was still so much that was still unknown about the Rifts or simply covered by layers of red tape.

"Milk and biscuits," Dillan teased as he placed his mug down and propped his feet on the desk, leaning back.

Jeffrey simply eyed the youngster's feet and shook his head before he continued. "As in provisions. Some Rifts get cleared within days or weeks; others take longer because of unforeseen circumstances." The public knew Rifters needed to take a lot of provisions with them, but most were blissfully unaware of just how complex this could be depending on each individual Rift.

"And what about the Rift in Paris? Do you think it had something to do with provisions, or was there another factor in play?" Ali asked suddenly, referring to the disaster of Paris where a Rift had occurred that was so abnormal that a full year had passed inside while only a week had passed on Earth. A group of twenty Rifters had tried to clear the Rift but failed in doing so. Only two Rifters had survived but had refused to explain how they had endured for so long. One of them had even taken his own life a few months later.

Later, other Rifters failed to clear it as well, which resulted in the Rift continuing to grow, culminating in the outbreak that destroyed most of Paris, flooding the city with monsters that remained even now. Jeffrey had no answer for the Paris incident. No one had an answer. His clearance within the GRRO was higher than the other two men, but even he could only guess what had made that Rift so cataclysmic.

Sensing that Jeffrey wouldn't answer, Ali asked another question. "Do you reckon anyone could've survived this Rift?" He then glanced outside, taking in the sight of the black orb of energy pulsating next to the destroyed hospital.

All three of them had read the missing person list and knew just how many lives the Rift had claimed. "Hard to say. I rarely try to speculate on these things. Most of the time, it isn't good news," Jeffrey explained. He had seen a few anomalies in his time as a site overseer. The GRRO kept statistics on the chance of survival in certain situations, although they didn't make this available to the public.

All three of them could only imagine the horrors that might've happened inside of the Rift. Dillan had seen a few Rifters exit a Rift with minor injuries but never witnessed any casualties. Jeffrey had seen far worse in his time with the GRRO, even remembering the early days of Rifts and Rifters.

Eventually, Dillan finally broke the silence in a less than tactful way. "It has been a long time since anyone even showed an interest in this Rift. Do you reckon they'll even try to send in a rescue squad or just pass it off onto a guild and let them clear it in a few weeks?"

Jeffrey shrugged as he placed his mug down. "A lot of time has already passed. Normally I'd say they'd hand it off to a guild, but a big hospital like this? There is still too much media attention. I'm not sure why there hasn't been a rescue attempt already. Perhaps there are more pressing Rifts at the moment?" Jeffrey offered as he rubbed his eyes.

Initial Rifts like this one were always horrible events, but they weren't always a pressing matter. It sounded awful, but they posed little danger after the initial incident. There was the immediate loss of life, but it did not compare to a Rift that was about to turn into an outbreak.

Jeffrey's weathered hand sifted through his silvered hair as he stole a glance at his watch, the ticking seconds drawing his attention. The nearing ten-hour mark signaled the arrival of the late shift. "All right, how about you youngsters finish your part of the report while—" Suddenly the Rift unleashed a cataclysmic surge of malevolent energy, engulfing the surroundings in a maelstrom of dust and debris. The violent eruption transformed the once-quiet location into a chaotic tempest, hurling projectiles of stone, dirt, and bodies in a relentless onslaught.

Some objects hit the nets, absorbing the violent momentum that had sped them outward. The force launched other objects outwards at a higher angle. Others even went straight through several layers of protective netting as they hurled into the nearby ruined hospital or the surrounding area.

Seconds later, the air was thick with the sounds of people screaming and the scent of blood. Jeffrey sprung to life at once, throwing his communication device towards Dillan.

"Call it in! Tell them we've a code red!" Jeffrey barked as he rushed out, dragging Ali with him as he grabbed his medical kit, simultaneously holding onto the pistol at his hip.

SAMUEL

An hour later, the site of Rift 97-B had transformed from a small monitoring outpost into a quickly constructed base of operations with state-of-the-art facilities. The GRRO had already brought in dozens of shipping containers that could interlock with one another to form a larger construct. They had done all of this with both haste and precision. Within an hour, the Rift-site now had a room for each of the survivors, surgery stations, a barracks, storage sections, offices, and several other rooms.

Military presence had increased alongside GRRO personnel. Already the perimeter around the Rift was being expanded and several teams were now combing the streets to look for expelled debris, since it could be valuable or dangerous. Usually, it was both.

They had taken dozens of readings of the Rift itself and the press was already lining up outside of the walls, some even daring to sneak closer to the walls to get a scoop.

"An unprecedented development has occurred just outside of Ealing Hospital," a woman said, looking directly in the camera as she gestured towards the hectic scene behind her, with just the broken hospital still visible over the protective walls.

"Reports have come in of several people surviving the Rift, unaided by external Rifter intervention. This despite the time that—" The woman went on, with other reporters next to her saying similar things. On the scene were people from major UK news stations, as well as journalists from foreign channels.

Three cars passed by the crowd with their windows tinted black. They reached the security checkpoint and drove farther onto the site and out of sight from the reporters. Samuel Jones was sitting in the middle car as he glanced outside, seeing the Rift still pulsating its black energy.

"Even after having feasted, you continue to mock us?" Samuel uttered, clenching his fists as he forced himself to stare at the Rift for a few seconds longer, suddenly filled with unbridled rage. As the head of the GRRO London branch, Samuel had the highest rank of anyone on site. They had called him out of his bed some forty minutes ago with a car already waiting outside. He didn't doubt that he wasn't the only one that had his sleep disturbed by an aide or a supervisor that night.

Lack of sleep matters little compared to the hell these survivors have gone through, he thought as he chastised himself. The initial reports were vague beyond that there were only a handful of survivors. Many were wounded, including two Rifters.

It had taken a while to figure out that the Rifters had been inside the hospital when the Rift had formed instead of them having tried to clear it on their own. Samuel's assistant had updated him that the wounded Rifters were Dieter Kühn and Daniel Wells. Samuel had dealt with them before, even before he had become the head of the GRRO London branch.

Stepping out of his car, he met with the site overseer, Jeffrey Oakfield. The overseer looked tired and stressed. Samuel didn't doubt that the man had spent the last hour frantically directing both civilian and military matters. Samuel interrupted him before the man could even utter a word. "Keep it short and compact, Jeffrey. We both have too much gray in our hairs already."

"Several survivors, including two Rifters and a Rift-hound. Many critical and already in surgery. Potential viable prospects would be less than half. The Rift appears to have dwindled in strength. All markers and measurements are showing an actual cleared Rift-event," Jeffrey stated as he led Samuel inside the building.

As the men moved further into the compound, Jeffrey handed him several documents and informed him they had prepared a personal office for him at the end of the hall. Samuel knew from experience that he'd also find several stacks of documents there regarding the Rift and the recent developments. "Abnormalities?"

Jeffrey paused for a second, the expression on his face clearly indicating that he was carefully structuring his thoughts. "None directly Rift-related, sir."

"Explain," Samuel demanded as he rubbed his eyes to wake himself up. As soon as they concluded the briefing, he'd order someone to fetch him coffee.

"One of the Rifters is in surgery now. The other, Daniel, is monitoring and supervising the other survivors. He has been . . . difficult in terms of cooperation. He's already made some threats, and so far he has refused treatment," Jeffrey explained, careful to choose the right words.

"I understand. I'll head over to them as soon as I'm done. Keep me posted," Samuel said, walking past the man as he grabbed his mobile phone. He could see the dozen messages that he would need to take care of. Glancing over the latest texts, he could see they were urgent. Several of them were from representatives of the prime minister, one from a spokesperson of a local Rifter guild, and another from a company offering to help with site security.

When there's blood in the water, Samuel thought, knowing full well where this was going. An initial Rift was horrible, and the media would always cover such a thing. But a Rift that was cleared by mostly survivors would draw much more media attention. The entire country would read or hear about it tomorrow morning, either focusing on the two Rifters, or the brave survivors.

Public opinion would matter especially. Even though the Rift was dormant for now, the government would no doubt want to see it cleared several more times in the following weeks until the Rift finally ran out of energy and collapsed. It wouldn't bring back the dead, but it would serve as a gesture of strength and leadership from the government, the GRRO, and the Rifters involved.

No doubt people will want to make a bloody movie about this nightmare in the coming years, he thought, as he reached his office and placed several folders and other items down on the desk. His phone was already ringing and beeping nonstop, but he switched it to silent. No doubt people would try to contact him through other channels, but he figured it would at least buy him a few minutes to think and plan.

Many countries, including the United Kingdom, treated Rifters with a significant amount of appreciation and respect. Even lower-ranked Rifters would get treated as local heroes deserving of adoration. Higher-ranked Rifters enjoyed a status akin to that of a celebrity. It was hard not to hero-worship them when some Rifters could single-handedly do things a small army couldn't manage.

First things first. I need to calm this Rifter down before I have another public incident on my hands. He then signaled a GRRO officer and instructed her to guide him to where Daniel was last seen.

CHAPTER TWELVE

Scotch and Shards

DANIEL

The one-armed Rifter walked farther down the hall, ignoring his pain and discomfort as he did so. Daniel watched the dozens of nurses and doctors rush in and out of rooms. Many of them were treating the wounded survivors on their beds while the heavily wounded were already undergoing surgery in specialized rooms. The Rift-hound had a private room as well, with no doctor daring to refuse the request from the blood and dirt-covered Rifter.

Daniel had checked in on every survivor, instructing the medical staff to not throw away the survivor's clothes or belongings, but to keep them secure. Every damaged bit of fabric was now infused with Rift-energy. It meant that it could pass through a Rift and that marked it as highly valuable. Even if the survivors wouldn't want to become Rifters, those items would be theirs to sell or keep, along with several black-shards that the Rifters had collected for them. It was a small reward, but Daniel wouldn't let the survivors lose anything else.

Come on, guys. You've endured so much. Just pull through, Daniel thought as he watched more nurses rush into another room for yet another emergency. The horde of monsters that had descended on them at the end had killed and maimed so many of the survivors. Although a few had escaped with their lives, the memories of that Rift would forever mark these people, both physically and mentally.

Daniel's body was bruised and battered, and he was fatigued beyond words. Still, he stood tall in that moment. Some of these people wouldn't survive the next few hours because of their injuries. The least Daniel could do was stand vigilant until they recovered or gave their last breath. He was also angry, however. Mostly because of the GRRO officers constantly trailing him, asking questions all the while. He knew why they were doing it, that there was strict protocol, but fatigue had drained him mentally. He didn't want to deal with them.

"Can you tell us more about how many people were with you? Do you have a—" a GRRO officer asked before Daniel interrupted him.

"No, I cannot. And the GRRO will get my report when I finish checking in on the others. Now back off," Daniel said fiercely as he rounded the corner. He wanted to check on the Rift-hound while Dieter was in surgery. He knew the bond that those two shared, even beyond what Dieter's Rifter Class gave him. The man loved that dog and would take a bullet for him. His German friend would've wanted him to check up on Little Hans.

"That won't do at all. Protocol says we need to debrief—"

With lightning speed, the Rifter's hand closed around the GRRO officer's throat in a vice-like grip, effortlessly lifting him off his feet with just one arm. Daniel's words exploded from his lips, laced with a venomous intensity. "The report can wait until I'm done checking up with the wounded!" His eyes widened, a turbulent storm raging within him. Every fiber of his being dared the GRRO officer to so much as tremble the wrong way.

Normally, Daniel was a composed and calm individual. Now he was just one question away from slamming someone through a metal wall. Like vultures, the GRRO came rushing in with their red tape, paperwork, and recordkeeping. He was once again reminded why he had chosen to not be a GRRO lapdog back when he was still an active Rifter.

"Let's give the man some room before someone else loses an arm as well," a tall and graying man said suddenly as he approached the group. Like the others, the man wore a GRRO uniform, although he clearly had a higher rank. One nod from him was enough of a signal to the others that the Rifter was to be left alone for now. The other men and women nodded respectfully and scurried away to check on other things. He took a proper look at Daniel when it was finally just the two of them.

After first letting Daniel check on the Rift-hound, the man, Samuel Jones, steered the Rifter towards his private office. "How about we sit down for a moment?" he said, offering Daniel a chair and grabbing two random mugs off a nearby shelf. Afterwards, he pulled out a small metal flask from his pocket. He poured a generous amount of decent Scotch in both mugs, handing Daniel one of them. "I seem to recall you preferring the same poison. So, did retirement not suit you, Daniel?"

The Rifter watched Samuel for a few seconds before he spoke. "I gave retirement a fair chance, but you know how work pulls you back in," Daniel said with a weak grin as he accepted the mug, raising an eyebrow at the text written on it: *#1 Mum!*

Samuel ignored the look and spoke his mind. "I can only imagine Dieter and your old guild will interpret this as a sign that your life as a Rifter isn't over yet and that you should come out of retirement."

"Bah! Dieter could see me putting on the wrong pair of socks as a sign of me needing to come back." Daniel took a generous sip of his drink as he savored the taste. It reminded him of his fight with the Rift-guardian. He knew Samuel could read him like a book. The man had worked with him and Dieter on important Rift matters before, and no doubt had read up on recent events.

Samuel smiled at the comment for a moment before the mood shifted. They both knew that it was only a matter of time before they would have to address the elephant in the room. The man narrowed his eyes and focused on the bloody Rifter sitting in front of him. "How is your friend doing?"

Daniel closed his eyes and lowered his head as he swirled the contents of the mug around. "Bad. Lots of fractures, lacerations, a ruptured spleen, and a collapsed lung. Still, he has been through worse. Last time I checked, they were still performing surgery on him. As soon as he is stable enough, they will transfer him and the others to St Lucas Hospital." Daniel said, taking another sip from the mug.

"Let's hope he will pull through. The same applies to the other survivors as well. I've rarely witnessed a scene as messy as this one," Samuel said, replying like an old friend. Daniel knew that the old man meant it. Samuel's position today was a delicate one. He was there to balance mutual respect between men while maintaining enough distance due to his position as the head of the GRRO London branch.

Daniel knew what Samuel was doing but didn't seem to get as irritated with him as he did with other GRRO employees. Daniel and his former guild had built up a bit of a rapport with Samuel, even taking on GRRO contracts for a few years until it had felt too constrictive. They had still clashed a number of times, but Samuel had built up a reputation within the Rifter population of being strict but fair.

Sensing the tension, Samuel then shared a bit of the information that the GRRO had already gathered. "From what we've learned, this Rift scaled somewhere between a Level Six and Level Eight Rift. We should have an exact measurement within a few hours. But even if we were assuming a Level Six, it is still miraculous that you guys cleared it at all while taking care of so many survivors," Samuel said, his words honest and respectful. The man knew what he was talking about. He had seen first-hand just how often an initial Rift could cause the deaths of everyone inside of it.

Daniel was almost hesitant to do so, but finally forced himself to ask the dark question that had loomed over him. "How many people?" He didn't want to know the answer but knew that he owed it to the fallen to bear witness.

"284 people were at the scene when the Rift occurred," Samuel said, stating the horrible fact. It was a current number, since time and further investigation might have shifted it up or down.

"Dammit," Daniel said, gritting his teeth as he closed his eyes. His thoughts wandered toward all those people who had died within the Rift. *Too many. There are always too many.* He still remembered the confusion that had taken place in the beginning, with his room suddenly transported into the Rift and breaking apart. It had taken him time to find his bearings and to equip himself before he could help the survivors. For every survivor he had found and protected, he felt like the monsters had killed a dozen more.

"I could only save a few of them. Two dozen at the most, in the beginning. I don't know how many will survive their injuries. I doubt there were over ten of us when the Rift-event closed," Daniel said, pausing afterwards. He tried to search for words he could utter to describe what he had seen. There were none. He remembered how he had forced the survivors to huddle against the Rift-event when it closed. Most of them had appeared heavily wounded or even at death's door.

Those that had died inside the Rift wouldn't be able to accompany the living as the Rift forced the survivors back to Earth. The Rift had claimed the bodies of the fallen forever, both human and monster alike. He sighed once more before he opened his eyes, seeing Samuel stare at a blank spot on the wall himself. He figured the old man felt the same way about the whole situation. They stayed quiet like that for a while, each of them coming to terms with the reality of what had happened and the state of the world they were living in.

Finally, Samuel broke the silence. "Despite what the press and the families of the fallen might say—"

"You mean the butchered?" Daniel interrupted, his voice calm and thick with the weight of loss.

"There wouldn't have been any survivors if it hadn't been for Dieter and yourself. It would've been another three days before a proper Rift team would have even been available. We had two simultaneous new Rifts forming, and an impending outbreak in Scotland," Samuel said truthfully. He eyed the thick stack of papers on his desk that would contain a summary of everything that had happened since this Rift had formed here. On top of those stacks were the letters of condolences, or drafts of those. Samuel's phone was buzzing again, new texts and calls coming in, so he had to wrap things up with Daniel.

"We can only look forward, lest we drown in the blood we've been wading through," the GRRO director said before he slowly got up and finished his drink. Afterwards, he made his way towards the door and turned around. "Daniel, you're still bleeding, and that infection needs to be taken care of. I'll get a doctor to treat you and give you some time to collect yourself. I'll let the GRRO vultures know to leave you alone for a while. We'll talk more tomorrow." Then Samuel left the room, closing the door behind him. He didn't wait for a response. What was there to be said? Samuel had only asked what he needed to finish his report. He didn't need to ask more, having seen all that he needed to know from Daniel's gaze.

Experiencing hell had a way of etching a permanent mark into someone's eyes.

LANCE

The following morning, GRRO representatives visited the survivors who were stable enough to speak. The occupant of room three, Lance Turner, was one of those survivors.

"The GRRO will take care of any further treatment and medical cost for the next twenty-four months. You will find all the information within the folder I've placed on the table next to you," the man in the black suit said as he pointed at the table with a soft and reassuring smile. He had practiced this smile before and knew how to calm people. Survivors of an initial Rift had been through untold horrors. The man knew from experience that a calm tone and a reassuring smile helped in these situations.

Still, the patient in room three paid no attention to what was being said. Instead, Lance was lost in his own mind as he focused on a single word: *Seven.*

"After they've moved you to St. Lucas Hospital, a GRRO employee will check up with you every few days to see if there is anything we can do for you in the meantime," the GRRO representative explained, trying once again to make eye contact. Everyone reacted differently when surviving a Rift, but the young man before him looked about as shell-shocked as could be. The nurse had told the representative that the patient had moments of clarity when Rifters or other survivors came to visit.

Seven. Lance continued to focus on just that number, blocking out anything else.

The representative hesitated, seeing the blank expression on the young man. He no doubt realized that anything he said would land on deaf ears. Still, he pressed on with all that he needed to explain before saying farewell and telling the nurses and doctors what he had discussed with the young man in case there were follow-up questions later.

As the representative left the room, Lance simply stared at the window, repeating "Seven" over and over in his mind.

He still couldn't deal with how many people had died within the Rift. He thought he had seen Hell, watching Rachel and the others die right there in front of him. But the reality was far worse. It turned out what he had witnessed was only a fraction of the death that occurred within the Rift.

Seven survived, Lance whispered again. Just seven people had survived the Rift, including the Rifters, Thomas, and himself. Of those seven, the hardships had crippled two survivors to the point of never being able to walk again.

"This isn't real . . . Hundreds had to die, so just seven could live . . . This is all a joke, right?" Lance said aloud, ignoring the nurse who had come in to change his IV fluids. He barely registered her presence or the look of confusion on her face as he argued with himself.

Seventeen hours had passed since he had returned from the Rift. He'd survived a fate that no person should've ever had to endure. He had seen the horrors of monstrous life-forms, the brutality of close combat, and the desperation of his own actions as he had killed living things to survive.

"What the hell was the point of it all?" he said aloud, ignoring the nurse who was asking him if he needed anything or if he was all right.

Lance just continued to stare at the window, or what was in front of the window, observing something that only he could see.

[You have cleared this Rift]
[You have now been registered]
[You have been awarded with a Level Up]
[You have been awarded with a personal Skill]
[You have 3 unspent Attribute points]

The words kept popping up no matter what direction he was looking at, blinking now and again to demand his attention. Daniel had explained these things to him when he had visited Lance, but it was still surreal to see a status screen pop up whenever he concentrated on it. There was far too much information being displayed on the screen to make sense of, so for now he had mostly ignored it.

Instinctively, he knew that his life had changed. He had changed. He wasn't the same person as he had been before he had entered the Rift. What he had endured physically and mentally had manifested within him, taking root and forever changing him in more ways than one. He wondered if his life would ever return to some sort of normalcy after all of this.

He had heard some of the other survivors make phone calls with their families, pouring out every emotion they had kept bottled up since they had entered the Rift. Thomas had broken down when he had spoken to his parents as well, weeping as he told them that he was all right and that they could see him when they were all stable enough and screened for any possible pathogens.

In time, Lance hoped he would feel the same way as his friend, to be grateful for surviving. For now, he simply felt numb. "What is the point of all this?" he whispered as he gradually got out of bed, ignoring his protesting body and making his way over to the window. His gaze focused on something past the floating letters and numbers. He was staring at his reflection that he barely recognized at this point.

"Has this truly happened?" he asked himself as he held out his hands, seeing smaller wounds that had already partially healed before he brought his hand to his unshaven chin. He drew soft lines through the messy hairs before steering his hand further downwards.

He pulled the hospital gown down a bit as he exposed his chest and the bright crystalline shard that was firmly embedded in its center. The white-shard had become active, marking him as a Rifter.

CHAPTER THIRTEEN

Learning to Heal

St Lucas Hospital
London, England

LANCE

Two days had gone by since Daniel and Thomas had made it out of the Rift in one piece. During that time, the GRRO had moved them to St. Lucas Hospital for further treatment. It had taken the two men some time before they had come to terms with what had happened to them. They had spent so many nights sleeping on the dirt, scrounging for food, and fighting for survival. Just having a warm bed and being able to listen to the radio felt almost alien.

Thomas's family visited them both every day. Although they both had their own rooms, they mostly stayed with one another. When they had the energy to do so, they also checked in on the other survivors, looking out for them as best they could. One was still in critical condition and would need further surgeries but most of them were recovering quickly. Even Lance's damaged ribs were healing at a remarkable rate, far beyond what was normal for an ordinary human. From what they had learned from Daniel, that healing ability would only increase in potency the higher their Level became.

"We'll never be the same again," Thomas said suddenly.

Lance looked to his right, seeing his friend standing in front of the mirror, having pulled off his T-shirt again. Thomas's athletic frame was thinner than before and covered with injuries that would no doubt turn into proper scars. The lack of food, constant stress, and brutal combat had streamlined his body. No doubt a few weeks of proper eating would see his former size return. But mentally, Thomas would never truly be the same again. None of them would. The

Rift had robbed them of their innocence. "I don't doubt that. I mean, you've been walking bare-chested every chance you've gotten."

Thomas smiled at his friend's comment as he ran a finger across the white-shard in the center of his chest. "I . . . I'm seriously considering it," Thomas explained. He was referring to their earlier discussion when Thomas proposed becoming actual Rifters. They both knew that Thomas's family would freak out if they heard it, although his father might be more understanding due to the man's military background.

Lance had argued that it was too soon to come to a decision on the matter, but even he had felt the pull of his friend's words. They were still recovering from the Rift, both mentally and physically. The hospital still had dozens of tests to run before the young men would get clean bills of health.

"I know," Lance said. A part of him knew it would be a waste of their medical background and years of training to become nurses. But he also felt like he needed to prevent this from happening to others. He could still remember the way Rachel had screamed as the monster had torn into her, or how the Rift-guardian had pulled Jacob apart. A sense of duty and survivor's guilt was slowly pushing him towards the path of a Rifter. Lance figured the same feeling was also driving Thomas onwards. *He's always hated bullies. I can't think of a bigger bully than a Rift-guardian.*

Not knowing what else to say, Lance changed the subject. "So, have you decided on where to spend your points?" Lance asked, referring to the three Attribute points they could freely spend on their stats. GRRO officials had been visiting them nonstop, answering any question the survivors might have had about the Rift or what it meant now that they had survived one. The officials were helpful and did their absolute best, but Lance and Thomas were more interested in getting information from Daniel whenever he visited them. In their minds, the GRRO hadn't helped them; the two Rifters had. This despite Daniel having fought one-handed while battling a severe infection that had robbed him of his strength.

From what the two friends had learned, their white-shards had activated upon surviving the Rift, awarding all survivors a single Level Up. Daniel had explained that no matter how weak or strong a Rifter was, clearing any Rift would always award a Level increase. At Level One, Lance and Thomas were as weak as a Rifter could be, but more capable than your average human. They healed faster, were slightly more durable, and would be less susceptible to minor issues, such as the flu. Each additional Level increase would boost all their Attributes by one point, as well as offering three more points to spend freely. In short, if they became proper Rifters, their potential for growth was enormous.

Thomas smiled as he put on his T-shirt again. Afterwards he sat down next to Lance. "Well, I figure Strength, Endurance, and Agility would be the smart choice for now."

"You mean exactly like Daniel said we should do?" Lance said with a knowing grin, only to receive a playful nudge to his shoulder. The two of them continued to sit there for a while, processing what had happened to them over the last
few weeks, as well as the crossroads they now found themselves at.

We'll never be the same again, Lance thought, his gaze focusing on the status
screen that only he could see. He didn't doubt Thomas was having a similar
experience.

Name:	Lance Turner
Level:	1
Class:	Survivor

Attributes

Endurance	10	Agility	10	Wisdom	10
Strength	10	Perception	10	Luck	10
Health	150	Mana	35		
Stamina	65	Inventory	5		

Skills

Mend Wounds	Lvl 1	Restores minor wounds	+10 Health +4 Stamina	−10 Mana

A few hours later, the two of them were having dinner with Daniel in Lance's
room. He was informing the young men that the government had contracted a
guild to clear the Rift until it collapsed in on itself. The sudden arrival of the Rift,
the destruction of Ealing Hospital, and the later clearing of the Rift by the survivors had made the news. Public outcry had demanded action, pressuring the
government and the GRRO to pour resources into clearing it.

"It will be good for the community. It might offer some closure to those that
have lost loved ones," Daniel said as he struggled to cut his food with the dull
knife the hospital had provided them. "It isn't the same as bringing a son or
daughter home, but at least there won't be a permanent black sphere of energy in
the spot where your loved ones died."

Lance nodded while Thomas directed his full attention to his own meal. Both
were dealing with their own grief, remembering friends, co-workers, and patients
that they had lost. They understood where Daniel was coming from, but it was
hard to come to terms with it. *How often has he been through something like*

this? Lance thought, as he tried to picture Daniel's life and state of mind before he had been a Rifter.

"Perhaps they'll build a new hospital?" Thomas offered between large bites of his meal.

Daniel shrugged as he placed the hospital knife down. "Or a monument. Who knows?" The Rifter then produced a dangerous-looking dagger out of thin air.

Even after having spent all those days with Daniel and Dieter inside the Rift, the young men still found it strange to see items stored or retrieved from a Rifter's Inventory system. At Level One, they had an Inventory capacity of five, allowing them to fill five individual slots with Rift-related items. It had taken them a little while to acclimate, but eventually they learned how to use it.

The Inventory could only store things classified as an Item. And these Items had to be found inside a Rift or made from Rift-materials. Most of Lance's belongings that had survived his first Rift were in an awful state. Only his backpack and phone were still functional, save for the crack on his phone screen. Lance and Thomas had spent several hours playing with their Inventory system. Lance enjoyed storing and retrieving his smartphone, while Thomas did so with a lighter and last remaining cigarette.

Lance watched as Daniel divided his meal into smaller pieces using the sharp dagger. The blade easily cut through both potatoes and meat, hinting at a sharpness that had proven its lethality on many types of monsters. *I'd hate to be the poor creature that has to square off with Daniel throwing one of these.*

"Have you been practicing your Skills?" Daniel asked, referring to the Skills they had gotten when they had gained their first Level. Each Rifter would get one starting Skill at Level One, and another Skill at Level Ten, at which point they would get their Class and no longer be a mere survivor.

The Skill at Level One was usually a hint of a Rifter's future Class, or something that matched their personality. Thomas had gotten a Skill called "Bullrush," while Lance had gotten one called "Mend Wounds."

Thomas nodded as he activated the Skill, his muscles suddenly tensing up as power poured through his body at the cost of much of his Stamina. It was a temporary increase in Strength for only a few seconds, but it drastically increased Thomas's combat ability. "I've gotten the hang of it now, but it robs me of most of my Stamina. If I use it too often, I can barely walk."

The older Rifter smiled as he carefully hovered his dagger above a piece of meat. "You'll get used to it in time. Skills usually either drain Mana or Stamina. These Attributes increase the higher your Level is, so eventually you'll be able to use your Skill several times in a row. Or—" Daniel said as the dagger gave off tiny sparks of lightning before he used it to stab downwards. Even though he only struck once, the meat showed two dagger cuts and appeared to be cooking from the inside. "—learn to combine it with other Skills. Provided you lads even want to become Rifters."

"We—"

"We've been practicing," Lance interrupted his friend. He didn't want to have Thomas go off on another rant about the pros and cons of becoming Rifters. Instead, Lance slowly reached out towards Daniel, carefully placing his hand against what remained of his amputated arm.

Mend Wounds
[You have used Mend Wounds lvl 1 at the cost of 10 Mana]
[Current Mana 25/35]

Lance felt the Skill activate as healing energies left his hand, seeping into Daniel's wounded side. A blue light enveloped Daniel's body for a few seconds. Lance's Skill allowed him to partially heal himself or others. He could only treat minor wounds or ailments, or at the very least, treat the symptoms. It couldn't remove poisons, restore limbs, or any other major feats, but it was still useful in restoring a bit of Stamina or speeding up the healing process. In Daniel's case, the man would no doubt feel a slight ease of the lingering infection in his arm.

Daniel had said that their Skills suited them both, since Lance had a caring personality and Thomas had a very physical and brash nature. Although their eventual Class could be something entirely different, their initial Skills hinted that Thomas could end up with a melee-oriented Class, while Lance might drift towards a healer or support Class.

"I still say it is weird that my healing Skill also temporarily blinds the person I'm healing," Lance said as he watched the blue light fade from Daniel's body.

"Every Skill has its strengths and weaknesses. It is up to the individual to figure them out and make it work for them. Still, a healing Skill is rare," Daniel said before explaining how a Rifter with such a Class or Skill could frequently find high-paying jobs in healthcare or the GRRO, treating injuries beyond modern medicine.

From how Daniel was carefully phrasing things, Lance figured Rifters who specialized in healing were rare because of the high casualty rate during an initial Rift. *It makes sense that those who were most physically strong and combat oriented would have the highest chance of surviving their first Rift.*

"And how many Skills do you have?" Thomas asked, putting his empty plate down before eyeing the bits of food that were still on Lance's.

The older Rifter smiled as he held up his dagger, making a slight gesture as if he were chastising Thomas. "A Rifter never tells, and it is rude to ask. Still, since we've just survived a Rift together, I'll indulge you. I've got seven Skills."

"Only seven!" Thomas exclaimed as his jaw dropped at the revelation.

Could you be even less tactful? Lance thought as he stared at his friend for a minute. "Sorry about the oaf next to me. Please continue."

Daniel smiled as he slid his plate to the side and stored his dagger into his Inventory afterwards. When that process happened it instantly dropped whatever bits of residue that had previously clung to the blade, hinting at how the Inventory system worked on things classified as Items. "It is fine. But you two must understand that Skills are rare. There are some Rifters out there who only have a few Skills but who are much stronger than I am. The reverse also applies, with weaker Rifters having dozens of Skills. We gain them from reaching certain Levels, from finding Skill-shards, or buying those Skill-shards from other Rifters."

"So why didn't you?" Lance's friend asked with the social grace of a blunt instrument.

"Because even a common Skill-shard gets sold for hundreds of thousands of pounds, if not millions. A rare one would be worth billions," Daniel explained, a small smile creeping across his face when he saw both Lance and Thomas's eyes go wide. "So, unless you've some spare family fortune lying around, I'd suggest you focus more on your Levels and Attributes for now." He then got up and said goodbye to them, explaining he wanted to check in on Dieter and the other survivors.

After that, the two friends spent a long time discussing all that they had learned about the essence of being a Rifter. That and lost themselves yet again in their status screens. With ten points in Strength, Endurance, Agility, Perception, Wisdom, and Luck, they began to imagine how twenty points might feel like, or a hundred.

Three free Attribute points per Level. Three points to spend how we see fit and specialize how we want, Lance thought as he remembered Daniel's style of fighting. He had much higher Perception and Agility Attributes compared to Dieter. *If I become a Rifter, how should I branch out? Should I go for a Strength build and overpower any threat? Or become like Daniel and focus on speed and precision?* Lance lost himself in his thoughts, feeling the burden of choice.

All of this is quite complex, and it isn't even factoring in what a Class could mean for a Rifter. Daniel told us that all Classes have unique traits and benefits. Eventually, Lance felt a hand on his shoulder as Thomas lured him back into the present. He wasn't sure if it was the survivor's guilt, the meetings with Daniel, or the obvious appeal of developing his body and mind beyond human limits, but he knew he had made his choice.

"All right," he finally said, feeling Thomas's grip on his shoulder lessen, as if the anticipation was getting to him as well. "Let's become Rifters."

CHAPTER FOURTEEN

Discount Grenade Launchers

September, 13 AR
St. Lucas Hospital
London, England

LANCE

Y ou boys should stop playing with that or you'll go blind," Dieter jested, eyeing the two lads beside him fixated on an arbitrary spot on the wall. He knew
they were checking out their status screen and were seeing something that most
ordinary people couldn't even fathom. Naturally, his remark jolted Thomas and
Lance into action, their faces reddening with embarrassment. It wasn't the first
time Dieter had seen the young men glancing at their Attributes, Levels, and
Skills. Rifters couldn't see each other's status screens, but Dieter knew the tell-
tale signs when someone was busy with their own.

Both Lance and Thomas had announced their decision to become Rifters a
few days ago, after having discussed it at length with one another, Daniel, Dieter,
and Thomas's family. There was still a lot of uncertainty and fear, but they had
sworn to one another to become proper Rifters and never feel as helpless as they
had felt inside their first Rift. Daniel had told Thomas's family that he would help
the young men in the beginning, to guide them through the basics and temper
any overly risky behavior.

They heard Dieter chuckling as he finished packing his bags and putting on
a clean shirt. His chest displayed an assortment of newer and older scars, with
many of them originating from the last Rift encounter. Meanwhile, Dieter was
now speaking to them in German. Lance and Thomas could now understand any
language uttered by a Rifter. This was due to their white-shards. In their minds,
it was as if Dieter was speaking fluent English to them, unless they forced

themselves to listen carefully. Lance and Thomas wouldn't be able to understand non-Rifters that spoke German, because the speaker having a white-shard as well was a necessity.

Daniel had explained that the ability to understand one another was universal for every Rifter. It allowed perfect communication with any Rifter, and thus better cooperation within the Rift. There were theories about why this was the case. A lot of Rifters figured this was an evolutionary process; others thought it was an innate ability; some even claimed it was by design. The latter was worrying since it would mean that the Rifts were intentionally rather than randomly created.

"I still don't see how you allowed that stubborn old fool to be the one to pick us up by car. You've noticed he only has one arm, right?" the imposing German asked, while doing his best to suppress a hidden grin. He grabbed his bags and whistled once to wake Little Hans, who was resting on the sofa.

Thomas was quick to break the silence, teasing the imposing man. "Well, we would've suggested you drive, but you were taking your sweet time in recovering. Speaking of which, do you need me to carry you downstairs?"

Lance rolled his eyes as he heard Thomas laughing, knowing full well that more comments would come next. He made his way out the door, letting the nurses know Dieter was checking out. They had taken care of the paperwork beforehand. The only thing they needed to do now was to help Dieter with his bags and get him and the Rift-hound back to his flat. It was more of a gesture, since Dieter was the strongest man they knew.

He would've been fine on his own, having mostly recovered these last few days, but Daniel had insisted on it. He had claimed that true Rifters could count on one another during war and peace.

By the time Thomas and Dieter reached Lance, he had already called for the elevator. A few of the staff said their goodbyes to Dieter and the Rift-hound, having spent a long time with the two of them. The hospital had discharged both Lance and Thomas earlier that week, after the young men had cleared several physical and mental tests. They would still have additional check-ups in the following days, all provided by the GRRO.

The young men had only needed a week before they were physically fine, despite having suffered injuries that would've taken an average person weeks to heal. Upon leaving the Rift, Thomas had suffered quite a few lacerations and Lance was still recovering from several fractures, but their elevation to Rifters came with sturdier bodies that were quick to recover.

"You do realize we're going to feed you some actual food, right? Not the hospital rubbish you've gotten used to. I was thinking of burgers or ribs. Something to clog those arteries of yours," Thomas said as he nudged Dieter in the side.

"Don't forget about actual hot sauce. Or chips!" Lance pitched in.

At the mention of ribs, the Rift-hound barked eagerly. The sound instantly drew the eyes of people within the hospital when the lift doors opened out into the lobby. Even though St. Lucas Hospital had a specialized wing for Rifters, and occasionally hired Rifters with healing abilities, a large Rift-hound was still an alarming sight.

"No, Hans. You're on a diet, remember?" Dieter said sternly as he locked eyes with the powerful creature. At that moment, they were sharing something that went beyond a mere bond. Dieter, with his powerful frame, blue eyes, and blonde hair, drew just as many eyes. His shirt was slightly open to expose his white Rift-shard. It was a style that Thomas was slowly copying as well.

"Burgers sound good," Dieter said as the men exited the hospital and spotted Daniel outside, leaning against his car. The green Range Rover looked expensive, but obviously within the price range of an experienced Rifter like Daniel. The man clapped Dieter on the shoulder and hugged him, leaving the younger men to place the bags in the car.

"You shouldn't be driving with one arm," Dieter said.

Daniel merely snorted before he retaliated. "So, when I'm driving a car, you turn into my overprotective mother. But you're more than fine with me jumping in a dangerous Rift with only one arm?"

"Yes, exactly. They're different things, and I've seen how you drive. Besides, you need your right arm to shift gears."

Daniel looked confused for a moment before he tapped the bonnet of his car with a grin. "It's an automatic. And you realize we have the steering wheel on the other side of the car, right?" Daniel responded, as his smile widened into that of pure mirth.

"I . . . argh," Dieter blurted out as he stepped into the car before slamming the door behind him, no doubt hoping to block out his friend's laughter and the two young men that were joining him when they realized what had just happened.

Two weeks had passed since the hospital had discharged Dieter. During those weeks, the young Rifters had gotten a crash course on how to be a Rifter from both Daniel and Dieter, focusing on strengthening their knowledge about Rifts, types of monsters, and a lot of physical training. After a while, Dieter had said his goodbyes to them because of obligations to his guild. Still, Daniel had kept them busy. The former nurses had gotten their GRRO Rifter credentials and had passed the physical and written tests. Afterwards, Daniel had taken the young men to the GRRO-sanctioned Workshop.

It was located a few miles west of London and covered the size of a large warehouse, with several floors and underground sections. It was a formidable place, with both military and GRRO security on site. People could only enter it with proper clearance from the GRRO or if they were Rifters with proper credentials.

Daniel had explained what the Workshop was but seeing it in person was something else. Everywhere they looked there were large shops filled with merchants buying or selling Rift-based items. There were weapons, armor, small vehicles, useful tools, and other devices on sale. On other floors, there were information brokers, Skill-shard sellers, alchemists, and medical professionals. The place smelled of leather, gunpowder, oil, and metal.

The GRRO documented every item that was bought, sold, or made within the Workshop, ensuring that any buyer would know the quality of the item, its properties, and how well-tested it was. Rifters frequently brought items back from the Rifts, selling them for a hefty profit. Still, most sellers offered items that were made on Earth. Anyone could smelt metals found in a Rift and make weaponry or armor from it, but an item made by a Rifter who had the Crafter or Smith class would usually be of a better quality and more powerful, as well as have slots to house upgrades.

Lance's eyes went wide at what he could see, but even wider at the cost of these items. He could see a shop that was selling electronic devices, including phones, charging devices fueled by Mana, and communication devices. Most of them were going for thousands of pounds, at the very least. Lance felt overwhelmed upon realizing just how valuable his cracked phone was. A few minutes later, he couldn't take it anymore, pulled it out of his jeans, and stored it in his Inventory.

[You have stored an item in your Inventory]

Lance knew Daniel had seen him store his phone as soon as he felt a hand on his shoulder, putting him at ease. The two of them then made their way over towards Thomas, who was ogling heavy weaponry.

"Dude! They have grenade launchers here! I want one . . . No, two!" Thomas said. Lance knew his friend had either missed the price tag or purposely ignored it, no doubt under the illusion that they could afford one soon. Luckily, Daniel was there to temper the eager redhead.

"You need some serious cash to pay for it, the ammunition, and the upkeep," Daniel said before he explained how much a single grenade would cost and how rare ammunition was. Rifters could only bring Rift-exposed materials, and there was a severe lack of raw resources to produce a lot of ammunition. Buying additional bullets or grenades could quickly lend a Rifter in serious debt.

Daniel then led the young men towards another shop. "Here, let's check this out." He pointed at an assortment of bows, crossbows, and throwing weapons. Every weapon looked quite durable and sturdy.

"Most Rifters use these types of tools, produced from ores found or mined inside the Rifts. They can take a beating and the cost of maintenance is manageable. And you can usually reuse a bolt or arrow," Daniel told the young men before greeting the shopkeeper, having done business with her on multiple occasions.

He then pointed at other stalls that had melee-oriented tools and basic protective equipment. "Most Rifters start out with minor jobs. Acting as either muscle in mining jobs or hauling equipment. They go by many names, but most people refer to them as porters."

"That sounds . . . glamorous," Thomas said with his mood deflated.

With a disapproving glare, Daniel swiftly corrected his companion's misguided statement. "It's better than bleeding out in some damn Rift just because you got cocky."

"Yeah . . . Sorry. I just got excited," Thomas quickly apologized.

Daniel nodded, since he could no doubt understand the excitement. He then led them past some booths that had recruiters for local guilds and spokespersons for local companies. The latter often hired Rifters for regular jobs as either porters or as muscle to keep the porters safe. Even the GRRO had people on site to recruit Rifters in their organization. They wanted experienced Rifters to help maintain order and to react quickly to dangerous Rifts.

"Come on. I want you to meet someone," Daniel said as he led them towards a recruiter for a company that frequently employed Rifters as porters. A company logo was visible on his jacket: *R.A.M.* When he later asked the R.A.M. recruiter if there were three spots open for the next Rift clearing, Daniel struggled to suppress a smile upon hearing the lads' reaction.

Four days later, the two friends stood in front of their second Rift, watching the pulsating black energy flare up now and again. Thomas narrowed his eyes as he observed it. "Does it look smaller compared to the one at the hospital?"

"I'd hope so," Daniel commented as he signaled the young men to follow him further towards the Rift.

It feels strange being so close to a Rift again, Lance thought as his eyes remained fixed on the mass of black energy. Daniel had persuaded the lads to join him inside a Rift. This time there would be a lot of Rifters backing them up and a lot more preparation. It had terrified the young men at first, but Daniel's words had made sense when he explained just how different an average Rift clearing would be for them. The experience would strengthen their resolve and educate them, as well as lessen the fear of a Rift. The quicker they did so, the easier it would be.

Like most Rifts, there were layers of security around it. Large nets and rope created an almost spherical protective layer, preventing major incidents when Rifters or objects exited the Rift. There were mobile housing units installed behind the cage of nets. These structures contained a small barracks, an office for the overseers of the site, and private cubicles for the Rifters.

"They ranked this Rift as a Level Two. It differs vastly from the Level Seven one that we experienced together," Daniel explained, pointing at the size of the Rift and how it even felt weaker than what they had experienced.

Each time Rifters cleared a Rift, its energy and size would decrease further until it collapsed in on itself. Companies such as Rift-based Advanced Metallurgy, or R.A.M., were one of many that profited from these Rifts.

Daniel pointed at the large metal bins that were near the main building. "The setup is quite simple. Companies like R.A.M. buy ownership of certain Rifts from the government in exchange for their guarantee that they will clear it, not risk public safety, and will occasionally help with other Rifts. In return, R.A.M. can let its Rifts grow a few Levels before clearing it for profit. This creates the opportunity to extract precious resources and harvesting rare items from the inhabiting monsters. When done with a Rift, the porters then drop collected resources inside these metal—"

Enthusiastically interrupting, Thomas blurted out, "So, it's like a farm or a mine, right?"

As the two men continued to discuss the situation, Lance thought about how he felt. It was easy to point a finger at companies such as R.A.M. and claim that they were seeking profit out of a horrible event, but he could also make the argument that these companies were supplying the raw resources needed to manufacture weapons, armor, and other tools. With them, Rifters could more reliably clear Rifts.

As one might suspect, the world isn't just black or white, Lance thought as he followed Daniel's instructions to check their gear one last time before they went in. They had gotten jobs as porters, meaning that they and a dozen others would mine and harvest rare resources within the Rift. Other more experienced Rifters would clear out the enemies.

Thomas and Lance looked under-equipped compared to some of the other Rifters, who were decked out in expensive plate armor, scale, and leather. The two friends were wearing the standard gear that R.A.M. issued porters for the duration of the event. The gear amounted to thick leather gloves and boots, and a sturdy padded green overall with the R.A.M. insignia on the shoulders. For extra protection, they got to wear a thick iron breastplate and helmet. It was all machine or non-Rifter made, meaning it lacked any specific boons. Even without upgrades, the quality of an item made by a Rifter classed as a Smith or Crafter was usually far better.

Feeling the weight of the armor, it surprised Lance at how easy it was to move within it. "It feels . . . lighter than I expected," Lance said.

"Most people think that wearing armor is cumbersome. They're wrong. It isn't that restrictive. And besides—" Daniel replied, as he pointed at Lance with a smile, "—you two aren't your former selves anymore. You're Rifters now and your power will only grow from now on."

His words rang true for the young men. As an achievement for surviving their first Rift, the encounter had awarded them the rank of Level One and gave them three extra Attribute points to distribute. As per Daniel's advice, they had spread the points out in their Strength, Endurance, and their Agility. A Rifter's base stats started around ten, slightly above your average non-Rifter.

[Endurance:] **[10]** (+1)
[Strength:] **[10]** (+1)
[Agility:] **[10]** (+1)

The effects of those additional points spent were subtle, but they were there. The increased stats helped them heal, mending wounds and broken bones in a matter of a week. Their bodies felt lighter and more energetic than ever before. Both were wearing the slabs of thick iron around their torsos and on their heads without really feeling all that bothered by it.

Daniel watched the two young men and nodded. "Good. Now, dig deep and find your resolve." Slowly, the Rifters moved towards the Rift. The combat-oriented Rifters rushed in first. The porters would head in after sixty seconds had passed. When it was time, Thomas and Daniel walked towards the Rift and entered it, with Lance at their heels.

Before Lance went inside, he picked up a pebble from the ground and threw it towards the Rift. He watched it disintegrate the moment it hit the violent mass of black energy. "Here goes nothing!" Lance yelled before he inhaled deeply and rushed into the Rift. It pulled his body inwards as everything turned dark.

CHAPTER FIFTEEN

Fresh Perspective

September, 13 AR
Inside Rift 2

DANIEL

Daniel's feet slammed into the ground, his momentum coming to an abrupt halt; he fought to maintain balance. Years of being a Rifter had taught him to adapt quickly if he wanted to live, so he scanned his immediate area for any hostiles.

Around him he could see other Rifters appearing. *Looks like the porters made it,* Daniel thought as he watched some of them fall on their faces, and others vomit because of the disorientation, while the more experienced porters remained standing. Daniel smiled as he noticed Thomas and Lance, their faces covered dirt, indicating how they must have landed. *They didn't puke, at least. That's a good sign.*

Daniel gave them a moment to adjust as he inspected his surroundings, an ocean of rock and sand. There was barely any vegetation and the sky had a brownish tint. *The gravity is different,* he concluded after taking a few steps and feeling his feet dig into the sand. Every world was unique. Some were like Earth; others were entirely oceanic in nature, a volcanic hellscape, or a desert planet like this one. *It shouldn't be too bad for them,* he thought as he watched the young men looking around with a mixture of awe and fright plastered on their faces. "Lads, with me."

Hearing him, they snapped out of it and rush towards him. Meanwhile, the other porters were making their way to the sound of fighting in the distance. "Just stick with me and you'll be fine. All right?"

"Yes, sir," the two young Rifters said, falling in line.

Daniel then led them up a sandy hill after the line of porters. It wasn't long before they spotted the fighters in the distance. Even without a heightened

Perception stat, it would be obvious to see that these Rifters were fighting monsters. "Most companies send in the fighters first. They clear and secure the entry spot or move the fighting away from it."

He led the two men as closely as he felt comfortable, allowing them to see the fur-covered monsters that were attacking the fighters. They stood on two legs and had a canine appearance. "You're in luck. These are intelligent monsters. See the weapons that they carry?" Daniel pointed at the slain monsters. Around them were crude spears, bows, and stone hammers.

"Isn't that more dangerous?" Lance asked, while Thomas's face lit up like a Christmas tree at the prospect of loot.

"It can be. Arm a monster or a Rifter with decent gear and they will become a bigger threat—" Daniel vanished suddenly as he activated his Dash Skill. He appeared in front of Thomas and caught one of the monster's stray arrows mid-flight. Thomas's smile instantly vanished, the gravity of the situation hitting him, as he realized the potential harm the arrow could have inflicted had Daniel not intervened.

"Exhibit A," Daniel said, his hold on the arrow growing tighter. "Danger's a given, no denying that. But there's a flip side, a shimmer of opportunity. We can collect their gear for ourselves or sell it and make a profit. We can exploit their intelligence and take advantage of their tactics." At that, he snapped the crude arrow shaft in half and placed his hand on Thomas's shoulder. "Are you all right?"

"Yeah . . . Sorry."

"Don't worry. Even experienced Rifters can get startled at suddenly being shot at." He then led the young men towards the porters who were setting up a temporary camp near a flat piece of rock while other porters were already cutting out black-shards from slain monsters.

"Shouldn't the porters help with the fighting?" Lance asked after a while as he watched each fighter battling two or three monsters simultaneously. Despite the numerical advantage, the monsters were clearly on the defensive and most of the fighters were quite relaxed, with some even smiling.

"Sometimes. But not in a weak Rift like this one. It's more efficient for the porters to set up camp and simply get to work. Higher-Level Rifts can be trickier, and any additional manpower would help. But the number of fighters we have at hand here is overkill," Daniel explained as he stepped closer to a fighter who was picking off monsters with a crossbow. "Lucie, how goes the fighting?"

Sporting a mischievous expression, the female Rifter nimbly fitted a bolt onto her crossbow, her left hand clutching five more. A moment later, all five spare bolts disappeared as she shot at a group of monsters. Instead of one bolt, six suddenly peppered the group in a horrible barrage of steel and wood. "First wave's as good as done. Need a hand over there, old man?" she quipped, a hint of playful mockery in her voice.

Daniel, clearly amused, shook her hand with a firm grip, his eyes examining her ranged weapon for a moment as if he longed to fire it himself. "I'll remember that comment for after the Rift. You can buy this old man a drink."

"You got it," Lucie said, reloading her crossbow as she spotted a group of six monsters trying to attack the fighters on their left flanks.

"Did you guys name them already?" Daniel asked as he watched her pick off one monster with ease, forcing the other five to scatter in fear.

"Sand-Gnolls." She immediately held up her hand before Daniel could even shake his head at that. "Not my pick, let me tell you. But you're acquainted with the caliber of imbeciles I'm stuck dealing with. Did you honestly reckon they'd have the wit to select anything better?"

Amusement danced in Daniel's eyes as he observed the battle alongside her, watching her occasionally picking off another one. "I could use a quick stretch, to be honest. Show these lads here how it is done," he quipped, directing his words towards her. His finger then singled out Lance and Thomas. "Think you can keep an eye on those two for a bit?"

"All right, consider them my own cubs. But don't come whining later when the rest of those fighters start feeling like worthless piles of dung cause you out-shine 'em by a bloody mile. Half of them barely scraped their way to the Veteran rank," the woman retorted, her tone laced with a touch of sarcasm. She positioned herself in front of the young men, as if to show that she took her temporary duty seriously.

Daniel pressed forward with a sense of purpose. Retrieving a throwing dagger from his Inventory, he clenched it tightly, resolved to make an impression. *These boys need to witness first-hand the stark contrast between their horrible first experience and a controlled Rift experience,* he thought as he flexed his neck and physically prepared himself. *To do that they need to see me at my absolute peak, and not withered away because of an infection.*

Daniel sprinted forwards as he closed the distance between him and five Sand-Gnolls. Compared to the monsters he was used to fighting, these Sand-Gnolls barely had time to grab their weapons and switch to a defensive stance before he was upon them.

Double-strike Imbue lightning.

With a swift flick of his wrist, Daniel released the throwing dagger, sending it hurtling through the air. The blade found its mark, burying itself deep in the monster's throat, producing two distinct wounds and a large spray of blood. A gurgled gasp escaped the creature's lips before its life force was consumed by crackling lightning, coursing through its body like a raging storm.

Dash.

Like a wraith, Daniel vanished from the monsters' sight, only to materialize behind them in an instant. Gripping his short sword firmly, he cleaved in a wide and merciless arc, painting the air with a spray of blood before he attacked once more. Empowered by heightened Strength and Agility, his blade sliced through their ranks effortlessly, encountering scant resistance. In a matter of a few heartbeats, Daniel had dispatched the group of monsters, his demeanor resolute and untroubled, not a single droplet of sweat marring his brow.

These boys need to experience this. His gaze shifted towards their awestruck faces. Lance's expression twisted into a mix of shock and astonishment, while Thomas, unable to contain his excitement, wore a grin that threatened to split his face wide open.

Dash.

Like a bolt of lightning, Daniel surged forward, seamlessly melding with the other Rifters as they confronted the remnants of the initial threat. Lance and Thomas stood rooted to the ground, their eyes wide as they watched Daniel unleash the staggering capabilities of a Rifter beyond the reaches of a mere Veteran.

In the heart of this Rift, monsters would taste the unbridled fury of an Expert-ranked Rifter who was fixated on proving just how scary Rifters could be compared to monsters.

Just as Daniel had promised the lads, their second experience within a Rift was vastly different. The Rifters had wiped out two-thirds of the monsters in the first few hours and hunted down the rest in the days that followed.

Most of the fighting was done in those first few hours. Afterwards, the porters kept Lance and Thomas busy with skinning monsters for their prized leather and harvesting valuable parts such as their claws, teeth, and black-shards. When the two men weren't on harvesting duty, they would follow other porters and learn how to find minerals and useful ores, mine them, and secure them for transport. It was seven days of constant hard labor, little sleep, and a lot of hands-on learning.

Daniel was constantly there, but he never helped them out beyond ensuring their safety or offering advice. The young men were smart enough to realize why he was doing things this way. It was arduous work, but the two men had slowly transformed themselves during those days. In the end, they were just as dirty as the other Rifters and even earned some respect from their fellow porters.

The Rifters had also moved their camp towards the Rift-event itself, having thoroughly scouted out the environment and secured the location beforehand. Trenches, dirt walls, and improvised wooden embrasures protected their latest camp from any monster incursions, although that had never happened.

The lure of joining the fellow fighters on their monster-hunting expeditions or in capturing the formidable Rift-guardian tugged at Daniel's heartstrings. Memories of his bygone days alongside Dieter with their guild resurfaced, evoking a yearning to embrace the lifestyle of a Rifter once again. A part of him wondered if he couldn't train himself to be a skilled one-handed swordsman or perhaps master the art of a single-handed crossbow. Yet, deep down, he acknowledged the sobering reality that his aspirations would render him nothing but a burden to his comrades, or worse, a liability.

Lance had asked him about it during their first night in the Rift, inquiring if he couldn't simply work as security for R.A.M. despite only having one arm. It was a valid question and Daniel had said that the line of work wasn't for him. Even now, he wasn't sure if what he had told Lance was the truth or not.

Despite having lost his right arm, Daniel still felt confident enough in his abilities to solo most of the monsters here in this Rift. His current Level was more than enough to compensate for the lack of his right arm. Still, that compensation would suddenly stop when he'd reach higher-Level Rifts.

I need to figure out what I want to do after this. Am I going to stay a Rifter or become a civilian? Daniel thought as he toyed around with a throwing knife, training his left hand to be as dextrous as possible. A short distance away from him, he could see Lance and Thomas getting a lesson from a few of the Rifters that were on guard duty that day. From what Daniel could hear, the young men were being taught the benefits of bolts and arrows over bullets, despite how effective guns were on weaker monsters.

But guns are cool, Daniel thought, silently mimicking Thomas's words as he deciphered the movements of the spirited redhead's lips. Thomas wasn't entirely mistaken in his assertion. Many Rifters resorted to rifles or pistols in desperate situations, but the costly nature of ammunition posed a significant hurdle. Moreover, the arsenal of Skills a Rifter possessed often didn't synergize as well with bullets as they did with swords or arrows. *I'll enlighten them about the advantages and disadvantages of modern weaponry back on Earth,* Daniel contemplated, catching sight of several fighters trudging back to the base, hauling something sizable in their wake.

"Lads, grab your stuff. It's time to leave," Daniel said as he made his way over towards them, pointing at the Rifters who were returning.

"Really?" Lance asked a few minutes later. He and Thomas watched the other Rifters pack up their equipment and store most of the ores they had gathered into netting or sturdy containers before securing them to a porter's back. "That's it?"

Thomas nodded in agreement, his shoulders slumping with disappointment. "I had imagined an epic final battle," he confessed, his voice tinged with dejection. "This . . . this is pathetic."

Daniel smiled as he walked up to the tied-up monster that lay at their feet. "Did you want some dangerous battle? Some heroic fight at the end of the Rift?"

Disappointment etched across their faces, the duo shared a collective sense of dissatisfaction, though it was the redhead who vocalized it more explicitly. "Yes and no? I don't know. It's a mixture of both," Thomas admitted.

Daniel nudged Thomas in the ribs like a father would do before squatting next to the monster and placing a finger on the creature's Rift-shard. It had a red hue to it, marking it as the Rift-guardian. It was like the other Sand-Gnolls but bulkier, in terms of muscle mass. From what Daniel had gleaned, the others had found the monster this morning after dragging it out of a small den.

"You guys have been watching way too many movies," Daniel scoffed, shaking his head. "Yes, there are some intense fights between Rifters and monsters, but the reality is quite different. Most of the time, we have a significant numerical advantage, higher Levels, and superior equipment. This is just a Level-Two Rift, and with the number of actual fighters we have here, we can even handle a Level-Four Rift without too many problems," Daniel explained, tapping the Guardian-shard once more for emphasis. "You see this?"

"The red hue?" Lance asked as he knelt next to Daniel, examining the shard.

"Correct. If the two of you are going to become proper Rifters, then you'd better develop a healthy amount of respect for the things that carry these. They are dangerous—"

"Because they're stronger, right? Like that big lizard creature you and Dieter fought?" Thomas interrupted as he balled his hand into a fist. Daniel wasn't sure if it was because the young man was remembering that horrible scene or if it was his conviction to become a Rifter.

"They can be. Or they have more intelligence. But no, the real reason is the sheer amount of energy these shards contain when compared to a normal black-shard. Enough energy for them to use Skills as well. And there is nothing scarier than seeing a monster that can use the same Skills a Rifter can," Daniel explained.

"But they are worth a lot, right?" Thomas blurted out. He poked the Guardian-shard, completely ignoring the bound, wounded monster that was attached to it.

Daniel nodded once as he answered. "Spoken like a true Rifter. Yes, they are worth a lot. Around a thousand times as valuable as a black-shard. But that number varies depending on the market."

"Who gets to keep the shard?" Lance asked finally, after having stayed quiet for some time.

"It depends on the Rifters. Working for R.A.M. means that the company keeps it and will sell it for profit. In smaller groups of freelancers, it's usually the Rifter who kills the monster that gets it. In m—I mean, in Dieter's guild, the MO was to store it for later use, in case there was an emergency," Daniel explained. He had gotten to know Lance well ever since their first Rift and their talks afterwards. No doubt the young man was deep in thought about the many guilds out there, types of monsters, and pondering what a guild might deem an emergency. Rather than let the young man drown in more questions, Daniel answered some he figured he might have.

"If a Rifter sells it, it means more cash to spend on better equipment. If a Rifter holds onto it, it means they can use it to enter or escape from a Rift." Daniel then explained in depth how a Rifter could use a Guardian-shard to stabilize a Rift temporarily to allow a single Rifter to enter it, or a Rifter could use the shard near the Rift-event to escape.

"So, a really expensive key that only works once?" Lance asked.

"Yeah, something like that. Larger guilds have more of them in store and it can help in the more dangerous Rifts, allowing other Rifters to enter and reinforce the team that is already inside. But enough questions for now. From the looks of things, we are about to finish here," Daniel said as he pointed to the other Rifters, who were nearly done with all their preparations.

The three of them then joined up with the others and stored as much ore as they could inside of their Inventory and backpacks, holding the remainder in their hands. Everyone assumed a position near the Rift-event and hugged it as tightly as possible while the party leader slit the Rift-guardian's throat and retrieved the reddish shard. As soon as the Guardian died, the world rumbled violently, signifying that the event would soon end.

"Get as close as you can. Keep your hands in front of you and roll into a ball when you get out on the other side and feel like falling down," Daniel said to the young men, standing behind them, hoping to reassure them as much as he could before an explosion of black light claimed them all and threw them all back on Earth next to the Rift they had entered.

Daniel skidded to a sudden stop, his feet kicking up small clouds of dust. He shook his head repeatedly, trying to dispel the dizzy spell that had overcome him. As his vision gradually cleared, he spotted Lance and Thomas sprawled on the ground, broad grins on their faces. Thomas playfully flung dirt into the air while Lance, having removed his helmet, ran his fingers through his tousled hair. "You boys doing all right?" Daniel inquired, concern lacing his voice.

"Yeah, we Leveled Up!" the two of them said in unison as their grins turned into laughter.

Daniel listened to the two friends' animated banter, thoughts of relief washing over him. *They're all right,* he silently reassured himself. Lance and Thomas continued to discuss their plans for allocating the three newfound Attributes points and eagerly speculated about the type of Rift they would tackle next.

Breaking into their lively exchange, Daniel said, his voice laced with a hint of amusement, "All right, hold onto your horses, heroes. Let's wrap things up here and head for a well-deserved shower. Thomas, once you're freshened up, make sure to give your family a call and let them know you're back safe and sound. I've had the pleasure of meeting your mother, and I'd rather stay on her good side." Daniel smiled warmly. Extending a helping hand, he guided them to the on-site R.A.M. office, where they would collect their first payment as official Rifters.

They'll be fine.

CHAPTER SIXTEEN

Shaving Accidents

One month ago
February, 14 AR
England, West of Sheffield,
Outside Rift 6

LANCE

As with many Rifts over the last few months, the thick black orb vibrated violently before exploding in the blink of an eye. When the energy settled again, it left a Rift that was smaller than it had been before. Suddenly standing in front of it were several dozen Rifters holding onto a lot of cargo.

"Back!"

"Jesus, I need a pint after that."

"Remind me to book a massage after walking around as hunched as that."

"Why don't you just stop being so freakishly tall?"

Laughter reverberated through the air, intermingling with the bustling symphony of diligent labor that echoed across the grounds of site 25-A1. The triumphant Rifters, now return to Earth after a prolonged absence, seemed determined to make up for lost time, their voices resonating with unrestrained exuberance. Despite their experience with working inside Rifts, the thrill of emerging unscathed was always cause for celebration.

One might have mistaken it for the average construction site if, that is, they ignored the spherical safety net and pulsating black Rift in the background. There was an exterior fence, a small office building, and several on site-cubicles where Rifters could store their clothes, shower, and get dressed in private. The Rift leader, Grace Hicks, ordered everyone back into formation the minute the excitement had lessened.

"All right! Ladies, line up," she said with a commanding voice that oozed authority. She stood in front of the twenty-five Rifters who had just cleared the Rift with her. Grace scanned each of the ten fighters and fifteen porters who she had commanded the last few days, checking them for any injuries. None had gotten seriously injured inside of the Rift, but exiting one could sometimes be even more dangerous.

Her smile spoke volumes about how well this run had been. A smile that was only marred by the two old scars covering the right side of her face. Blood and dirt covered her oak brown hair, making her green eyes stand out even more so. Even after weeks inside the Rift, her focus remained as sharp and as vigilant as ever.

"You guys know the drill by now. Return the company equipment and tools, drop off your items, and try not to drink away all your earnings in one day," she told the Rifters before dismissing them with a wave.

The other Rifters were looking forward to the prospect of getting paid. Even a Level-Two Rift like this could be quite profitable for a new Rifter. Other jobs might have offered substantially more, but it also required basic gear and a deeper understanding of a Rift.

Lance was well aware that a significant portion of their newfound wealth would likely be squandered in various pubs or clubs if Thomas had any say in the matter. While monetary gain hadn't been their primary motivation for leaving behind their nursing careers to embrace the life of Rifters, he couldn't deny his satisfaction with the substantial increase in income.

This had been the sixth Rift that they now had under their belt. In doing so, their confidence in their Skills and Abilities had increased. Their second time inside a Rift had been with Daniel who had pressured them into joining him. Compared with the brutal struggle for survival during their first one, the second had been a walk in the park. They had seen a one-sided battle, Rifters cracking a joke while clearing it. The young men had gotten a crash course in how lethal Rifters could truly be when they made the correct preparations, had decent equipment, and worked together in a group.

The two of them had debated whether to take on more jobs to speed up their Leveling. They ultimately decided not to, rather only taking on one job every few weeks. The time off they would spend training with Daniel, who had taken his role as mentor seriously. Their decision to pace themselves was also to appease Thomas's mother. She had been the most vocal opponent to them becoming Rifters but had eventually given in.

The two friends finished hauling and storing the heavy steel crates they had carried with them. The crates contained spare tools, camping equipment, and empty food and water containers.

"Come, let's drop the items next," Lance said as he lead the way to the side, where they waited in line until it was their turn. Both men held out their hands above large containers as they retrieved items from the Inventory, letting them materialize into this world.

[You have retrieved an item x4]
[You have retrieved an item x9]
[You have retrieved an item x3]

Not a bad haul for this trip, Lance thought as he watched his friend deposit a similar amount as he had. They had partially filled up both containers with lumps of iron and copper ore, coal, and monster scales. Lance had also deposited a size-able chunk of Mana stone. The stone glowed blue when infused with Mana and could hold a small amount of it.

The young men then removed their backpacks from their shoulders and produced several more lumps of iron ore and bits of needle bark they had retrieved from the local vegetation inside the Rift. As he felt the fabric of his own back-pack, he was once again reminded of his luck.

I was fortunate to have kept my backpack on me during the first rift, Lance thought, knowing that modern backpacks were expensive items to purchase. There were cheaper alternatives, but Thomas had decided not to go for that option just yet. This forced the redhead to rent a sturdy R.A.M. backpack each time he went in a Rift. Thomas had insisted that he was saving up for something more practi-cal as well as to financially help his parents. *No doubt that muscle-brain is saving up for a rocket launcher or something like it.*

The aide that was helping them quickly went over the items and registered each of them. The man flashed the occasional glance at a more expensive item, such as the Mana stone and needle bark. When the aide was done, he uploaded all the data to the system and handed both Rifters a printed-out sheet of the transaction.

"All right, lads. Nice haul this time. I take it we can rely on you two gentle-men for another run in the future?" the aide asked, taking photos of the items in the container on his phone before sealing the boxes. Although not a Rifter him-self, Jack Delby was the on-site liaison for R.A.M. Industries.

Before Lance could even reply, Thomas had already beaten him to the punch. "Hell, yeah. You can count on us. I take it we will hear from you within a few weeks, or do you want us on another site?"

"I think it will be this one. If something else comes up, I'll contact you. All right?" Jack asked as he entered their names in the ledger that he kept on his mobile phone.

"Sounds good. Thanks, Jack," the young men replied as they left the liaison to process the items from the other Rifters. They then mingled with some of the other porters and fighters, enjoying hot tea, coffee, and some warm meals that employees were handing out. The food wasn't all that special, but after several days of eating flavorless Rift ration packs, it resuscitated their tastebuds. After their meal, they went to their private changing rooms. Although most of the Rifters looked dirty, covered in dried up blood and direly needed a shower, everyone was in good health and spirits.

[You have cleared this Rift]
[You have been awarded with a Level Up]
[You are now Level 7]
[You have three unspent Attribute points]

Lance ignored the floating message in front of him as he stepped into his own private cubicle. The inventors of the cubicles had designed them so that a truck could easily transport them and drop them off at a site. Inside of these cubicles was a shower, a security locker to store items, and an open spot to get dressed. Lance stepped into the shower for what was to come next.

[You have stored an item in your Inventory 5x]

In a mere second, his R.A.M.-issued armor, helmet, thick overalls, boots, and gloves were gone. Old blood, dirt and grime fell to the shower floor, no longer having any clothing or armor to cling to. Rifters could quickly clean their gear just by storing and retrieving it, since the Inventory system treated the equipment and the filth on it as separate Items.

The equipment he had borrowed from R.A.M. was sturdy, protective, and made from Rift- material. Beyond that, it was as ugly as one could imagine. He was also saving money to buy some decent gear for when they finally reached Level Ten. He figured it would make sense to wait until then, since he could tailor his gear to suit the Class he'd get at that Level. *I wonder what class that'll be?* Lance thought before his friend dragged him out of his contemplations.

"What are you going to spend your new Attribute points on?" Thomas asked, shouting from his room to Lance's, no doubt oblivious to the fact that he was being a nuisance to the other Rifters.

Lance knew it was best to answer him lest the man raise his voice further. "Earplugs . . ."

"What? I couldn't hear you. What are you going to spend the points on?" his friend continued, clearly unconcerned by his volume.

"I don't know," Lance said, ignoring the Level-Up status as he turned on the shower and stepped underneath the stream. He could feel the warm water wash away all the dirt and grime he had collected over several weeks inside the Rift. As the cabin filled with warm steam, the air vent powered up automatically. Even a low-budget cubicle like this felt like a five-star hotel compared to roughing it out in a Rift. The warm water was as relaxing as it was stimulating, allowing his mind to ponder about his recent growth.

Level Seven already. Clearing six Rifts awarded six Level Ups. I gained the other Level Up when we killed those rat monsters the fighters had missed. He clenched his fist and felt the surge of power flow through his veins.

"We're going to a club or pub tonight, right?" Thomas asked, once more interrupting Lance's train of thought.

"Er . . . Sure. I could use a pint," Lance said before he heard the impulsive redhead slap his hand against the steel wall, showing how pleased he was.

"Now we're talking! How about we visit my parents first? Get some decent food and some padding before we tackle a few pints? Who knows, we might meet some impressionable girls who are into Rifters!" Thomas exclaimed despite the fact that they'd just eaten. Anyone could tell that his real plan was to drag Lance on another pub crawl, or worse.

Although Lance enjoyed a pub just as much as anyone, his friend was inexhaustible ever since they had survived their first Rift.

It's probably his way of coping with what has happened to us. At least it's probably better than keeping it all bottled up like I've been doing, Lance thought as he turned off the shower. He then made his way over to his locker to grab a fresh towel and his civilian clothes. After placing them on a small bench, he went over to the mirror to shave. Having been inside a Rift for three weeks, his facial hair had grown into an unkempt patchwork that needed to be trimmed.

A few minutes later, he inspected his now clean-shaven face. He could finally recognize himself again, no longer hidden underneath all the stubble and filth.

A small drop of blood trailed a small line down his chin where he had nicked himself with his razor. He placed a hand on his face and concentrated for a second, making use of his personal Skill, which he had gotten at Level One.

Mend Wounds
[You have used Mend Wounds lvl 1 at the cost of 10 Mana]
[Current Mana 81/95]

A blue light flowed from his fingertips onto his face before it enveloped his entire body in a soft blue healing light. It blinded him briefly before it disappeared. The slight cut on his chin had closed during that time. The Skill couldn't handle larger wounds—only minor cuts and bruises.

His friend had no doubt noticed the flash of light coming through Lance's air vent and could smell an opportunity. "Shaving accident again?"

"Oh, shut up."

Thomas then laughed loudly as his friend had all but confirmed it by telling him off. As soon as the other Rifters heard what was going on, they were quick to join in with the laughter. A few of them even began teasing Lance, asking him if he had hit puberty or if he needed help with tying his shoelaces afterwards.

Although Lance knew what they were doing, he still felt the need to retort. "Remind me to be out of Mana the next time one of you sprains an ankle or wrist while we're in a Rift," he replied, although that only increased the playful laughter coming from the other Rifters. In the end, he himself was laughing the hardest.

Lance had already passed the main gate and was waiting in the car park with a bored expression on his face. After their shower, the lads had made a coin toss. Thomas lost, forcing him to be the one who had to return the clothes, tools, and other equipment they'd rented. Leaning against Thomas's motorcycle, Lance peered upwards and summoned his status menu.

Now, where to spend these? he thought as he looked at the notification that he had three unspent Attribute points.

He had learned much these last few months about his new abilities and how Leveling seemed to work. He had Daniel confirm all of it whenever they spoke, just to be sure of all the facts.

Each Rifter starts out with ten points in each of their Attributes, such as Strength, Wisdom, or Luck.

Each Level Up automatically adds one point to all Attributes.

With each Level Up, a Rifter also gains three points to spend however they want. To tailor a build further.

Daniel had advised them to spend their first few points in Endurance, Strength, and Agility. That way, they would have an easier time working as a porter and be able to better defend themselves in the beginning without relying on Skills.

The last run went well. I had enough speed and energy to get the job done. The only thing that remained difficult was finding the rarer resources. Perhaps I shouldn't increase those further?

Due to him being Level Seven, his base stats were now at Level Sixteen, with Strength, Endurance, and Agility raised to twenty-two from additional points. The Attributes themselves were quite straightforward, with most of them like what you found in a classic RPG game.

I already increased my Endurance by six additional points to take less damage, while increasing my Agility and Strength by the same amount, he recalled. Even with those few points allocated in those three Attributes, he could already notice a sizable difference from how he had been before.

Perception is lacking as of now. Three points should help with my sight, smell, and hearing while in the next Rift, he thought as he mentally agreed to raise his Perception stat three times.

[Perception:] [16] (+3)

It might not be much, but it should help with the little things. Or at the very least, make me a bit more rounded. I think it's better than just dumping everything in Strength as Thomas had been doing as of late. He closed his status menu and noticed his friend making his way towards him. "All done?" Lance asked before the red-head rewarded him with a sly grin while waving a wallet.

"£9700!" Thomas explained, throwing his wallet up in the air only to snatch it again at the last minute. He then gave Lance a fist bump to show how pleased he was.

"Nice! I didn't know you could count that high," Lance said teasingly. Thomas was Level Nine already, due to him having killed more monsters whenever he had the chance. The higher-Level gap also meant that Thomas could hold more items in his Inventory, thus get paid more. Each increase in Level meant another two Inventory slots. There were some porters out there that had a high Level and could carry dozens or even hundreds of items within their Inventory, making a job as a porter quite lucrative. Still, most high-Level Rifters tended to work as freelance fighters and clear Rifts for an even higher cash flow.

Looking pleased, Thomas continued their talk. "Should be enough to buy us a few drinks, right?"

"Again, how much were you planning on drinking tonight?" Lance shook his head at the hangover he would no doubt feel tomorrow morning, or the week after that.

Although Lance was at a lower Level than Thomas, he still got the occasional extra payment after using his "Mend Wound" Skill whenever an injury happened. Healers were a rare breed amongst Rifters. While the "Mend Wound" Skill could only treat minor injuries, it still meant that a person would recover faster. Healthy Rifters meant a Rift would get cleared faster.

Thomas then crammed his wallet back into his pocket before he continued. "You want to stay over at my place afterwards?"

"Sure, if your folks will have me," Lance replied, watching Thomas drag his motorcycle with ease. It was almost comical, as if the man were pulling a child's bicycle, and forcing it to face the right way. The display of strength was all the proof Lance needed to confirm how his friend had been spending his points.

That guy needs to stop spending points in just Strength alone, Lance thought as he grabbed the spare helmet and got on the back of the motorcycle.

Thomas then revved the engine and sped up quickly, leaving the sight of Rift number six behind them.

Status Compendium

Name:	Lance Turner
Level:	7
Class:	Survivor

Attributes

Endurance:	22	**Agility:**	22	**Wisdom:**	16
Strength:	22	**Perception:**	19	**Luck:**	16
Health:	450	**Mana:**	95		
Stamina:	155	**Inventory:**	17		

Skills

Mend Wounds	Lvl 1	Restores minor wounds	+10 Health +4 Stamina	–10 Mana

CHAPTER SEVENTEEN

Ginger Sanctuary

Walker Residence
London, England

LANCE

It was nearly sunset when Thomas drove onto the rocky road, wheels slowly spinning to maintain grip. As the engine slowly died out, Lance jumped off. He then stretched his long legs and arched his back. Riding the motorcycle was fun, yet it did a number on your posture, even for a Rifter. *I should've spent those three points on Endurance.* He had considered using his healing Skill to lessen the soreness in his back, but he knew he'd never hear the end of it if Thomas had anything to say about it.

"Much better!" he commented as he glanced at Thomas, seeing him pull the keys out of the ignition. Although Lance wasn't a motorcycle person, he could understand his friend's fascination with the old Triumph.

According to Thomas, the motorcycle had been custom-made by his father, Jacob, several years ago. The matte black finish and worn brown leather seats complemented one another. Lance watched him as he ran his hand across the machine, briefly massaging it with his fingers. Lance simply rolled his eyes before he interrupted. "You need a minute . . . or a room?"

"Sod off. You don't understand that there is a delicate balance between rider and machine. There is a sense of respect and trust," Thomas said gravely. He got off the bike and threw the keys in the air before snatching them with his other hand. He smiled as he walked towards his friend, who was ready with a retort.

"Right . . . Still, if you treated a girl with the same care and attention that you give your bike, you might make it past three weeks of dating."

"I'll have you know that the record stands at five," his friend replied playfully.

Lance, both bewildered and amused, simply stood there for a minute before he did a slow clap. "I stand corrected. I didn't know I was in the presence of a love-sage."

"You realize I'm at a higher Level, and I could box your ears in, right?"

Lance was sure of two things: Thomas was a loyal friend who would protect him with his life, and Thomas would also be the first one to instigate a playful back-and-forth. Most of the bruises Lance had suffered in his life had resulted from Thomas's idea of friendship. But he couldn't recall a confrontation in his time in London when Thomas wasn't there to back him up or stand in front of him as a shield when necessary.

Lance replied as the two men made their way to the back of the house. "I know, you keep reminding me. Huh, that is new." There were several empty pots discarded left and right and the place smelled of fresh flowers and soil. It was clear to see that the Walker household had been busy gardening the last few days.

Thomas noticed the same and shared his thoughts on it. "I think Mum has another project going on. I swear to God, the amount of her hobbies has only increased since I became a Rifter. Perhaps it is some sort of stress-related thing?"

"Who knows? I'm not a shrink. What was it last time again . . . Bees?" Lance asked, shrugging his shoulders.

Thomas chuckled, the two men stopping near the door as they heard voices from inside the house along with sounds of movement. "God . . . yeah. The bee thing. It ticked dad right off when he got stung a dozen times." The smile on his face hinted at fond memories.

"Well, his fault for marrying a redhead, right? All that rusty red does something to the brain," Lance commented, quickly knocking on the door.

When Thomas clocked the verbal jab from Lance, he was about to move towards him when the door opened and a sturdy woman rushed outside. She pulled the boys into an embrace with enough force that even these young Rifters had no choice but to submit.

"My darlings. My sweet, sweet boys," the woman said, her voice split between maternal strength and dissipating fear. Her bearlike embrace silenced the two friends as they hugged back. Lance's nose caught the scent of rosemary and fresh earth. In his mind, it smelled of home.

The Walker family watched as the two young Rifters devoured what was on their plates. Upon receiving her son's text message that he was returning, Caroline Walker had sprung into action and mobilized the rest of the family. They had warmed up yesterday's lasagne and added some extra pasta. Thomas's father had retrieved a few cold beers and set the table as per his wife's instructions.

Next to Caroline was Kate, Thomas's older sister, and his younger brother, Oliver. Both siblings had the same auburn hair as Thomas, and their eyes were bright green, a color that simply demanded one's attention. Although a shade darker than the bright red hair of their mother, it was unmistakable where the children had gotten most of their genes.

Caroline smiled as Thomas finished his plate, looking quite pleased with himself. Lance had tapped out after his third serving, now massaging a stomach filled to the brim. "Do you boys need anything else? Dessert?" Caroline asked, seeing Thomas's eyes light up at the word "pudding" before he figured out just how full he was.

"Perhaps later, Mum. I'm beyond full. God! I needed this," Thomas said honestly as he leaned backwards into his seat.

Lance nodded at that, agreeing with his friend. Although the GRRO took care of the supplies and rations, the meals they provided were neutral in terms of taste, nothing compared to a mother's home-cooked meal. "Thanks for making us a feast, Mrs. Walker."

Hearing the boy's approving words, Caroline smiled even wider. She took pride in running a tight ship and the least she could do was to whip up a little feast for the returning heroes.

"Oh, think nothing of it. It is just some leftovers and something I made in a hurry. But, dear, I wish I could find out sooner when you two are done with . . . work," she said. Everyone knew she hated the words "Rift" and "Rifters." She had told her son how proud she was of what he was doing and how he was helping people, but it was no doubt hard for her to accept him fighting literal monsters.

Lance could only imagine what the poor woman had been through when she had seen the state of her son in the hospital so many months ago. From what Lance had learned, the family had first been told that Thomas would likely be dead, like the others. Weeks later, the miraculous news arrived that they had both survived. *The rollercoaster of emotions must've been awful for them,* Lance thought, feeling guilty that he had agreed to become a Rifter with Thomas, putting the Walker family through even more worry and uncertainty.

Thomas nodded reassuringly. "I would if I could, Mum. But it's hard to know when we clear the bugger and how long it takes to mine all that we need—"

"That and reception inside the Rift is horrible. I mean, our mobile phone providers should really do something about that," Lance interrupted. He smiled as he heard a soft chuckle coming from Thomas's father.

Caroline simply shook her head before she continued, "You boys . . . Even after all you've been through." Her eyes met them with a look only a worried mother could produce.

"Caroline, let them be. At their age, they're still idiots and not open to reason. Remember how foolish we were back then," Jacob mediated, letting the young men have a little freedom.

Caroline's gaze shifted towards her husband, letting him feel the weight of it. "I hardly think we can compare their situation with ours, Jacob."

"You're right, as always. Still, let the boys be idiots when they're home and safe. You know how I was back in the army at the beginning of my career," Jacob replied, standing up and groaning as he supported his lower back. Afterwards, he went to fetch the young men and himself another beer.

The youngest of the family looked anxious, as if he had been waiting until dinner was over before he could bombard the Rifters with questions. "Is what Thomas said last time true?"

"About what?" Lance asked, seeing the bright-faced Oliver nearly trembling with curiosity. He looked a great deal like Thomas, and he was already showing the same stocky shoulders. *The Walker family sure does build sturdy men,* Lance thought as he looked at the boy.

"Thomas said that he fought off a troll last time he went inside the Rift. Was that true?" Oliver asked, wonder in his voice.

Lance immediately glanced at Thomas, seeing his blank expression before he exploded in laughter. "The closest thing to a troll Thomas faced was when he last looked in the mirror."

At that, the family joined Lance in laughter, Thomas grinning before he replied in a grandiose manner, "You see, Oliver, we Rifters are a tough breed. The world needs us to be. Sadly, this toughness has robbed us of our once handsome looks." Thomas held up his hand as if he was preaching the truth from his own personal gospel.

His father snorted at the comment while his mother placed a hand on his cheek at which point Thomas's older sister replied, "I don't think that rule applies to all Rifters. I know of at least one of them that is quite attractive." Kate gave Lance a knowing smile. It wasn't the first time she'd flirted with him, but Lance still turned a shade closer to red when he felt her lingering gaze.

Thomas immediately countered, pointing his finger at his sister. "Dammit! No one wants to hear those kinds of things from you! We just came back from a Rift and the last thing that Lance needs is to meet something even worse than a monster."

"Oh, stop being such a prude. I was only joking," Kate commented as she shifted her gaze towards her brother. The two of them frequently argued, with Kate's quick wit usually deciding the outcome. Although she was eager for a verbal confrontation, it didn't change the fact that she had immediately left her flat and raced home when she heard her brother had cleared another Rift. Still, Kate would no doubt have denied that fact had Thomas ever found out.

"Hilarious, sis. How about you do us all a favor and throw yourself off a bridge?" Thomas barked. Kate knew just which of his buttons to push.

She sighed as she gave him a dramatic slow clap. "Oh, what a brilliant retort, Thomas. You're lucky there isn't an IQ requirement for becoming a Rifter."

"Either you think you're a comedian, or you think calling me stupid is a wise idea," her brother replied, leaning closer and using his size to his advantage.

"Well, do you see me sitting on a stage with a mic in my hand?" Kate countered, giving him a smile that simply dared him to take another step.

Thomas was still slowly moving towards his sister before his mother interrupted, suggesting that the girls and Oliver go back to the kitchen to clean the dishes.

Thomas's father had been mostly quiet throughout all of it, sipping his beer and enjoying the chaotic nature of the household. Despite the bickering and the name-calling, anyone could feel the layers of love woven throughout the home. Lance could've sworn he heard Jacob whisper something about "combustible redheads."

Jacob then addressed the lads when it was just the three of them. "Are you boys all right?" Jacob's gaze focused on his son, as if truly seeing him in that moment. It was hard not to be honest when Thomas's father looked right at you.

Jacob had served in the army for many years before his back had gone out. The man had seen first-hand the aftermath of Rifts and the horrors it forced upon survivors. He knew better than anyone in this house what the boys might have been facing, having seen footage of Rift outbreaks.

Thomas nodded before he spoke. "Yeah, Dad. We're okay. The last run went well. The biggest danger we faced was Lance's snoring."

"Sir, you can trust the group we've been running with. We all work well together," Lance said, putting his bottle of beer on the table and watching as Thomas and his father had a moment with one another. He loved seeing these types of moments and knew just how lucky his friend was to have a family like his.

Finally, Jacob nodded as he placed a hand on his son's cheek and patted it gently. "Thomas, you know that we only want one thing from you, right?" Jacob asked, his features softening a bit.

"Yeah, I know, Dad. Just come back home," Thomas answered with a grin before he nudged his old man in the rib playfully but still allowing his father to feel the strength he now possessed. It was to show his dad that he was no longer the crying mess they'd found in the hospital a few months prior.

Jacob smiled, acknowledging his son before shifting his attention towards Lance. "And the same goes for you, Lance. God only knows why you befriended our boy, but we're grateful for it. You'll always be welcome at our house. You understand?"

"I do. Thanks for that. It means a lot," Lance said honestly. The sentiment hit him harder than Jacob realized. After his mother had died, the Walkers had been the closest thing to family he had.

"Good to hear. Now, onto more important questions. When are you going to ask my daughter out on a date?" Jacob asked before the house exploded with commotion and noise, Thomas causing most of it.

[You have retrieved an item]

"Really! I can have this?" Oliver asked Lance, looking down at the strange, glowing rock that the teen was now holding in his hands. Fifteen minutes had passed since dinner and the three young men were now relaxing in Thomas's room. Oliver's emerald gaze admired the blue light coming off the Mana stone. Lance infused it with even more Mana, increasing the light it was giving off. It would slowly lose its charge over time, like an inefficient battery.

"I said it was a gift, did I not?" Lance said, seeing the young man tremble with excitement. He liked him a great deal. Oliver had all of Thomas's positive traits sans the blunt personality.

"Bloody hell! Dad!" Oliver yelled as he rushed out of the door and down several flights of stairs.

Thomas smiled for a moment before he faced Lance. "You know you're going to spoil the little bugger, right?"

"Oh, I know. But can you imagine the look on his friends' faces when he shows up to class with a Mana stone?" Lance asked, remembering how in awe he had been when he had first collected them in a Rift. The blue ones weren't all that rare. Still, a little chunk like the one he had given Oliver would be worth at least a few hundred pounds.

"Could you have imagined how different our childhood would've been if we had one of those?" Thomas asked, imagining the outcome of such a thing.

"Well, having a Rifter as an older brother doesn't hurt either," Lance replied as his friend snorted. He knew how proud Oliver was Thomas. It was hard not to want to live up to those expectations. Thomas then stood up as he closed his laptop, having sent a bunch of emails to Lance's phone.

"Really? Even more?" Lance asked, sighing as he felt his phone vibrate several more times. Each mail would no doubt hold a number of music files. It was one of Thomas's greatest irritations concerning Lance since they had become Rifters. Lance had been lucky enough to have made it out with his phone somewhat intact, but he barely used it.

"I figured it was high time you got some decent music. If I have to go through one more Rift listening to that same album you have on your phone, I swear to God I'm going to throw you through a Level-Twenty Rift," Thomas threatened as he rummaged through his closet to find some clean socks.

"Come on. It can't be that bad, right?" Lance asked, both himself and Thomas.

"Lance, a senile cat with rabies has better taste in music than you do," Thomas explained. A few seconds later, they could hear Jacob knocking on the door before opening it.

"You boys finished applying your makeup or whatever you youngsters do now?" Thomas's father asked as his son quickly rewarded him with two middle fingers. Shaking his head, he then continued, "So, where am I dropping you two miscreants off tonight? And I take it you will stay over tonight, Lance?"

"The usual, Dad," Thomas replied as a matter of fact.

Lance nodded. "Yeah, that would be great, sir."

The two friends grabbed their phones, wallets, and did the last-minute hairstyle check in front of the mirror. The latter took too much time, so Jacob intervened again.

"No amount of hair gel can fix the two of you. Now, how about you boys head out while the night is still young?" Jacob asked, clapping his hands before he pointed at the stairs to get the young men to move.

One by one, they passed him and went downstairs, Jacob smiling as they did so. The man was glad to have Thomas back under his roof. He closed the door behind him as followed them downstairs, no doubt hoping that he'd have a thousand more of these encounters with his son and Lance.

CHAPTER EIGHTEEN

Kebab, Beer, and Death Threats

Mr. Chang's Kebab
London, England

LANCE

The kebab shop smelled of meat, spices, and just a hint of sweat. Time had stained the once-sparkling white floor tiles gray and dull. There were a dozen benches and tables inside the shop, supporting groups of people eating a less-than-healthy late-night snack.

Lance watched Thomas continue to dig into his meal, stuffing his face with kebab, potatoes, salad, and plenty of garlic sauce. Just the idea of eating again was almost enough to nauseate Lance.

Observing his friend's wide grin and the fork poised for yet another indulgent bite, Lance couldn't help but shake his head, a hint of disgust and discomfort nestling in the pit of his own stomach. "You know you're a pig, right?"

Thomas simply gave a food-stained smile before he replied, "A man has got to eat. Like Mum said, I'm a growing lad."

"Horizontally perhaps. We just had an enormous meal with your family forty minutes ago and a smaller one at the Rift before that," Lance said, although the stubborn redhead didn't answer. The man simply took another bite before he added some more sauce and destroyed the delicate balance between food and garlic. Knowing that attempting to change the ravenous entity that was Thomas would be a futile endeavor, Lance shifted his gaze towards the television.

The quality of the old device was horrendous. It surprised Lance that it even displayed color at all. He could still make out the commercials that were being shown on the TV. Watching them was clearly a waste of brain cells, but he figured it was better than losing even more of them by watching Thomas.

Most of the commercials were about beauty products, perfumes, or cars. The one that particularly stood out was for a new beverage that was being promoted by a well-known British Rifter. The woman was ranked somewhere in the top 200 in the UK and she held a position within a good guild.

Lance shook his head at what he was seeing as he felt Thomas's elbow nudge him in the ribs. "Come on, it's not that bad. Professional athletes do it too. Why not Rifters?"

"Because athletes don't fight monsters or store items in the ether, or whatever is linked to our Inventory system," Lance replied, shifting his gaze from the television to his friend, who had finished his plate and was looking quite pleased with himself.

With a sly grin, Thomas then leaned closer and spoke, his garlic-tainted breath doing unspeakable things to Lance's nostrils. "People like symbols. It can be a logo on your shoes, a celebrity you fancy, or an athlete you wish you could be like. Sure, it's just a money grab, but that is the way things are. Why shouldn't Rifters have a slice of that pie as we—" Thomas suddenly stopped talking as Lance's eyes went wide, knowing full well how that reptile brain of his worked.

Desperately, Lance tried to stop his friend. "Thomas, don't—"

"Pie! Lance, I want some pie," the redhead demanded, interrupting Lance as his smile widened. He then jumped out of his seat and made his way over towards the glass cabinet housing the assortment of desserts. Lance shook his head before returning his attention to the television. The commercials were over now, and the regular news program was on.

At the bottom of the screen, Lance could see the lines of text slowly crawling from right to left. The news ticker gave information about the stock market going down, the French president having to answer to parliament, and the weather forecast, as well as an update of a Rifter who the Japanese government had finally caught and imprisoned.

Lance had heard of this incident but only vaguely. The man had been a high-ranking Rifter who had gone rogue and raised a horde of the undead to terrorize one of Japan's many islands. A force of skilled Rifters had taken out the horde and subdued the man.

His Class, Necromancer, was a rare one that allowed a user to revive corpses temporarily into undead minions. Rifters classed as Necromancer could be great boons inside the Rift because they could fight numbers with numbers. But they had a bad rep because of working with corpses and, of course, situations like the one that occurred in Japan. This convicted Rifter worsened the Necromancer Class's reputation even further.

"Are you ready?" Thomas called out.

Lance blinked as he spotted Thomas standing next to him, licking some pie crumbs from his fingers. Sensing a change in the man, Lance figured it would be best to find out what the plan was. "Yeah, I'm ready. We were going to take it easy tonight, right? A few pubs?"

"Of course. Nothing too fancy. I promise," the redhead said, no doubt lying through his teeth as he led Lance out of Mr. Chang's place.

The outside air relieved Lance's nostrils of the pungent odor of garlic. His sharpened senses could now identify the unique scents that lingered in a city such as London. It still amazed him how much more of the city he could experience through his senses the more his Perception increased. He could only imagine what a person such as Daniel experienced with a Perception in the triple digits.

He inhaled once more to remove the last of the garlic taint before he followed his friend into the night.

"You know you're lucky, right?" Thomas asked a few minutes later as he looked over his shoulder and spotted Lance browsing through the gallery on his phone. Most of the pictures he had taken were of the monsters they had encountered in their previous Rift. Most were harder to identify because of the injuries they had sustained during the fights. Only a few still had their features intact.

A working mobile phone that someone could bring into a Rift was a rare commodity, so Lance was indeed lucky. "I know, you keep reminding me every day. Jealous?" Lance asked, although he already knew the answer.

"Hell yeah. So, are you going to send the pictures to the GRRO or sell them to an information broker?" Thomas asked, watching his friend zoom in on a picture of a small rat-like creature. They had faced several of these in the past. Although still a monster, they were a minor threat and wouldn't be all that interesting to other Rifters.

Someone could usually sell pictures or recordings of monsters to brokers. Rifters that wanted to prepare for a new Rift would usually pay a premium to learn more about the monsters inside that Rift if the GRRO didn't have full documentation of it.

"I doubt it will be worth more than a few pounds," Lance said as he opened the GRRO app on his phone. Through this app, he had access to dozens of features and thousands of documents. He quickly filtered through the known list of monsters and found that there were already hundreds of pictures and documentation about the rat-like monster he had captured on camera. "Perhaps even less than that. Do you think your little brother would like a picture?" Lance proposed as the two men slowly made their way further down the street.

"The little brat is obsessed with Rifters. So, he'd love a picture. Mum would probably have your hide if she found out," Thomas said. Cleary, he had a deep understanding of the fury his mother could unleash.

"Good point," Lance countered, not wanting to chance it.

"So, what did you think of the music selection I emailed?" Thomas asked, as the two of them crossed the street and passed a taxi.

"You mean the torrent of spam? I'll check it out later. Besides, I don't see the point."

"Dude, it's outdated and boring. Who even listens to classical?" Thomas replied, doing his best to educate his musically stunted friend.

"Those are fighting words, my friend," Lance said as the two of them rounded the corner and spotted the nightclub that they were heading to. Thomas had heard about it from his sister and wanted to check it out. Apparently, it was hard to get into. Judging from the line of people outside, this seemed accurate.

"Speaking of music! Come on," Thomas said, playfully jabbing his friend to get him to follow.

"That queue looks way too long. We could still head back to our usual place. All right?" Lance asked as he realized just how long he'd need to stand in line.

"I'll be fine. Besides, I'd rather not spend my first night back on Earth drinking lukewarm beer in a boring old pub. Come on, you promised me a night of drinking," Thomas said as he applied more pressure until his friend finally caved. "I guess . . ."

"That's the spirit. Besides . . . I have a plan to get us in," Thomas said with a childish grin as he led the way towards the nightclub, passing the long line of people who were waiting outside and stopping in front of the bouncer, casually asking him to open the door for them. Some onlookers were curious, others simply annoyed at the arrogant two men who looked like your average blokes on a night out. Still, Thomas oozed confidence when the bouncer asked whether they were on today's guest list, leaning in close.

With his right hand, he opened a button on his shirt to reveal the Rift-stone in his chest. "I was under the assumption that this club treated my people decently. Was I misinformed?" Thomas asked, enjoying the look of shock on the bouncer's face. His soft smile turned into a wolfish grin as the bouncer quickly stepped to the side, allowing the two men in. Moments later he alerted the staff through his earpiece that the VIP room would have to make space for two Rifters.

Lance was still shaking his head as he followed his friend inside, praying that the redhead wouldn't make an even bigger scene inside.

"Come on, do the thing!" the girls requested, watching Thomas with anticipation. He got up, after a show of hesitation, grabbed a chair with both hands, and lifted it with ease. The girl who was sitting in the chair at the time giggled with glee. Even at a Level considered abysmally low compared to more experienced Rifters, anyone could see that he was no ordinary human.

Lance observed from his seat. Surrounding the two of them were several men and women who had enough social credits to be allowed entry in the VIP section. Lance thought he recognized at least one actor and a singer. Still, all eyes were on his friend at that moment.

Thomas, you're just one step away from performing in the circus, Lance thought, sipping his beer and leaning backwards on the sofa. He ignored the loud dance music in the background as he focused on the conversation his friend was having with a blonde woman.

"Does it hurt?"

"Hmm? Oh, the Rift-shard?" Thomas asked her as he glanced downwards. Within the blink of an eye, he opened another button to better show off the white crystal-like shard embedded in the center of his chest.

"It does, but you get used to it," Thomas said, pretending it wasn't a big deal. All lies, of course. The shard had appeared in their chests the moment they had were thrown into their first Rift. It had been a painless process, and most of the survivors had only noticed it after some time. It didn't hurt or cause discomfort beyond the skin around it itching when they got near a Rift. "I'm sorry if the scars might bother you."

Bloody hell, mate. Could you smear it on even thicker? Lance thought, grinning as he finished his beer and placed it on the table.

Ignoring the first Rift that they had been in, Lance and Thomas had only been performing porter jobs. Tagging along with other Rifters to clear Level-Two or Level- Three Rifts. A small group of regular Rifters could clear these on their own. Their group usually had about twenty lower-Leveled Rifters who did the mining while ten higher-Leveled Rifters ran security. It was pretty much overkill, but they could clear out a Rift quickly with minimal or even no injuries.

The only actual fight we've been in was squashing those rat things. And even then, the idiot had felt grossed out because of the way they were wriggling on the walls, Lance thought, remembering the way Thomas had acted afterwards.

Still, the people with them in the VIP section wouldn't have been able to tell whether a Rifter was just a beginner or a veteran of a hundred Rifts. Thomas was counting on their naivete. Rifters could sometimes feel out another Rifter's strength, but it was hard to measure properly and more akin to guessing. The only accurate way of knowing was either to have it measured by a machine the GRRO used, by a Rifter who had a specific Class allowing such a feat, or when there was an enormous gap between the two Rifters' Levels.

This could've been fun, were it not for everyone staring at us, Lance thought, noting several individuals looking at them from a distance. No doubt there was a mixture of curiosity, jealousy, and resentment among them. He couldn't blame them, seeing as a Rifter was such a curious thing. It wasn't something you trained to become or inherited. It was a pure chance of ending up in an Initial Rift and surviving it.

"It could have been worse," he said to himself as he slowly got up, signaling to his friend that he was going to get them another beer. Years of drinking together had created a perfect non-verbal system between the two of them regarding ordering drinks.

In some places, people treated Rifters with scorn, linking them to the horrors of the Rift itself. Other, scarier places forced Rifters into work camps, charged to clear Rifts all at the whims of a despotic government, with the threat of imprisonment or worse hovering over their families and loved ones.

At least here we can still have fun, earn cash, and spend it on ridiculous things such as staying in a VIP section of a club, Lance reflected as he made his way over the bar, evading the occasional person who nearly bumped into him on the way.

Seconds turned into minutes as Lance waited for the bartender to notice him, rather than help each attractive woman who wanted to order first. *This is going to take all night,* he thought, his irritation slowly building until he finally had enough. He steeled his mind and activated his Skill.

Mend Wounds
[You have used Mend Wounds lvl 1 at the cost of 10 Mana]
[Current Mana 85/95]

Instantly, a blueish light radiated from Lance, making him temporarily stand out like a sore thumb. Those closest to him were still adjusting their eyes while those further away glanced over, shock on their faces. The startled bartender blinked a few times before he recovered and put two and two together. The man instantly dropped what he was doing and rushed over to help the Rifter.

"Two beers," Lance ordered, placing a few pounds on the bar, and waited for his drinks. He felt anything but calm at that moment, not fully understanding why he had done that. It was so out of character for him. Still, it proved quite effective.

Nearly everyone close to him continued to stare, fascinated by the unknown. He could understand why, remembering the same feelings he had when he had first met a Rifter in the hospital. It felt weird to have the roles reversed. Compared to his friend's display of strength, Lance figured what he had just done was far worse. Anyone could understand raw strength or speed, but to illuminate yourself like a blue candle . . . No doubt the number of eyes on Thomas and himself would only increase.

Dammit . . . I'm slowly turning more and more into Thomas, he thought, grabbing the beers when they arrived before making his way back to the VIP section. He handed one of them to his grinning friend, knowing full well what would come next.

"Nice," Thomas said, complimenting his introverted friend for finally showing off a little. He had seen Lance's little show. It was hard not to, seeing as he had lit up like a silly blue torch.

Unlike the eager redhead, Lance preferred not to shout to the world that he was a Rifter. "Sod off," he said, suppressing a smile before knocking his beer bottle against that of his friend, creating a satisfying sound before both started drinking again.

All right, perhaps I could learn to enjoy the benefits of being a Rifter, he thought, taking another sip before he decided they should hit the dance floor after their beers. "Hey, do you want to—" Lance stopped, seeing his friend staring at his phone with a frightened, pale expression. The man's mouth was slightly ajar as the phone gradually slipped from his hand.

With the mobile now on the table between them, Lance could read what was on the screen, seeing an open text message.

Talk and training, starting tomorrow at 7. Same place as always. Looking forward to seeing your progress. —Daniel.

Now Lance understood why his friend had turned pale, as he suddenly felt the same. That feeling increased as his own phone vibrated. He knew Daniel had sent him the same message.

"He's going to kill us," Thomas said.

CHAPTER NINETEEN

Educational Bruises

Three weeks ago
February, 14 AR
GRRO Training Facility
London, England

LANCE

Two figures were sprinting and jumping over obstacles within Training Room Twelve. The large chamber housed many obstacles to get over, under, or go through to better prepare a Rifter for an actual Rift. Artificial rain, temperature, fog, lighting—all of it was available to re-create different climates and weather.

"Faster," Daniel said, watching the two men from the sidelines. His left hand cupped his right upper arm, massaging where the arm abruptly stopped.

"Thomas, pick up the pace," he ordered as he observed the two young men on the obstacle course, throwing themselves over logs, climbing up ropes, tackling heavy sandbags to the ground, or kicking them away.

Daniel watched Thomas force a heavy sandbag to the side with one kick. His Strength-fueled frame allowed the young man to bulldoze through the course. The added power even increased his speed, as his strong legs allowed him to propel himself forwards with great momentum.

As Daniel sifted his gaze to the side, he spotted Lance scaling a wall with ease. He could see his increased Agility and Perception at play, with the lad instinctually knowing where he could find the best grip or at what angle he should plant his legs.

He smiled softly as he observed the progress the two friends had made these last few months. The lads had transformed from nurses into capable porters. As he suspected, the experience of clearing minor Rifts had steeled their resolve and restored their confidence.

"Lance . . . Are you letting Thomas beat you again?" Daniel inquired as he watched Lance throw his sandbag to the side. Everyone could see just how much further Thomas had kicked his own. It was clear to Daniel where the redhead had been spending his points. No doubt Daniel was already blaming Dieter for the bad influence he had had on Thomas.

"And time!" Daniel shouted as he stopped his stopwatch and waited for the two young men to join him. He handed each of them a bottle of water before scribbling down his notes on a pad.

Both Lance and Thomas had taken off their shirts and were wringing out large amounts of sweat. They'd changed a lot over the course of the past six months. Thomas's strong build had gained more definition, rippling with primal energy. Lance's lanky frame had bulked up and, coupled with his tall stature, had an explosive element to it. There were bigger and more impressive individuals out there, but the progress they had made in a relatively short span of time was significant.

"So . . . how did we do?" Lance asked Daniel, panting as he finished his water.

Daniel checked the numbers once more before he replied, "Faster than last time. Still, you guys have room for improvement. Next up, the weapons room," Daniel said, leading the tired men there. Like last time, they would have to use many sorts of weapons and tools. Some days Daniel trained them with blades or blunt weaponry, other times they were at the shooting range, using pistols, rifles, or bows. Thomas was usually most excited when it came to firearms.

Although there were a lot of Rifters who used firearms, most preferred melee weaponry, bows or crossbows. Daniel had demonstrated this for them a few weeks ago, letting them see just how much further an arrow could travel through a few sandbags compared to a bullet, even without using his Skills. It was a good lesson in how every weapon had its pros and cons.

Beyond that, guns rarely synergized with a Rifter's Skills, limiting their usefulness when facing tougher foes. Daniel had illustrated this by imbuing both a bullet and a throwing dagger with his lightning Skill before using them on a wooden log. The bullet did decent damage, but the dagger utterly wrecked the wooden log. It was a far better tool at channeling Daniel's Skill.

Daniel wanted them to have as much experience as possible with various types of weaponry. This was to help them learn which weapon suited them best, and to keep them flexible and adaptive. It had made sense to the young men. No single weapon was suitable for every type of monster. Sometimes you needed a cutting tool or a blunt weapon. Other times, you wanted a ranged weapon on your side.

Today it was throwing weaponry. Daniel instructed them how best to throw knives, axes, and bits of rock while jumping or moving left and right. Daniel awarded each successful throw with a thumbs up, while rewarding each miss with another set of push-ups.

"Don't overthink it. Your brain will follow your eyes through experience and practice," Daniel coached them while occasionally showing his own throws. He wasn't a fan of the throwing axe but knew the benefit of learning how to throw various types of weapons.

They spent two hours like this, with the men learning how to throw in a straight line, in an arc, and even how to ricochet a shot to hit something behind cover. When the timer rang once more, they could see Daniel smiling.

Thomas was the first one to take the bait. "What? Why the cheerful expression?"

"I'm proud of you, lads. So, I figured you have earned a treat," Daniel said. But Thomas and Lance grew more and more uncomfortable the longer they stared at his smile. It was almost an instinctual response, like when prey could sense a predator nearby.

This isn't good, Lance thought, as he felt the need to back off.

Daniel ignored their reactions as he placed a hand on Thomas's shoulder and squeezed it softly. "The treat is a sparring match with yours truly," he said, still smiling at the redhead before his left hand suddenly shot out to the side, gripping Lance by the neck when he made a run for it.

A while later, the air was thick with the smell of sweat and the sounds of bodies hitting the training mat. Daniel had planted himself in the center, his one arm held outwards in an offensive position as he glanced at the two battered Rifters who he had knocked down mere moments before.

"Ever heard of pulling your punches?" Thomas asked as he rubbed his jaw, slowly climbing to his feet. Lance followed afterwards, sporting a bloody nose and a nice bruise on his temple. This was due to Daniel's "generosity;" he had knocked both men on their rears within a few seconds.

"I have. And I was," Daniel answered the redhead before he shifted his gaze towards the moaning Lance, seeing the man wipe away a bit of blood.

After the beating he had just taken, Lance was keen to share his thoughts. "I think Dieter might be a gentler soul compared to you. You realize you outrank us by quite a bit, right?" he said, hoping to get a reaction from the older man. *Even holding back, he outpaces us with ease,* Lance thought.

Daniel shook his head at the young Rifters. It was true. There was a vast difference in terms of ability and experience, but that was precisely why he was training them. To get them used to fighting more dangerous enemies. Far better to endure a brutal training than to be ill-prepared in the field. "Come on, lads. Youth is on your side. Not to mention a second arm." He flexed his muscles, an amused expression on his face, as he signaled that they should try again.

Lance thought about ways to beat his more experienced foe as he watched him get back into a fighting stance. *Although Daniel said his Class relied mostly on Agility and Perception, he still hits like a truck. We need to try something else,* he thought as he struggled to plan their next move.

"Thomas, you got this," Lance said, getting his friend's attention.

"I got this?" Thomas said, his head snapping towards Lance's.

"Yes."

"Are you mental? I'd have more luck fighting a pack of gorillas. You saw how he literally tossed me around like a rag doll, right?" Thomas exclaimed.

Lance held up his hands to calm his friend. He had to get him on board. "Yeah, but I think—"

"Lance . . . He threw me around the room like he was my stepdad, and I'd just spilt his beer. What do you think I could do?" Thomas asked him, as he circled around Daniel. He could see a dozen of potential openings but knew full well that all of them were traps.

Lance recognized the necessity of sparking Thomas's determination; without it, the red-haired warrior would approach the task half-heartedly. Leaning closer, Lance planted a seed of possibility. "His ego. Think about it, Thomas. It's his vulnerable spot. The two of us haven't even reached Level Ten, but he's in the triple digits. How do you reckon he'll react when one of us manages to land even a single?" Lance artfully manipulated the conversation, skillfully selecting the right buttons to push in order to stir up his friend's resolve.

Daniel relaxed his posture and let out an amused chuckle as he tried to pitch in. "Well, a sense of pride—"

Thomas's interruption was swift, his blue eyes alight with a surge of newfound vigor. "Yes! He'd feel bad, perhaps even shameful. Imagine if Dieter or his guild discovered the truth. Him losing to us would be akin to losing a battle against toddlers, wouldn't it?" Thomas's words conveyed a glimmer of exhilaration, reigniting Lance's energy as his mind focused on landing just a single blow.

"I believe you're all failing to grasp the purpose of our sparring sessions," Daniel remarked, his tone laced with admonishment. But before his words could fully sink in, the two young men abruptly lunged at him from opposite directions. Despite their inferior abilities, their teamwork was spot-on.

Lance executed a swift leg sweep, aiming to destabilize their opponent, while Thomas focused on attacking Daniel's right shoulder. Thomas even activated his personal Skill, Bullrush, temporarily boosting his Strength but draining his Stamina at an alarming rate.

Still, Daniel maintained a calm posture as an amused smirk appeared on his face, displaying both mirth and pride. He then lifted his leg to dodge the sweep while ramming his shoulder into Thomas's chest. Without missing a beat, he kicked Lance backwards, sending both men down onto the training mat again.

Wincing, Thomas struggled to his feet, his hand gingerly touching the tender spot beneath his eye. "All right, I felt that one." He had face-planted the floor with force, leaving a nasty bruise on his face. He didn't doubt that it would swell and transform over time, showcasing an array of hues.

Daniel noticed the newly formed bruise and checked in with him. "Are you all right there?" he asked, genuinely concerned. He was rough with them during training, but he was always careful not to go too far.

"Yeah, thankfully, my face cushioned my fall. So, nothing vital got hit," Thomas explained, casting a glance at his best friend, who was still dry heaving on the mat. It wasn't the first time Lance had experienced such discomfort today, and it certainly wouldn't be the last. A soft jab from Daniel could knock the wind out of someone. A kick was a different kind of agony.

Thomas watched his friend's gradual recovery for a few seconds before he spoke to Daniel. "You know you're a freak, right? Two on one and you look like you're as fatigued as if you had been doing a crossword puzzle."

"Come on now, lads. This is good practice for the two of you. You need to understand your limits and know how to spot a trap or a dangerous situation," Daniel said to the men as he watched Lance slowly getting up again, groaning as he did so. "But we can stop this any time you want. I'll never force you two to become Rifters—"

"Not a chance," Thomas interjected, his eyes ablaze with determination. "Lance and me, we're destined for greatness as Rifters. And mark my words, before this day is through, you'll be tapping out on this mat."

A surprise might work, Lance thought, forcing himself to appear as calm as possible when he addressed Daniel. He felt anything but fine, but he could at least breathe again. He knew Daniel would give him a few minutes to recover. "You're right. We still have much to learn from you. Thanks for doing this for us," he said as he walked towards his friend. Lance noticed the bruise that Thomas was sporting as he placed a hand on him. He then activated his Skill.

Mend Wounds
[You have used Mend Wounds lvl 1 at the cost of 10 Mana]
[Current Mana 17/95]

A blueish light slowly flowed from his fingertips into Thomas, covering his entire body in a soft blue glow, almost to the point of it blinding him, before it vanished. Once the light had faded from his body, his bruises had also lessened.

"Thanks," his friend said with a grin as he felt the soreness leave his body as he suddenly experienced renewed vigor.

Once again, Lance was glad to have gotten this Skill. It made sense according to Daniel, considering Lance's background as a nurse, his affinity for the healing arts seamlessly aligned with his personality. The path of a Healer or Cleric seemed increasingly likely for Lance as he approached Level Ten, given the fact that the initial Skill bestowed upon an individual often hinted at their eventual Class.

"No worries. I'm glad that my Skill is useful. Here, this is the least I can do to thank you," Lance said as he held out his hand and walked towards Daniel, placing his hand on the man's chest in a nonthreatening manner as he used his Skill again.

Mend Wounds
[You have used Mend Wounds lvl 1 at the cost of 10 Mana]
[Current Mana 7/95]

As with Thomas, a soft blue light enveloped Daniel's form, its gentle radiance weaving through his body, mending minor injuries and alleviating discomfort. Lance's Skill only possessed the ability to mend minor injuries, but it also offered temporary respite from the persistent infection coursing through Daniel's veins.

Now! Lance thought as he quickly reacted.

As Daniel was about to thank Lance, an undercurrent of unease prickled his senses, his keen hearing attuned to the abrupt shift in Lance's movements. The cause remained shrouded in Daniel's conflicted thoughts as he instinctively recoiled, his body swaying backward in response. A faint whistling sound brushed past him, barely audible yet laden with menace.

A second later, the blue light vanished from Daniel's body, along with the blinding effect. In an instant, he realized that, in the time that the healing effect had taken hold, Lance had used it to try a sneak attack. The young man had been healing with his right and going for an uppercut with his left, banking on the disorienting side effect to secure the upper hand.

A malevolent smile crept across Daniel's face, an amalgamation of pride and the need to remind Lance of his place as the teacher. In a fleeting moment, Daniel's body blurred into motion as he invoked his Dash Skill, vanishing from Lance's sight. Abruptly, he reappeared by the young man's side, his left fist finding its mark in Lance's midsection, launching him upwards with such force that the impact sent him careening into the ceiling before bouncing back down.

The last thing Lance heard was a cacophony of comical sounds—his own body colliding with the ceiling and then the floor, accompanied by Thomas's piercing shriek.

"You killed him! You bloody killed him!"

"Here you go," Daniel said a while later, handing Lance another ice pack to ease his throbbing abdomen; meanwhile Thomas was nursing a black eye. "The two of you are really shaping up."

"Well, I feel somewhat bent out of shape," Thomas retorted while his friend simply groaned in agreement, feeling the ice soothe his pain.

Lance's mind wandered towards what they had been doing. *Kickboxing, wrestling, judo, MMA, even some exotic variants. Daniel has been training us beyond just getting us ready for the next Rift,* Lance thought, remembering all the push-ups, sit-ups, and cardio Daniel had forced them to endure each time they had cleared another Rift and had some free time.

Daniel noticed how quiet Lance was and verbally nudged him back to the present. "Should I contact your next of kin, or are you still with us, lad?"

"Still here . . . in spirit . . . perhaps with a shattered ribcage and pride," Lance groaned, slowly crawling up to a seated position as he glanced at the black eye Thomas had on display. Not sure why, but the sight slightly lifted his own spirits.

Daniel had explained to them that Attributes amplified a person's body and mind. An already fit or developed individual would get far more out of a Strength or Agility improvement than a weak or unhealthy individual. Daniel was training them hard because of this, to make their foundation as sturdy as possible. It was easier to build it in the beginning, when a Rifter couldn't rely as heavily on the boons that came at a higher Level.

"Mate, can you fix my eye?" Thomas asked as he massaged his bruised face.

"Can't, out of Mana," Lance said as he lied through his teeth. Already he could feel a bit of Mana replenish itself. No doubt Thomas was aware of this as well. The higher your Strength and Endurance, the more health replenished each hour. The higher your Agility and Perception, the more Stamina replenished. A high Wisdom and Luck would aid Mana recovery.

Daniel handed Lance a bottle of water before he inquired further. "So, what are you youngsters planning next?"

"R.A.M. offered us another spot in the next clearing. The last Rift we did still hadn't increased in Level, so they wanted us to assist in another Rift," Lance said.

Daniel simply nodded, weighing their choices for a moment. "That sounds like a good way to earn some cash and to Level Up further. R.A.M. has been treating you lads decently. How about we get something to eat when you get back from your next Rift? My treat," Daniel offered, no doubt pleased at their recent developments and how well they had been sticking to his advice to not rush into more Rifts.

"Hell yes!" Thomas said, seeming to have miraculously recovered at simply the prospect of eating free food. Sensing danger, Daniel quickly attempted to limit the offer to just a few burgers. Lance, however, knew that this was a fight that Daniel couldn't win. The only option the man had left was pray that Thomas's hunger wouldn't bankrupt him.

In the end, the true victor would be Thomas's stomach.

CHAPTER TWENTY

Hazard Pays

Two weeks ago
February, 14 AR
Outside Rift 7
Liverpool, England

LANCE

"Grace. Oy! Grace!" Jack said. Seeing as there was no reaction, he kicked her feet off the desk, forcing her into a sudden seated position as she opened her eyes. Her scarred features exposed her fatigue and an obvious hangover. Still, her emerald gaze quickly flared awake, watching Jack Delby.

"What do you want?" she asked, her voice still hoarse from her fight with last night's bottle of rum.

Jack sighed once, in disapproval. "The Rifters have all arrived. We've got twenty porters in total for this run."

"That should do for now. What about security?" she asked, rubbing her eyes as she slowly got up, mentally preparing herself for another Rift clearing. She wore a padded R.A.M. uniform with a ram avatar on the right sleeve. The green-dyed uniform had been machine-woven from sturdy fabrics harvested from within the Rift. It wasn't as good as a uniform made by a Rifter, but R.A.M. preferred to order in bulk.

"The usual ten fighters have all arrived. Because of the Level of this Rift and the short notice, we had to hire five outsiders. They're all veterans and ranked above Level Forty. One of our regulars was familiar with one newcomer and will vouch for her. The rest are unknown, save for one with a chip on his shoulder. Apparently, he is the younger brother of some big shot from the States. He claims to be here on holiday and to see how we do things across the pond," Jack said, his words drenched in disdain. "So, two Americans, two Brits, and one French bloke." Jack then handed Grace a tablet loaded up with all the information on the five outsiders. "Frenchie has a stiff stride. Probably ex-military."

Grace read through it while accessing her Inventory at the same time. She summoned items out of thin air, letting them hug her body in a perfect fit as they encased her in additional armor. Jack ignored it, having seen this countless times already. A somewhat worried expression was clearly visible on his face. "I still don't see why we couldn't just go for a Level-Two or Level-Three Rift. Why wait until it's a Level Five?"

Grace glanced outside, seeing the groups of Rifters make their way towards their cubicles to get dressed and prepare themselves.

"Profits, Jack," Grace told him while double-checking her wrist guards, then equipping her sword and slinging it across her shoulder.

"R.A.M. has been seeing a steady decline in profits over the last two years. There is more competition, and the lower Rifts don't hold enough ores to make them worthwhile anymore. Letting the Rift grow until it's a Level Four or Five increases the difficulty while also increasing the number of precious metals we might harvest," Grace said as she placed a hand on his shoulders, signaling that it was above their paygrade. Jack mostly took care of the logistical side of things, while Grace was a party leader of dozens of men, but none of them were high up the corporate ladder.

Afterwards, the two of them stepped out of the complex and made their way over towards the group of Rifters who would join them today.

[You have equipped an Item: R.A.M. Steel pickaxe]
[You have equipped an item: R.A.M. Padded work clothes]
[You have equipped an item: R.A.M. Leather boots]
[You have equipped an item: R.A.M. Leather gloves]

Swinging his pickaxe a few times, Lance tested its grip until it satisfied him. He swung his backpack over his shoulders and left the private cubicle that the company had assigned to him. He had already stored away his clothes and belongings in the locker there. The lockers were quite secure and there was security on site to guard them. Lance usually traveled light, but it was always good to have some fresh clothes when you came back out of a Rift.

A bright-faced man made his way towards him as Lance stepped out of the cubicle. "Hey, Lance."

"Hey, Matt. What's up?" Lance asked, looking over at the man, a gentle smile visible on his features. Matt Chapman stood out amongst most Rifters, being even taller than Lance. He'd shaved his brown hair at the sides, no doubt hoping to look more professional. Sadly, his soft brown eyes ruined any chance of that happening.

Matt had been a fellow porter on a few runs but had finally gotten a position as a fighter. During the last run, Matt had provided security as well. He was several Levels higher than Thomas and Lance. Some Rifters of his Level would seek employment elsewhere, or work as a freelancer. Others, like Matt, preferred to work a steady job and clear Rifts they were familiar with and those of a lower Level.

"Good, good . . . But are the rumors true about Thomas? You know, about the black eye?" Matt asked in a hushed tone before glancing back at Thomas in the distance. The redhead was speaking with Jack near the entrance, still signing the contract that allowed him to rent the uniform, pickaxe, and the backpack he would use inside the Rift.

Lance noticed several of the other porters and fighters talk amongst themselves as they stared at Thomas. Some were even smiling outright. The more Lance thought about it, the more his mind put two and two together. *I don't know what they're talking about, but I know it will ruin Thomas's mood.*

"Completely true. I was there when it happened," Lance said, lying through his teeth while being clueless about what he had just confirmed. He just knew that it would be hilarious.

"I knew it! I bloody knew it," Matt said, nearly bursting out in laughter as he slapped Lance on the shoulder playfully. The two of them then joined up with the other Rifters. Lance could've sworn he heard hushed whispers coming from Matt and the others, explaining that Grace had punched Thomas in the face after the redhead had tried to flirt with her.

It's these moments that make me glad to be friends with him, Lance thought, remembering how often Thomas had asked him to heal the black eye he had sustained after sparring with Daniel. It had been a few days, but faint traces still lingered.

Although there was a relaxed atmosphere on Rift Site 47-C4, there was no mistaking that they were about to enter a dangerous environment. All around him, Lance could see people double-checking their equipment, helping one another out with straps or simply going over the information they had involving this Rift.

Most of the porters were wearing the typical R.A.M. equipment, while the fighters had equipped their own gear. It made sense, seeing as the fighters were several Levels higher, had more experience, and got paid more.

Most of them had tailored steel armor, with thick padding or chain mail underneath. Others wore flexible leather and scale or a mixture of both. There was a blend between a historical design that was tried and tested throughout the ages and a more modern style. Had they not been standing in front of a pulsating angry Rift, the sight of a bunch of grown men and women dressed up in armor might've seemed funny.

Nearly everyone had a cutting or blunt weapon at the ready, some even several of them. A few Rifters used shields; others carried bows, crossbows or throwing weapons. The wealthier Rifters had actual pistols and rifles. The latter was quite effective in smaller Rifts, seeing as a bullet would take down just about anything if hit in the right place. Apparently, higher-Leveled monsters could shrug off bullets. Lance didn't even want to think about such monsters.

Spotting Thomas in the distance, Lance held up his hand, signaling where he was.

"All good?" Lance asked, getting the nod from Thomas before the two of them rechecked the contents of their backpack. Upon opening the average Rifter backpack, one would find several steel containers filled with clean water and tightly stacked food bundles. These would last them a few weeks if they rationed them wisely. Manufacturers made their meals from things that were brought back from a Rift. Some Rifts had water, edible plants, or even wildlife inside, while others were devoid of anything supporting life.

"All good. And you?" Thomas asked, bending his neck sideways until it produced a nasty popping sound.

Lance could see the change happening within his friend already. From what he had heard from Daniel, most Rifters reacted to it. A Rifter's body would tense up and they could feel the Rift-shard within their chest throb as their heart pounded violently. Fear, excitement, confusion, joy. Rifters could feel everything and anything at such a time when a lot of adrenaline coursed through their veins.

Lance nodded reassuringly. "Rift Seven, here we come! Seven is a lucky number, right?"

"Hell yeah. Maybe I get lucky and Level Up during the Rift itself. Level Ten, baby!" Thomas said with a grin as he wrapped an arm around his tall, introverted friend and pulled him in for an awkward hug before the two of them made their way over towards another group of Rifters that they enjoyed hanging out with.

As Thomas spoke with the others, hinting at a surprise he had bought for this Rift, Lance thought about what this Rift would mean for them. *Even if Thomas kills nothing inside the Rift, just clearing and surviving it will award him a Level Up. He'll go from Level Nine to Ten. That will elevate him from being a mere Survivor to an actual Veteran,* Lance thought, as he considered what that milestone would mean for them. At Level Ten, they would get their Class, and in doing so, gain several boons. Depending on what their Class was, they might even get scouted by important companies or even some major guilds. *I've heard that most of the fighters in this Rift were between Level Ten and 100. Perhaps we'll get promoted to Fighters when we get our Class, like Matt?*

"Hey Lance, what are your plans—" Matt asked before they could hear a large beep from the speaker system installed near the Rift. It announced that they would enter the Rift in a few minutes.

Every Rifter on site had been through this before and knew what it meant for them. One by one, they all lined up and waited for the Rift leader to make her appearance.

"All right, ladies! You know the drill," the Rift-leader said. Her back was towards the Rift, the strange black energy dancing in the background. Grace's gaze fell upon the Rifters before her, seeing the twenty porters and fifteen fighters all standing at the ready, waiting for her to continue. "Site Forty-Seven-C-Four. Others before us have dubbed it 'The Cave.' Other R.A.M. parties have cleared it thirteen times already. They usually let it fluctuate between Level Two and Three. It is now registered as a Level-Five Rift."

Whispers formed at that, yet Grace quickly snuffed them out. "We've increased our security by fifty percent. More than enough to see us through the Rift with no problems. We'll clear this place step by step while collecting and mining what they pay us to do," she barked, her no-nonsense tone instantly stopping any further whispers or doubts. Her fist pointed at the Rift, her singed steel gauntlet showing signs of having encountered immense flames at one point.

"Everyone has read the information surrounding this Rift. We know it has breathable air and drinkable water and that some creatures inside are edible," she said with a grin, knowing full well that most Rifters preferred additional rations, not to mention fresh meat now and again.

"Inside, we'll encounter mostly canine types of monsters and smaller humanoid creatures. Both are dangerous in groups, but less so one-on-one. They might have crude weaponry and tools at their disposal," Grace said, stepping closer towards a nearby crate that the Rifters would bring with them inside.

"So, I say we show them some of ours. I had the boys over at the Workshop build us something special for this Rift, and I'm itching to test it out in the field," she said before spinning on her heels and making her way closer to the Rift. The fighters lined up behind her, carrying equipment slung over their shoulders. Two porters carried boxes.

A timer near the Rift was slowly counting down to the zero mark. Upon reaching it, a beeping sound rang out. Grace then calmly walked forwards, disappearing in the black energy of the Rift while simultaneously activating one of her Skills. The fighters then waited five seconds before the next beep came. Upon hearing it, they then rushed forward, intent on supporting Grace, or dealing with what remained of the monsters.

Lance watched the fighters disappear from his sight as he pondered what they might find inside. *It's a brave thing to be the first person to go inside a Rift. Still, judging by the rumors about Grace Flame-Fist Hicks, she might be able to survive on her own inside a Level-Five Rift.*

Lance felt a nudge from Thomas, snapping him out of his reverie. He knelt and grabbed the crate on one end while his friend picked up the other. Even for two Rifters, the box was heavy, being full of equipment.

The timer once again displayed a countdown, this time from thirty seconds. The longer they stayed on Earth, the more time passed within the Rift. There was a window of a few minutes until the Rift would become violent and not allow entry anymore, so they would have to time it correctly. The safest way was to enter within a minute after the first person had stepped inside the Rift. After that, Rifts varied, with some staying stable for many minutes, while others' stability lasted only a few more seconds.

He could hear some porters counting out loud. It was customary to send the fighters in first before the weaker porters went in. They did this in order to take the brunt of the fighting and have to worry less about protecting the weaker party members. This didn't mean that porters wouldn't see any action when they stepped through the Rift. After all, there was always the threat of another monster lurking nearby. Sometimes they came in waves, other times they hid and tried to ambush Rifters.

Gripping the container more firmly, Lance moved forwards with Thomas. He could feel his friend's gaze shift towards him. They nodded to one another as they neared the violent black entity that was the Rift. This would be the highest-Level Rift they had been in, besides their first one.

Thomas and I are still Class-less, meaning we could take on Rifts between Level One and Three in larger groups. Three would push us to our limits. A Level-Five Rift like this would be something else. It would mean that we can't beat the Rift-guardian or the more challenging monsters on our own, Lance thought as he went over many scenarios that might occur before he felt the crate that he was carrying hit him in the side.

"Don't get lost in that head of yours. We'll be fine. This isn't like the hospital, nor are we the same people. And anyway, compared to Daniel's training, how bad could *this* be?" Thomas said with a grin, forcing a chuckle out of his friend. It helped ease the tension they were both feeling.

Thomas was right, for once. They had trained hard and had Leveled Up since that horrible day all those months ago. They had Skills, decent equipment, and a lot of training. So, Lance nodded and replied confidently, "Compared to Daniel? A walk in the park, right?"

"A picnic. Come on, let's do this," his friend said before the two of them got ready for the timer to run out. When the beep finally sounded, the porters all rushed forward, tightly holding onto their cargo and weapons before the Rift-energy finally swallowed them all up.

CHAPTER TWENTY-ONE

Graceful Hot Dogs

Inside Rift 7

THOMAS

Porters appeared one by one in flashes of black energy. Many of the more experienced porters were already on their feet while the others were on their knees or had fallen over.

Once he could finally breathe again, Thomas's lungs felt like they were burning. He shook his head to get rid of his disorientation. From the corner of his eyes, he could see Lance already up on his feet, his higher Perception stat helping him adjust much faster. A moment later, Lance was holding out his hand and checking in with Thomas. "Are you all right?"

After a moment, Thomas grabbed it and raised himself up. "I'm fine." He was taking in what was happening all around him. The air was thick with the sound of conflict, death, and the unmistakable sounds of Rifters using offensive Skills.

Thomas could see a line of fighters a short distance away. Those combat-tested Rifters had established a perimeter and created improvised barriers or elevated positions from where to shoot. The porters could see a horde of wolf-like monsters rushing towards them. No doubt this had been happening ever since the fighters had entered the Rift. Many of them were using ranged weapons to keep the horde at bay and to thin out those that dared approach them. Occasionally, a Rifter would throw a cheap Molotov cocktail at a large group of monsters, spreading chaos as the flames stretched out across multiple foes.

Arrows, bolts, javelins, axes, and daggers all hit their marks, staining the rocky soil red with gore. It was quite effective, although the sight of an automatic rifle showering the enemy was something else entirely. Even with lower-grade gunpowder and ammunition, the bullets still wreaked havoc on soft, unarmored flesh.

When some monsters got close enough, a Rifter who specialized in close combat would be there to meet them and make quick work of them, ripping or smashing with a brutality only a higher-ranked Rifter could muster.

A fighter stood behind a large stationary weapon. It drew inspiration from the historical ballista used in ancient Greece and Rome, although heavily modernized. It spat out sharpened, thick steel rods in quick succession, violently hurling them towards the incoming monsters. A single rod could impale several creatures if they were behind one another.

After all its ammunition was used up, the operator glanced backwards, seeing the newly arrived porters and the crates they had brought with them. A smile appeared on his face, and he pointed at Thomas and Lance before shouting, "Right on time, lads! Bring the crates here. The rest can help with the defensive line."

Not needing any further encouragement, the young men picked up the heavy crate assigned to them and made their way towards the fighter.

This Rift had formed on a construction site back on Earth, and its inside bore remnants of it. Thick steel beams lay strewn around the place. Old chain-link fences were half stuck in the dirt, as well as smaller objects one might find on such a site. Beyond that, the environment appeared to be an underground cave system with several side passages. No doubt those tunnels would lead to other larger chambers. Smaller Mana stone deposits scattered around the rocky surface added some light to an otherwise dark underground system.

Thomas helped Lance carry the crate towards the smiling Rifter, dropping it near him as they undid the latches. Inside the crate were large steel canisters that contained sharpened steel rods stacked on top of one another. It was not unlike a pistol magazine, only designed for larger objects.

Lance wasted no time in grabbing a canister, and positioning it correctly so that the fighter could quickly slide it inside the contraption. It was moments like these when Lance impressed Thomas the most, resulting in the redhead pondering which one of them was best suited for a life as a Rifter. *I might be the better brawler and have a knack for fighting, but Lance is more adaptive. The fact that he spread out his Attribute points more evenly makes it easier for him to adjust to a new environment, not to mention figure out how he should position the containers. He always had an affinity for things rather than people, so I suppose this is right up his alley.*

The siege weapon pulled Thomas out of his train of thought when he heard it fire again, spewing forth sharpened steel imbued with the fury and ingenuity of humankind. One of its shots had impaled two monsters and wounded another due to its sheer momentum. It also disrupted the enemy advance when they saw a large rod of metal kill several of their numbers in one swoop.

"Hell yeah!" Thomas had no choice but to yell loudly as he clapped his friend on the shoulder. At that moment, even Lance was quite giddy, seeing the second steel round leave the weapon and imbed itself in the charging monsters.

The fighter wielding the siege weapon simply loaded another rod and armed it as he turned his attention to the young men. "I need one of you here to help me with reloading and changing the magazines. The other one gets to help at the front lines."

Before Lance had even the chance to discuss who should do what, Thomas suddenly sprinted past the siege weapon and towards where the fighters and other porters had taken up a defensive position. "I owe you one!" Thomas shouted as he put some distance between him and his friend. He knew it was a bit of a nasty move, but Lance would understand, hopefully.

The fighters had taken up a position behind steel beams and old cement bags, and inside improvised trenches. Being flanked was nearly impossible because of intense and constant flames on the left and right. The Rift-leader, Grace, had produced those with one of her flame-based Skills.

The wolf-like monsters were quite agile and did occasionally dodge a ranged attack, but only a few of them ever made it near the front line. One wounded monster had gotten up to Grace. Before it could even react, however, she had already grabbed its throat and lifted it up high with one arm. An amused grin painted her features as she activated one of her Skills.

"*Ignite.*"

Flames rushed out from the palm of Grace's hand, engulfing the brown fur in a sea of bright red flames. The power in her fingers had already crushed the monster's neck, so it remained limp. More and more heat poured out of her, engulfing the beast until the intensity obliterated the corpse. In the end, only a pile of ash remained.

Glancing at her sides, she could see the defensive line strengthened by Thomas and the other porters. "Ah, the reinforcements," Grace said. Her right gauntlet was still glowing red from the heat she had produced. She watched the enemy numbers quickly dwindling while her numbers held firm. It wouldn't be long before they completely routed the enemy or slaughtered them to the last.

Thomas watched her scanning the scene, no doubt making mental notes in her mind for after the fight. Grace then began barking orders, instructing Thomas and the other new arrivals to take up specific positions where the chance of a monster breaking through would be low.

Thomas took position next to a Rifter who was using a bow to pick off those that came close. Ice-imbued arrows left the woman's bow and embedded themselves within the wolf-like monsters, exploding in a cold white mist, stunning or slowing other monsters due to the area of effect.

Emboldened by his allies, Thomas gripped the pickaxe firmly in his dominant right hand while relaxing the left. He then concentrated on his Inventory before retrieving the item he had recently purchased from the Workshop in secret. Only his family and Dieter had seen it.

[You have retrieved an item]

A large, crude, and thick steel shield materialized in his left hand. It was far more than what a normal man might feel comfortable carrying, but Thomas's increased strength allowed him to handle it just fine. It wasn't Rifter-made, so there wasn't anything special about it. But a shield did not need those things when it was essentially a solid, thick steel plate. Grabbing it, Thomas held it out in front of him. With both shield and weapon, he felt like a proper fighter standing on the front lines.

The bow-wielding Rifter near him gave a thumbs-up, approving of his shield. Thomas could feel Lance's eyes burning a hole in him from a distance, no doubt envious and upset that he had bought his first item in the Workshop without telling his best friend about it.

And that envious expression made Thomas's recent purchase even more worthwhile.

It had been a few hours since the battle, but already the place looked vastly different. The Rifters had created a sturdy temporary wall from steel beams, dirt, and old bags of concrete mix that they had found half-buried. Although this Rift had only existed for a short while on Earth, inside it seemed like many years had passed. There was a lot of rust on the steel beams and decay on the once-sturdy bags that held the concrete mix.

The Rifters had set up a temporary stockpile behind the walls near where they would be sleeping. Nothing would be there permanently—a few days at most until they had scouted out the other tunnels and found the center of the Rift.

It made sense to establish a more permanent base at the Rift-event itself. Doing so would mean that you had the stockpile close at hand when the Rift ended, allowing you to take as many items as you could carry. R.A.M. was a company first and foremost, so it made sense to maximize profits.

Thomas dropped off the claws, teeth, and black-shards he had pulled out of the wolf-like monsters, placing them all in a neat pile. Dirt and dried-up blood covered his outfit, tainting his uniform dullish brown. This was mostly from harvesting the monster parts. He noticed Matt making his way over towards him, carrying a few bits of cooked meat and a steel canister with water.

"And how goes it, O brave warrior?" Matt asked, displaying his tribute to Thomas.

"Better than these mutts. Thanks," Thomas said as he tried to wipe his hands clean on his outfit. The two of them took up a seat on a nearby steel beam as Thomas started on his meal.

Matt glanced to his right and spotted Lance in the distance, sitting on a pile of old cement bags with his eyes shut, no doubt listening to music. Smiling, Matt tried to steer the conversation towards Lance. "So, is the missus still upset?"

"Lance? Ah, we're fine. Sure, there's a bit of irritation, but he enjoys spending time by himself. He's probably just in his head again. You know how he can be," Thomas replied, waving his hand as if to signal that it was indeed fine between the two of them. *He'd have pulled the same prank on me,* Thomas thought as he lied to himself.

"True. Still, from what I heard, it was a bit of a jerk-move on your end," Matt said as he waited for an explanation, only to see the man shrug his shoulders and continue to eat. A few minutes passed before Matt tried once more, only to be cut off.

"He'll be fine. Look," Thomas said as he grabbed a small pebble and threw it towards Lance, hitting the man's leg. He waited for Lance to open his eyes and pull out an earbud before he shouted at him. "We're cool, right?" Thomas asked, only to receive the middle finger and have Lance ignore him again. Thomas chuckled and shifted his attention back towards Matt. "See, best friends. No reason to worry."

"You guys are weird."

"I know better than to dispute that statement," Thomas said with a chuckle.

"So, how much do you reckon we got today?" Matt asked as he shifted his gaze towards the stockpile, seeing thick sheets spread out on the floor with items stacked on top of it. There were piles of canine teeth, claws, and even their raw pelts. Another pile consisted of precious Rift-shards while others contained bits of ore that the porters had already mined out and collected. Each porter had shifting duties. Sometimes you had ore duty; other times you had to harvest corpses or assist the fighters in sentry duty.

"Well, not bad for today. Enough to fill three or four backpacks. I'm not sure what we'll end up taking with us, but Grace will have to decide on what to prioritize," Thomas said. When exiting a Rift, the Rifters would bring with them what they carried or held onto. There was only so much Inventory space a Rifter had available internally because of their system, so most of them carried crates or large backpacks with them. Anything larger than that would be quite dangerous when they returned to Earth.

The Inventory system was impressive, but there had some obvious limitations. Rifters could only store and transfer things that were classified as Items, so they couldn't just store a monster corpse or something similar. Harvested things from a monster such as teeth or a pelt would work, as that counted as an Item. Some might see this as purely a downside, but it was also efficient. It removed the need to get rid of the gore and blood from a pelt or claw. You simply stored the Item and watched as the other bits fell on the ground, no longer attached.

The Inventory would allow some Items to be stacked together and only take up one slot, such as arrows or bits of ore. Larger items such as a helmet would take up an entire slot. Anything that was heavier than the Rifter himself would take up more slots, but this was rare. Essentially, it became a balancing act between what a Rifter stored internally and what they carried with them.

Matt glanced at the bloodstained outfit the redhead was wearing and shook his head. "Imagine how much easier it would be if we could just store the corpses in our Inventory and drop them off back on Earth."

"Yeah . . . It would probably save a ton on the cost of dry cleaning. Still, I can't complain all that much. Skinning a monster, pulling out a few claws or an eye? That still beats the internship I did at the geriatric ward. I'll take monster blood over your nan's filled-up diaper any day," Thomas replied, grinning as Matt simply burst out into laughter.

The rest of the Rifters were relaxing as well. They had blocked most of the cave tunnels, and several fighters would be on guard duty. Those that had finished their assignments were busy cooking meat, getting their tents ready, or simply chatting with one another.

One of the Americans, Connor, had even brought a guitar with him and was busy tuning it before he set the mood for their first evening inside this Rift.

If one were to ignore all the armor, weaponry, blood, and dirt all around them, one might even have assumed that they were all friends camping in the wild. The camp had slowly established itself within a few hours, followed by the sounds of laughter, warm food, and people bonding with one another through shared hardship in this lifestyle they had chosen. Even the foreigners gradually found their place within the group.

Matt finally patted Thomas's knee as he got up, knowing he had the next guard shift in a few minutes. Still, before he left, he wanted to bring something up. "You're at Level Nine, right? Did you want to ride this one out and get your Class at the end, or do you want to tag along with a patrol tomorrow? Perhaps a few stragglers might be all you need to reach the next Level?"

"Really? That would be awesome," Thomas said, his eyes betraying his eagerness to finally reach Level Ten.

"Yeah, no worries. I'll discuss it with Grace later. Be sure to bring that stubborn friend of yours as a peace offering. Because you, sir, are an idiot. Besides, your nice shield needs a few nicks and dents on it. Proper equipment shows signs of wear and tear," Matt said before they nodded to one another, Thomas still grinning like an amused child.

The grin on the redhead's face only widened when he found out Matt had to spend the next four hours staring at rocks if nothing exciting happened during his guard duty.

CHAPTER TWENTY-TWO

Class Act

THOMAS

Matt and a few of the other Rifters watched as both Lance and Thomas fought against the wolf-like monsters. The other Rifters had subdued two of these creatures after dispatching a small pack of them. Afterwards, they had released the two monsters inside a narrow tunnel, blocking off any chance of escape. The monsters knew that the only chance of survival was to fight, forcing them into an aggressive, feral state.

Some eggheads in the GRRO had decided on a fancy Latin name with a number that matched its first Rift sighting. Unsurprisingly, no Rifter worth his shard would ever use it. Instead, each Rifter preferred his or her own nickname when encountering them. The most creative one would usually stick around and end up as the accepted term. Currently, it was a tie between Cave-wolves and Rock-biters. The former was more factual, while the latter simply sounded cool.

"Nice!" Matt said, grinning as he watched Thomas bash the Cave-wolf in the face. Wanting to tease the lads further, he shared his encouraging thoughts with two friends. "You two know you're supposed to fight it, not cuddle it, right?" He was both amused and proud. Lance and Thomas were doing rather well. The average Cave-wolf was quite agile, beyond what most porters could handle. In terms of raw power and fortitude, the monsters were not all that threatening. Basic armor would mostly negate their agility, seeing as a Rifter could just tank it.

"Put a sock in it," Thomas said as he kept his thick shield between him and the monster. He was trying to steer it into unfavorable terrain. The monster finally felt its hind legs hit the wall behind him as it realized the Rifter had trapped it. One last rage-induced attack was all that it had left before a thick steel shield bashed its skull in, followed by a pickaxe to the torso.

"There! Are you not entertained?" Thomas exclaimed, rising to his full height, his hands held aloft like a victorious gladiator of ancient times, appealing to the spectators for approval.

But Thomas's triumphant display met a sour reception. Matt offered a sarcastic slow clap, while the others half-heartedly raised their thumbs, their expressions teasingly devoid of emotion.

Suppressing the urge to make a rude comment, Thomas shrugged it off and joined the others, allowing him to see how Lance was doing. Even now, with a mere two-Level difference between them, one could see the difference in what those extra Attribute points made.

The ludicrous amount of Strength Thomas had at his disposal allowed him to pressure his opponent into a corner. Each Level would increase a Rifter's base Attributes by one point and grant an additional three points extra to spare. The more you factored these things in, the easier it became to accept how Matt and the other fighters could defeat several of these monsters at unfavorable odds and capture two monsters, sustaining no injuries save for a bruise or two.

Still, Lance is doing rather well, Thomas thought, seeing his friend narrowly evading the creature again and again, causing it to slam into the wall behind him. The lack of a shield meant Lance had to be more creative. What Lance seemed to lack in offensive Strength, he made up for in letting the monster damage itself through its charges.

"Come on! You got this," Thomas said encouragingly as he watched his friend slowly put some distance between him and the monster, not responding to the growls the Cave-wolf made.

At first glance, it seemed like Lance was backing off, apparently pressured by the monster. As Thomas focused on the details, he noticed something was off. Lance wasn't holding the pickaxe properly, letting it dangle downwards at a weird angle. It went against everything Daniel had taught them over the last few months.

Sensing weakness, the Cave-wolf rushed forwards, presenting its razor-sharp teeth. Suddenly, Lance moved, dragging the pickaxe across the ground in a shovel-like manner before launching large amounts of fine dust and smaller pebbles at the monster, peppering its face and temporarily blinding it.

Seconds later, Lance was upon it, tackling it to the ground as he grappled it in a chokehold, keeping its back pinned down against his chest. Lance's legs had ensnared the beast's hind legs while trained arms quickly went for its throat. As he cut off the Cave-wolf's circulation, it panicked and struggled like mad. This only made the chokehold more effective and sped up the process. *Although not a violent person, he sure can conjure up brutally effective strategies,* Thomas thought, seeing his friend calmly squeeze the life out of a monster that at this point wasn't posing any threat anymore.

A minute later, it went still, either killed or unconscious from the lack of oxygen. Not wasting any time, Lance pinned it down on the floor while grabbing its neck and applying force, causing the neck to snap with a bone-chilling crack.

"Clever," Thomas said as he made his way over towards his friend. Both were grinning from ear to ear at their victory. The Cave-wolves were a lot stronger than the monsters they had faced in previous Rifts. When the others joined them, they congratulated the greenhorns, even earnestly praising Thomas.

"Are you lads ready for another round, or have you seen enough action?" Matt asked before noticing Thomas acting weird, his eyes wide, as if seeing and going through something incredible. The more experienced Rifters quickly understood what was happening: Level Ten! For some, this moment was over in a split second. Others went through something longer as they received their Class. It was hard to describe to someone who hadn't been through it as well. Some experienced it as a memory or a dream of sorts; others felt as if their souls had left their bodies and a bright light illuminated them from within. Whatever a Rifter went through, each one would recall a strange and unnatural voice letting the Rifter know what Class it had assigned to them.

Thomas grabbed Lance and Matt by the shoulders and squeezed hard to keep himself upright. One moment he had checked his status screen, the next he had heard metallic voices screaming in his mind while his whole body had felt like it was on fire. It had lasted a split second, and he could only recall bits of it, but he knew he had become something *more*. "Lance . . . I Leveled Up . . . I bloody did it! I'm Level Ten," he said proudly before facing a barrage of questions from Lance and Matt, the other fighters speculating on what Class Thomas had gotten.

Matt prodded the redhead in the side. "What Class?"

"Come on, tell us!" Lance demanded, his own excitement no doubt matching that of his best friend.

"I am . . ." Thomas said as he stalled for a dramatic effect. He was browsing through all the notifications he had gotten, explaining what his new Class was, what new Skills he had gotten, and what other benefits came with his new Class. He quickly spent the three Attribute points he had also earned and dumped them into Strength before shifting his gaze towards the others.

"Warrior!" He threw his arms in the air, yelling incoherently, as his best friend joined him in mad celebration. It might've looked weird to the others, but the friends' jubilation went beyond simply cheering at a new Class or Skill. They were echoing an oath they had sworn to one another after they had survived their first Rift. An oath that Thomas now had partially achieved: to never be as helpless as they had felt during their first Rift.

When the scouting party returned, word quickly spread that Thomas had finally popped his cherry. Most of them could understand the importance of that and were quick to congratulate him, offering words of wisdom or simply compliment him on the good Class result.

Thomas's grin never left his face, and all of this did wonders for his pride. He had already pestered Lance for a few photos to commemorate the event. Most of them were of him standing over the corpse of the monster he had slain as he posed with Matt and the other fighters.

"Dude, enough!" Lance said, his annoyance palpable in his tone.

"Come on, one more picture. For my family," Thomas asked his friend, poking and prodding to demand his attention. Lance eventually gave in, no doubt realizing Thomas was beyond saving at this point. One second his hand was empty, the next a smartphone was suddenly clasped in it.

Widening his grin, Thomas then quickly took up his position on top of a small boulder, spreading his arms in a T-pose with his shield and pickaxe in hand.

Lance's smartphone flashed once, capturing the moment. "And done," he said with as much enthusiasm as a stale piece of bread. His phone was bursting at the digital seams from all the pictures it now contained.

"You sure you got my good side?" Thomas asked, moving towards his friend to take a better look at the photo.

"You have a good side?" Lance feigned shock as he noticed the redhead trying to sneak a glimpse. With a knowing smile, he moved backwards, preventing Thomas from snatching the phone from his hands.

"Mate, let me see," Thomas protested.

"Honestly, it's fine," Lance replied. A moment later, the phone transferred back into his Inventory. A new Rifter started with a base five Inventory slots and gained an additional two slots per Level. At Level Seven, Lance now had seventeen slots. With Thomas's Level now Ten, it meant that he had a sizable twenty-three slots.

Although the young men didn't have that much in terms of Items that they could carry with them, each slot potentially allowed them to store an Item without ever worrying about it breaking, rusting, or getting stolen. Lance's phone would also never run out of power within his Inventory, as if frozen in time.

"Relax. Even if I did mess it up, I could just send your family a photo of a random monster and they wouldn't notice the difference," Lance said reassuringly, getting a dig in to his pride as only a best friend could.

"Not funny. Be sure to send it to me when we get back, okay?"

"Sure," Lance said. He knew how important this was for his friend. Although the man was arrogant, Lance knew that most of these photos would go to his family. Thomas's younger brother, Oliver, had half his room covered with Rift-related articles and photos of his older brother, the Rifter. His father, meanwhile, had made a small shrine in the living room, next to Thomas's childhood boxing and rugby trophies.

"I'm sure even my old man is going to be proud of this one," Thomas said, satisfied.

Lanced nodded in agreement. "And your sister as well."

"Yeah, she would . . . wait . . . why did you mention my sister specifically?" Thomas asked, only to see his friend grin knowingly before the two of them burst out into laughter. Afterwards, they made their way over to the edge of their camp, sitting on one of the steel beams that functioned as a part of the defensive wall.

"So, do you feel any different?" Lance asked. He was curious to hear whether his friend had felt any changes to himself in Leveling Up. Thomas had already explained that upon reaching Level Ten, he had gotten two new Skills related to his Class. Beyond that, his ascension to a Warrior Class had also boosted his Stamina recovery and Health pool.

"Stronger, perhaps more durable? Obviously even more attractive," Thomas said jokingly.

"I doubt a Level Up could fix that mug of yours."

Thomas grinned at the comment, but he knew what Lance had meant. There was a heated debate within the Rifter community about whether a Rifter would gain a Class depending on his personality and nature, or if the Class would shape the Rifter's nature over time to better suit it. Holding up his hands to stop his introverted friend from frying his brain, Thomas continued.

"I feel like I've always done. I've always had a short temper, and I act when faced with danger. The Class of Warrior is a natural pick for me. I don't know what else to tell you," he said, sharing what he could. He knew Lance would already be deep in thought, speculating about this or that. Thomas nudged him in the side.

"I don't know what the effects of this Class might do to me, but for now . . . I'm happy about it. I feel good, got new Skills and honestly . . . a Warrior Class is the best pick for me. Besides, look at Grace. She is a Mage, a Class known for long-distance fighting and being calm and calculating. Does that sound like Grace?" Thomas asked.

"No."

"Hell no. Grace is anything but that. She is hot-headed, prefers fighting up close and is better at using a sword than anyone in this group," the redhead said before he activated his Inventory.

[You have retrieved an item]

"Like our party leader, we make our own fate, right?" Thomas asked as he opened his hand, showing a cigarette pack, with one remaining. He jiggled it before throwing it to Lance. "Let's just focus on getting you to Level Ten as well. After that, we can finally have that one," he said, reminding Lance of their promise.

Ever since Daniel had been training them, Thomas had stopped smoking regularly, save for the odd cigar with his father. The one cigarette now in his friend's hand was the one that had survived their first Rift. It was half-broken and dirty, but it held meaning for them. Thomas had agreed to stop smoking and Lance had agreed to smoke their last cigarette when they both got to Level Ten, marking them as true Rifters.

"You know that is going to kill you one day, right?" Lance asked with a disarming smile before he handed it back to him.

"Yeah, I know," he said as he stored it back inside his Inventory and watched what was happening around them. He could see Rifters patrolling their surroundings and checking the barricaded sections. "Speaking of bad habits, has that icy heart of yours finally opened up a bit to your brother?" Thomas asked. He could've sworn he heard Lance rolling his eyes.

"Marcus and I need a bit more time," Lance replied.

"Beyond the years already spent ignoring him, you mean?"

"Probably," Lance countered as he sighed. He hated discussing the topic.

"Well, you already had a lot of time to defrost. And let's be honest, you wouldn't even have replied to his text or brought him up to speed about you surviving a Rift if it hadn't been for me. Well, Daniel helped as well, but it was mostly me," Thomas said, hoping to keep the tone somewhat lighthearted by sprinkling some of his narcissism around. He knew he had failed when he clocked that Lance's face remained as expressionless as always when someone mentioned his family. Thomas could understand the bit about Lance's father, but he felt like his friend was overly harsh towards his older brother.

"Give the guy some slack. Your old man had his talons in him for years. Besides, you said that the divorce was nasty, and Marcus was about to graduate. I'm sure he tried his best," Thomas offered, hoping to make some progress. He knew full well how deep Lance's resentment ran, losing half his family and moving to a different country, only to lose his mother a few years later to a horrible illness.

That he didn't immediately reply with his classic line that he could've at least made it to her funeral is alone proof that Lance's warming up to the idea, Thomas thought, somewhat proud of his friend. The redhead liked to tease and bully those that he loved, but he never ever made a jab at Lance's family. He could still remember his friend's face during his mother's funeral—that empty gaze. Seeing that had hurt Thomas more that any physical blow he had ever received.

"People change, mate. That I'm saying this inside a monster-infested hellhole instead of a clean hospital proves my point," Thomas said, throwing an arm around his friend and pulling him close. "Just give it a chance. You're already a part of my family, so best-case scenario, you simply get an additional brother. And besides, if Marcus messes up, I'll toss him in a Rift for you. Deal?" he asked as he noticed a small smile forming on his friend's face. Lance was about to say something when Matt jogged up to them, suddenly interrupting their conversation.

"Lads! Grace needs us at the camp. She is going to explain the plan for securing the Rift-event and setting up base there," Matt said, as he collected them and led them back to the camp.

When the three of them reached the others, they found Grace standing in the center, drawing lines in the sand to create a map of the tunnel system they had already mapped out and comparing it to the information they had gotten from R.A.M. When she finished it, she looked each party member in the eye, letting them see her resolve.

"Listen up, ladies. In two days, we make our push to the Rift-event. There will be hostiles there: both the Cave-wolves we have fought until now and even tougher foes. Information suggests that they're intelligent, crafty and can use weaponry," Grace explained as she let the words sink in.

Opponents such as those would be dangerous but collecting the weapons and armor from them would be highly profitable.

"You've read the reports about them and know what to expect. And, by popular choice, you dimwits have named them Cave-goblins. Too bad for them, we outclass them in terms of skill and equipment. And beyond that, we have a trick up our sleeves," Grace said before she lit a small fire on her palm, twisting her facial features into a dance of light and shadow. It made the scars on her face that much more pronounced and turned her reassuring smile into something diabolical.

CHAPTER TWENTY-THREE

With Friends Like These

Several hours ago

THOMAS

"*The Count of Monte Cristo*," Lance said as he offered his thoughts on the matter. "*Dirty Harry*," Thomas said proudly, answering Matt's question of what the greatest movie ever was. In Thomas's mind, he was the clear winner.

Matt smiled, realizing that he didn't need a sociology degree to see that there was a clear connection between the two of them. One of them liked to plan out things and didn't like sharing his past, while the other wanted nothing more than to be a badass and stand out. "Good choices, although I would've gone for *Rambo*," Matt said as he leaned backwards against a comfortable dirt heap that was functioning as a chair. He had placed his steel axe and shield next to him.

Thomas got up and shook his head as he did so. "No way. Dirty Harry's gun alone is enough to beat Rambo."

"I think a machine-gun would beat a handgun, not to mention the downsides that go along with revolvers," Lance said, no doubt already regretting his words as he noticed Thomas getting worked up.

Slowly, Thomas pointed at his friend, using his right hand to mimic a revolver. "Bam," he breathed softly, as if winning the discussion in that moment alone. "There are more factors at play in terms of a fight. Style, intimidation, and elegance. All of it is important. Sure, five or six rounds have their limitations, yet it also makes it far more . . . intimate. Each round that's chambered would carry a clear meaning, a specific task . . . an oath that demands to be kept," Thomas said, drawing the attention of the other two men.

"That . . . That is . . . deep. You surprised me there," Matt confessed before he shifted his gaze towards Lance and nudged him in the side. "Hey, you told me

Thomas had the intelligence of a rusty bucket with a dent in it. Look at him now, stringing complete sentences together." His accompanying smile was both disarming and teasing.

Thomas replied with his own smile while simultaneously flipping him off as he shifted his gaze towards the surroundings. The party had established their new base right near the Rift-event, just as planned. A large host of monsters had guarded it, but the Rifters had driven them out in one quick, coordinated attack.

They established their new base on a small island in the middle of an underground river. There were several ways to reach the island, from smaller rock formations that stood out above the water, to an improvised steel bridge that the Rifters themselves had built.

Large Mana stone formations dotted the rocky ceiling, casting the entire chamber in an extraordinary blue light. The chamber was quite spacious, easily dwarfing any of the others they had explored, including where they had started. At the center of their camp was the Rift-event, giving off an intimidating, pulsating feeling when you got close to it.

Around the event were stacks of resources that the Rifters had collected, most of them neatly spread out or already secured in one of the many crates and boxes they had brought with them. Protocol dictated that the Rift-guardian should be subdued, not killed, allowing the Rifters enough time to collect resources and maximize their profits. Should the Guardian accidentally get killed, they would at least be able to grab the materials they had already prepared and packed. No matter the strange environment, fauna, or monsters, this was still just a job for the fighters and porters.

Thomas noticed Grace in the distance heading towards them, with three porters and four fighters following her. She, like the rest of the Rifters, was practically just as much dirt as human by this point. She clearly took care of her weaponry and armor, but inevitably, filth would build up after two weeks of roughing it out in a Rift. Seeing her making a straight line towards them rather than one of the other porters or fighters meant that the two friends were up next for excavation duty.

Nearly every Rifter here respected Grace because of her leadership, ability, and her higher Level. Those that had doubts before would've had them shattered after having watched her at work in the last two weeks. Her Class as a Mage and unique set of Skills made her an incredibly proficient wielder of fire spells. Most had seen these Skills at the beginning of this Rift, yet inside a place like this, Grace could truly shine.

Small cavernous tunnels became death traps for monsters when Grace flooded them with large streams of fire and heat. Some turned into ovens that incinerated everything, while others became smoke-filled nightmares. Grace did more work in those two weeks than most Rifters could do in several Rifts.

"Gentlemen," Grace said as she reached the two friends. Her emerald-tinted gaze inspected the young men before she continued. "I want you to grab your gear and join Squad B. You're to take the northern pass and collect a bit more coal if you can find it. If not, tin, copper, or any other metal beyond iron. We have more than enough with all these steel beams lying around. Understood?" she asked, waiting for both to nod before continuing on her way.

A few moments passed as Lance and Thomas equipped their gear and double-checked their weapons. Then they joined up with the fighters and the other porters. Thomas felt a surge of excitement at the prospect of seeing the fighters in action. Three of them were foreigners, which meant that he might learn a lot of new things from them.

"All right, gang. Let's head out. Hopefully, we run into something fun along the way. I'm bored out of my mind," Connor Moore, one of the Americans, said as he led the group across the makeshift bridge and toward their task.

Thomas clenched his jaw, both upset and in awe at what was happening. His steel shield and pickaxe were at the ready but remained unused. During their excursion towards the northern tunnels, they had run into several of the Cave-goblins. At first, it seemed like it was going to be a tough fight, seeing as how Matt had struggled against them, but the reality was rather different.

The four fighters in Squad B held off the goblins with relative ease. Each fighter was several times stronger than Matt, and it showed. Connor Moore managed to keep most of them at bay alone. His Warrior-Class Skills allowed him to draw the aggression and attention of many of the monsters. Anything that came too close to him ended up hacked to pieces by the axes that he was dual-wielding. His large build and charismatic nature had secured him the role of squad leader during their task. Thomas felt both drawn to him and irritated. Connor's blue eyes, blonde hair, and chiseled jawline were all just a tad bit too perfect. That he also was the brother of a high-ranking American Rifter only made his claim to leadership that much stronger.

Those that dared skirt past Connor would have to face the Frenchman. While some goblins wore crude iron armor or carried improvised shields, the Frenchman knew just how to take advantage of a small crack in their defenses. The man went by the name of Louis Vidal and was a former sniper. His skill and experience with a rifle, coupled with his Class as an Archer, essentially turned him into a Grim Reaper in these tunnels. He usually used a bow when fighting the wolves but switched to a compact rifle when facing the armored goblins. Ammunition was expensive, yet Louis made every bullet count. He was the perfect person to act as support and damage dealer, seeing as he picked off the biggest threats, allowing the other fighters to maintain their advantage.

Connor and Louis stood out the most, the other two fighters seeming quite average by comparison. One was Steve, whom Lance and Thomas had met before in some of their earlier Rifts. The other was another American. Unlike Connor, she mostly kept to herself and didn't bother making an introduction. Still, the two friends had overheard Connor addressing her as Kira at one point.

At this Level, I can only stand here and watch, Thomas thought, seeing the four fighters slowly pushing back and picking off the goblins one by one. Lance and the other three porters were busy, dragging some of the fallen goblins to the side and removing their armor, weaponry, and Rift-shards. The latter was always a tricky thing. The black-shards had fused with these creatures' bodies. Arteries passed through the shard in certain areas, infusing the blood with Rift-energy that spread throughout the body. No matter how skilled a porter got with extracting these shards, they would always end up covered in blood and gore. Luckily for Thomas, his friend was on shard-retrieval duty today.

"They're retreating!" Connor yelled as the remaining goblins slowly backed off, using their shields to protect themselves from the incoming fire. Before long, their tactic turned into a mad dash, rushing to the place where the tunnel would split off into several other pathways. Their leader then looked over towards his teammates to see how they were doing before he issued his command: "We need to follow them now that we have the advantage." His voice was calm and composed, but the look in his eyes spoke of an eagerness to prove himself.

"Connor, we can't. The side passages lead to terrain that the scouts have yet to explore," Louis said, reloading his rifle as he moved towards him and the others.

"Yeah. And besides, we're on an excavating job, not a hunting one," Steve added, rubbing his left shoulder, which had taken a beating during the encounter.

Their words of wisdom seemed to fall on deaf ears. Connor was determined to push the party forward, to sate himself in the fight and the prestige that came with it. "Come on, guys. You all noticed how scared and wounded they are. It would only take a few minutes, tops. Worst-case scenario, we find other monsters or run into unstable terrain. If so, we simply head back and share the intel with Grace and the others."

Kira simply nodded once, but Louis hesitated for a while. It was only once Connor placed a hand on his shoulder and flashed the sort of infectious smile that only someone that attractive and charismatic could pull off that he finally agreed. Steve was the only one who voted against it but he ultimately agreed to help when the other fighters voted to go on. They simply ordered the porters to follow and keep quiet, never offering them the chance to vote on the matter. Thomas felt an uneasiness about the whole affair. There was something in Connor's eyes that made him reticent. He had seen that look before on individuals being led by dreams of glory. These types of people rarely cared if their ambitions burned up anyone around them.

Thomas noticed Lance silently stand there, no doubt lost in his thoughts. Placing a hand on his shoulder, he smiled warmly. "Get out of that head of yours. We'll be fine. Besides, if we play our cards right, we might get away with snatching you a decent shield from a goblin," Thomas said, whispering at the end. It would be against the rules, but he figured R.A.M. would survive without one more goblin shield.

The group then began moving again, Connor leading the charge as they followed the trail of blood leading them into the unknown.

"Lance, stay behind me," Thomas said as he fought off two Cave-wolves with his shield and kept a goblin at a distance with his pickaxe. He had lost count of how many monsters they had already killed, but it came at a steep price. He wasn't sure how much time had passed because of everything that had happened. Two porters and the fighter, Steve, were already dead. Lance and Thomas had stuck together as best as they could, but they were against overwhelming numbers.

"You're bleeding," Lance said, pressing against Thomas's shoulder to help him hold his position and not get pushed backwards by the monsters.

"Everyone is bleeding!" Thomas snapped. Things were bad . . . Terrible, even. Lance's lower Level would make him a liability and he didn't have a shield to defend himself. Beyond that, his condition was quite critical. Lacerations covered his friend's arms and the thick iron armor he wore had large dents in several places. "Just stay behind me," Thomas said, grunting as he felt another arrow nick his shoulder, further sapping his strength.

The fighters and porters were defending on all fronts on unfavorable terrain. They had run into an ambush when they'd chased after the wounded goblins. They found them near a tunnel that led to a large, cavernous space. Shortly after that, they noticed additional monsters. A large group of wolves had surrounded them while more and more goblins came pouring in to reinforce them. Several of the newcomers carried bows and arrows and took up positions on higher ground. In a matter of minutes, the monsters had blocked off their only means of escape. The only option was to fight their way through or fall off the sides of a cliff to certain death.

There were too many creatures to fight on all sides. It was only a matter of time before they would be wounded or killed. When the first porter fell, the victim of a stray arrow, the balance of power quickly shifted. Had it been just the initial enemy force, the fighters might've been able to crush one side and get the porters out before they were all surrounded. Connor could've made that decision, yet his pride kept him there when he spotted a heavily armored goblin that stood a head taller than its brethren and was rippling with muscles. It was a clear sign the monster was a Rift-guardian.

Connor's greed and pride had forced the party to engage both sides instead of retreating when they still had the chance. A goblin archer had killed the first porter while wolves had dragged off a second one a few minutes later. The fighter, Steve, had taken out a fair share of the goblins before more had ganged up on him, stabbing and pushing at him until they all lost their balance and tumbled off the edge, falling into darkness, their lives ultimately claimed by the unforgiving hard rock below.

Beyond the devastating loss of life, the three dead Rifters also meant that their defense became significantly harder. Although all three remaining fighters were experienced veterans, their Health, Stamina, and Mana were slowly getting chipped away. The Frenchman was a mess of sweat and minor injuries while Connor's once-impressive armor was covered in blood and dirt. Kira looked winded but showed no actual signs of any injuries beyond a slight cut on her leg.

This isn't good. It's only a matter of time before they overrun us, Thomas thought as he watched Connor bash the Goblin leader against his helmet, knocking it off to the floor.

The sight of their leader getting injured appeared to halt the goblin horde for a few seconds, as if waiting for him to recover and give them the command to attack. Although the small moment of respite was welcome at first, Thomas quickly noticed the shift in the fighters' behavior. Earlier, they had spread out to cover all their sides, but now they moved closer to one another.

No! They wouldn't, he thought, seeing Kira talking to Connor, the man shaking his head several times before going still. Then, almost in slow motion, Connor glanced around him, inspecting the horde of goblins and the fallen porters, and finally making eye contact with Thomas while Kira made her way over to Louis.

Thomas could only shake his head, pleading with Connor. He couldn't utter any words, fearing that it would only hasten the betrayal. He watched Connor tear his eyes away from him and the other porters before the three fighters suddenly began slashing, bashing, and shooting their way through on one side, surprising the goblins. The sheer brutality of the surprise tactics allowed them to retreat but left the remaining three porters stranded.

"No! Wait!" Lance shouted. The other porter suddenly rushed towards where the fighters had retreated to, hoping that he could escape with them. He barely made it ten paces before a dozen weapons and claws tore him into pieces.

"Lance . . . Lance!" Thomas shouted, nudging his friend in the ribs to get his attention. "Hold onto my armor and don't let go," Thomas instructed hastily as he placed all the Attribute points he had gained from Leveling during this battle. All of it went into Strength and Endurance as he activated his Bullrush Skill to increase his Strength further for a few seconds. His muscles were struggling to contain all the power flowing through him. "Hold on!" he shouted, suddenly speeding forwards like a projectile.

Although not on a par with the speed of Daniel or Dieter, the sheer increased Strength the redhead displayed was enough to overwhelm mere goblins. He used his shield as a ram to fling several of them to the side as he rushed towards the leader. He slammed into the monster with enough rage to mimic his fiery hair. Before the Rift-guardian could retaliate, it found Thomas's pickaxe slammed into its shoulder. And then the young man activated his Skill again.

Bullrush

He felt his muscles straining to the point of nearly ripping. His joints were inflamed and protesting, but he ignored them. The heavily armored goblin skidded to a halt at the cliff's precipice, emitting a thunderous roar as it barked orders to its kin, commanding them to assault the two Rifters. Seizing the moment before the horde could intervene, Thomas ignited his Skill once more, channeling every ounce of his being into one final charge.

"*Bull . . . Rush!*"

The last thing the other goblins heard was Thomas's defiant roar as he forced himself, Lance, and the goblin leader off the cliff and into the abyss.

CHAPTER TWENTY-FOUR

Blood Knife

THOMAS

Thomas groaned as he got up, his mind foggy and his body protesting through-out the process. The ground beneath him felt unstable and soft. As he looked down, he realized that he had landed on a pile of corpses. He could see Steven's broken body alongside dozens of dead goblins. Light barely reached this low into the cavern, making the small Mana stone deposits appear like small blue stars in the night sky. There was a dampness to the caves in this region, collecting in certain spots to form small puddles.

Thomas slowly recalled what had happened, his eyes searching his surroundings until he spotted Lance behind him. His friend was unconscious and still. At first, he feared the worst, but when he placed two fingers on his neck, he could feel a pulse. Thomas nearly broke down in tears at that, struggling to keep his breathing under control. His knees buckled. He dared not move Lance, fearing his friend might've broken something.

Everything hurts, Thomas thought, his gaze drifting until he noticed his discarded shield to his right. The defensive tool contained a lot of dents and had bits broken off at the bottom. It barely resembled the shield that he had bought from the Workshop. *Maybe I could place Lance on top of the shield and drag him back to camp?* he thought as he stumbled towards the shield and grabbed it. He was about to return to Lance when he noticed movement a few paces away from them.

An armored figure slowly rose from the ground, its left arm hanging limp and mangled at its side. The monster's once-impressive armor was broken in several places. The Goblin-leader roared as it rose to its full height, its yellowish eyes wide and filled with rage. It had claws for fingernails and opened its mouth to reveal broken teeth, drooling as it snarled angrily. It was almost comical. But there was nothing funny about its intent. It was vicious, enraged, and now had its eyes set on Thomas.

Fearing for his friend's safety, Thomas faced the Goblin-leader head-on. He crawled and stepped over the corpses of the fallen before he rushed towards the monster but stopped just in time to dodge a swing from its right arm. The claw slammed into his shield, screeching as it slid over the metal. Thomas tried to block as best he could, but the creature simply kept hammering him, barely giving him time to respond. Eventually, the monster hit him with enough force to send him flying backwards. He landed a few inches away from Lance.

This won't work, Thomas thought, realizing that the shield was useless against the Goblin-leader. It was stronger, and it had obviously fought people with shields before. Thomas got up to his feet, ignoring the pain in his knees and at his side. He dropped his shield, letting it fall to the ground with a loud clang. A second later, he stored his damaged breastplate in his Inventory.

[You have stored an item in your Inventory]

Thomas watched his opponent. The monster had a strong build, and there was a sizable gap in their Levels. Still, the redhead had him beat in terms of height, reach, and the use of both his arms.

He took a fighting stance. Thomas knew he had no choice but to use his fists, seeing as he was without a proper weapon. His boxing experience as a teenager and the times he had trained with Daniel would be vital now. The monster glanced at him before it took on a defensive stance with its working right arm, clearly displaying caution and intellect. Thomas made the first move, rushing the Rift-guardian. He threw a left jab, striking the monster against its arm, momentum forcing the goblin's own claw to slam into its face.

Enraged, the beast lunged at Thomas. He narrowly dodged it in time, stepping in closer as he did so. Thomas pivoted to his right, then threw a powerful uppercut that hit the monster right in the gut. The punch passed between an opening in the armor. A split second later, Thomas's left fist slammed into the monster's temple. He then backed off quickly. The brutal combination from Thomas had nearly forced it to drop to its knees, but it forced itself to keep standing, letting rage fuel it.

How's this thing still standing? I can barely keep my arms up, Thomas thought. The sheer tenacity of the monster surprised him. He knew from experience that those punches should've landed it on the ground for a few seconds at least, but it continued to stand and radiate hatred. The monster lunged once more, which Thomas ducked underneath, rushing past it.

[You have retrieved an item]
"Bull . . . Rush!"

When the monster turned around to face him, it was already too late to react. Thomas rammed his thick iron breastplate at its face, using up all the Strength he could muster behind the strike. His attack ruined both the armor and the monster's face in a bloody union.

The severely disoriented monster wobbled backward as Thomas rushed in again. This time Thomas went in low and delivered an uppercut to its chin, sending blood, spittle, and teeth flying. Judging by the pain he was feeling in his own hand, he knew that he had done a great deal of damage to the Rift-guardian. The monster fell to its knees this time, its legs too unstable to support its own weight after the last blow.

Thomas might not have been at the same strength Level as the monster, but he knew perfectly well how damaging a blow to the chin could be. He was about to go for the finishing move when he felt a sudden sharp pain in his left side. Looking down, he could see a knife embedded there, right up to the hilt. A bony green goblin was holding onto it.

The smaller goblin let the knife go with a yelp as soon as Thomas made eye contact with it. *Another goblin? Did it fall as well?* Thomas understood that the smaller goblin could've been a survivor of a fall, or it was a scout that was roaming at this level. It might be just one, or the creature could represent an entire horde of them that would arrive at any minute. Thomas gritted his teeth as he shifted his focus to the fight, knowing that overthinking things at this point would be no help to him.

The fighter in him wanted to yank it out and stab the goblin with it, but years as a trained nurse suppressed that urge. *Pull it out and I bleed out and die,* he thought, telling himself that repeatedly. He took an unsteady step towards the smaller goblin when he heard the Goblin-leader slowly get up again. Its broken jaw and mangled face weren't enough to stop it.

"Lance, I need you to wake up right now!" he shouted desperately as the two goblins advanced on him from both sides.

CONNOR

Connor led the others towards the camp. All three of them had been silent until now, each dealing with their own thoughts and emotions about what had happened. Cold sweat ran down Connor's back as he did his best to push down his feelings of disgust at himself. Disgust at having left people to die; disgust at not having been strong enough to defeat all the monsters on his own. The latter weighed the heaviest. Just as they neared the large clearing where the camp was located, Connor's attention shifted to Louis, as he noticed he'd stopped moving.

"We . . . We need to go back. We need to help them," Louis said, his eyes downwards, not wanting to face the others.

"No," Connor said. He moved towards Louis and grabbed him by the shoulder before continuing to speak. "We made our choice. They're dead. All of them."

Louis swallowed the lump in his throat. They had lost six people today. Most of them had died because they'd made bad decisions or even ran away. All three of them had gotten to know the people they had abandoned. It was easy to see how Louis felt about all of it, his face displaying the conflicting emotions he was struggling with. No doubt the man felt sick to his core. The lifestyle of a Rifter frequently flirted with death, but this would obviously feel different to all of them. They had sacrificed people just to save their own hides.

Kira remained silent as she watched their interaction with a blank expression on her dark visage. She held one hand behind her back, her eyes scanning Louis.

Connor's grip tightened on Louis's shoulder. "We made a choice and will have to accept it and live with it," Connor said, lying to Louis as much as to himself. "They saved us. We can make up for their sacrifice by saving others in the future."

Louis nodded, but he didn't agree. They had made a choice. One that resulted in six casualties. Connor was right about one thing, however. They had no choice but to accept it. Louis finally nodded, looking Connor in the eyes for a moment before averting his gaze as if he had felt a piece of his soul wither away.

The three of them then continued walking toward the bridge. After crossing it, they made their way into the camp. It didn't take long before other fighters and porters rushed towards them. The bloodstains, the damaged equipment, and the look in their eyes spoke volumes about what had happened: they had lost people. A lot of people.

Grace arrived seconds later, taking in their current state. "A report, now!" she barked as her mind went over a dozen scenarios while trying to prepare for each of them.

Not trusting Louis to keep to the story, Connor spoke first. "We suffered casualties. The monsters ambushed us. The Rift-guardian was amongst them. We were overwhelmed right from the start."

Louis remained silent while Kira confirmed the story with a simple nod.

"Did anyone else make it out? There were five porters with you. And what about the other fighter?"

"They . . . They all died," Connor said, swallowing dryly. He suppressed his guilt as he faced Grace. "There was nothing we could do. They were everywhere. We tried, but we had no choice but to pull back and save who we could," he stated, hoping his words were enough. Grace was a hard woman to convince.

A minute passed before she finally nodded and instructed the porters to help the three wounded fighters. The rest of the camp was on high alert, with Rifters searching for a potential enemy force and preparing equipment and cargo in case the Rift-event closed on short notice.

Connor made his way back to his bedroll and slumped down, feeling the weight of his conscience on his shoulders. He could see Louis just up ahead, staring into oblivion. A part of him worried that he might become a problem, but he didn't even want to consider the situation where he might need to decide how to prevent that.

This isn't supposed to happen to me, Connor thought, biting down hard as waves of shame and humiliation washed over him. This task should've been a routine job. His brother had sent him to scout Kira. He was supposed to observe her in action and assess if she was worthy to join the guild. Instead, he had only proven to Kira his own inadequacies as a Rifter and a leader.

At this stage, he knew only the basics regarding Kira, had lost several men under his command, and would no doubt lose some of his brother's trust. The latter worried him the most, knowing what it represented. If there was one thing Connor feared more than anything, it was what his brother thought of him.

It was hard not to, seeing as his brother was the fifth-highest ranked Rifter in the United States.

LANCE

Lance could hear the commotion near him as he opened his eyes, feeling disoriented as he looked up into the darkness of the cave. He rose slowly, the sounds of combat ringing in his ears. He thought he could hear someone calling his name.

Mend Wounds

He activated his Skill, letting a wave of healing, invigorating energy spread throughout his body at the cost of Mana. As the pulsing light washed over him, he could feel the minor wounds staunching, moistening, then closing. Slowly, he returned to his senses. The pain in his body came back to him but wasn't nearly as intense as it had been before.

When he could see what was going on, he immediately rushed forward, stumbling over corpses. "Thomas!" He spotted his friend's broken shield along the way and grabbed it as he closed the distance. A moment later, Lance charged into the smaller goblin, using Thomas's shield as a battering ram. The momentum sent it flying before it crashed into the ground a short distance away.

Lance then tried to assist Thomas as he watched the Goblin-leader slash at his friend. Thomas shifted underneath the swing before retaliating with a flurry of gut punches on a spot where the monster had no armor. That Thomas was going toe-to-toe with the Rift-guardian was amazing. The two Rifters weren't even in the same league as the monster, but Thomas proved just how much raw talent and years of experience could help in a fight.

Lance slammed the broken side of the shield into the Rift-guardian's unarmored leg. He tried to sever it with the jagged pieces but lacked the raw power to complete the task. Still, he had wounded and distracted it for a few moments as Thomas launched another barrage of punches. Lance wanted to attack the monster again when the smaller goblin latched onto his back. He could feel a bony arm wrap around his neck as the creature tried to strangle him.

Lance desperately tried to pry off the goblin's arm but lacked the strength. Although bony, the monster had him in a tight chokehold. Lance rammed his head back a few times, hitting it against the side of its head, but never enough to lessen the grip.

As he grew more desperate, Lance dropped the shield and rushed towards a small rock. He climbed up on it. Then he used his legs to propel himself backward in an arc before slamming down hard. Lance had used his entire weight and the kinetic energy of the jump to smash the goblin into the ground.

Lance could hear it groan and hiss, its grip on his throat slightly loosening. Still, it wasn't enough to allow him to escape. Lance could already feel himself nearly passing out as he realized it would be over in a few more seconds. *I'm sorry, Thomas,* he thought, knowing that if he passed out, then his friend would have to fight two monsters and would probably die as well. His vision grew dimmer, and he felt his strength leave him.

"Lance! Use it!" Thomas barked as he threw the blood-stained knife near where his friend was.

Lance's mind, starved of oxygen, fought to maintain function as he extended his trembling hand towards the knife. His fingers fumbled and fidgeted, desperately seeking the reassuring touch of the hilt. At last, his hands recognized the unyielding texture of cold steel wrapped in leather. With every ounce of willpower that he had left, he clenched the blade tightly and, driven by a primal instinct for survival, drove it deep into the goblin's exposed neck.

Instantly, its grip loosened and he felt the fight leave the monster. Lance took in a huge gulp of air, then held his hand over his throat, wincing in pain. He gasped for air, but it only made it worse. He forced himself to his feet, seeing the slain goblin before staggering towards Thomas.

He saw his friend standing over the unconscious Rift-guardian. His right hand was holding onto a rock he'd clearly used to bash the monster's face in. His other hand was pressing against his left side.

"You look terrible," Thomas remarked, a pained smile playing upon his lips, his gaze fixed on Lance's frantic approach and the unmistakable fear etched across his friend's face. They shared an unspoken understanding, fully aware of the cause behind Lance's distress—a cause that manifested itself through the crimson stream seeping from Thomas's left side, staining the ground beneath him in an ominous red hue.

"Don't move!" His voice strained through a ravaged throat as he reached Thomas. He caught his friend just as he crumpled to his knees, his complexion draining with every passing moment. Jerking off a glove, Lance pressed the fabric against Thomas's left side, the sight of the deep, ugly wound making his stomach churn. "Tell me, when did—"

"The little . . . stabbed me earlier," Thomas said while wincing. He had to force himself to get the words out. "Had to make a choice." A soft, forced smile crossed his pale features. "Not really . . . a choice . . . for me."

Lance could feel his friend's blood soak into the glove. Thomas's slurred words were getting weaker. He could tell that he was going in and out of consciousness. He didn't need his medical training to know that his best friend was going to bleed out in a matter of seconds.

Mend Wounds

Lance activated his Skill, forcing energy through Thomas's body. It instantly began staunching and knitting as much as it could, but the damage was too severe. Still, it earned Lance a moment to tear his sleeves off. He forced some of the fabric into the open wound, while the rest he tied together and wrapped around Thomas's waist to apply more pressure. His mind desperately searched through every bit of experience and training he had at his disposal from working in a hospital for years.

Mend Wounds

More energy flowed between them, delaying the inevitable. He could see Thomas's eyes focus again, borrowing the paltry amount of energy he had given him. Panic filled Lance's mind, knowing he was about to lose his best friend. He had to do *something*. His current Skills weren't enough to help him. Thomas needed a Rifter with healing Skills.

He finally noticed the Rift-guardian on the floor a few paces away from him. It was badly beaten, but still alive. Either Thomas had lacked the strength to finish it, or he knew that killing it so far from the Rift-event would lower his friend's chances of survival.

I have to do this, Lance thought, helping Thomas to the floor before he rushed to collect the shield. He spun it in his hands, holding the sharpened, broken side above the unconscious monster, lining the shield up with its neck.

This better work, he thought, remembering how close he was to reaching Level Ten. He prayed that this would be enough to get his Class as he slammed the shield downwards, screaming as he did so.

CHAPTER TWENTY-FIVE

Taking Inventory

LANCE

After he slammed his shield down, Lance suddenly found himself in nothing-ness. Everything was pitch black other than one small source of light: the soft glow emanating from within his chest. At first, it was internal, embedded within his white-shard. A layer of flesh, cloth, and broken armor contained it. Over time, however, it left him, passing through those barriers until it hovered before his eyes. It blinded him in a way that went beyond cognition.

He tried to reach for it, to keep it contained, but realized that he was but an observer in this realm. He was a puppet without its strings, floating into nothing-ness. Time flowed in a way that he couldn't describe or fathom. Eternities passed within a singular thought or flowed backwards from fragments of emotion. He felt undone.

The light started pulsating as it illuminated this dark realm in a light that went beyond brightness. Sound accompanied the light. It was a strange sound that was hard to describe. It was like metal twisting and groaning, like lightning being wrenched apart. Lance had never heard anything like it before, so alien and absurd. Yet somehow he could understand it perfectly.

[Calculating Experience is done]
[You have reached Level 10]
[Calculating Class]

Lance felt the light overwhelm his mind, nearly undoing him as it searched within. He could feel his personality, nature, and memories being observed, tested, and weighed. All of it in the span of a nanosecond and a century. Within his mind, he found several memories constantly repeating themselves. Memories of him adapting to survive a Rift, using the tools at his disposal back in the hospital, be it flame or acid.

[Calculations are done]
[Weapon Smith is a 56.44% match]
[Your adaptive nature is recognized]
[Starting Class adaption]

The light pulsated even brighter as it got ready to imbed itself within Lance. He felt a sense of relief. The light suddenly felt far more natural, as if it had been further tailored to him as a person. The chosen Class felt right. He had always been more interested in tools than people. It was perfect, but . . .

I refuse, Lance thought, remembering the blood-stained knife. He forced that singular memory outwards, slamming it into the light and pushing it backwards. The more he thought about it, the more that memory burned both himself and the light.

[Error . . . Class adaption refused]
[Anomaly . . . Deviating from protocol]
[Adapting. Restarting process]

Once again, the light overwhelmed his mind as it searched within. It felt less stable this time, as if the light were rushing the process this time. Lance's personality, his nature, and memories were once again being measured, this time more brutally. It suppressed certain elements of him, forcing a different outcome. Memories overwhelmed him. Memories of the people he lost. A torn Rachel, lost survivors, a dying best friend. It tore at his darker memories, of the survivor's guilt he had, about how he had wanted to reverse their fates, to undo their deaths.

[Calculations are done]
[Necromancer is a 32.29% match]
[Your desire to undo death is recognized]
[Starting Class adaptation]

Not like that, he thought as he slammed the entirety of his will against the light, chipping at its core. Lance somehow knew it would burn him up as well, threatening to undo him if he wasn't careful. A single memory fueled his will: a young Thomas with a bloody nose standing between a younger Lance and several bullies. *I won't desecrate his memory like that. Never like that!* Lance thought, his will roaring until it nearly scorched him from within.

[Error . . . Class adaptation refused]
[Warning. Core instability is 47.5%]
[Adapting. Restarting process]

The light that enveloped his mind was delicate this time, uncertain of what it was looking for. Memories passed through without latching on. It radiated without direction, without a set path that it was used to follow.

I'm going to heal Thomas, Lance thought, forcing his will to latch onto the light, dragging it closer to the fire that was burning him up from within. He forced more memories inside of the light, memories of Thomas and him surviving six Rifts together.

[Adapting . . . Healer Class preference is incompatible with your goal]
[Warning. Core instability is 59.3%]

He didn't let go of the light, forcing more memories inside of it until fractures appeared within it. His will latched onto a single memory finally: the memory of Thomas taking care of his younger brother, Oliver. *He will not die,* Lance thought as he forced his will upon the light, fracturing it further.

[Warning. Core instability is 73.12%]
[Warning. Core instability is 89.9%]

More and more memories flowed through it, burning the light from within. The cracks turned into fissures, allowing the heat from Lance's will to pour out. The light was uncertain and desperate. It grasped at anything it had experience with, suggesting Class after Class. It failed, only fracturing further.

Lance instinctively knew that he was hurting himself, that he was losing something in doing this. One could not produce such defiance without burning up some vital part of himself. He knew, on some level, that this could cause his own demise.

He continued sending more and more memories into the light. Memories of a young Thomas comforting a young Lance as he watched a casket go in the ground. *This won't be his fate. He is coming back with me. He will be leaving by my side!* Lance roared at the light, forcing everything he had and would ever be at it.

[Warning. Core instability is above 95%]
[Deviating from protocol . . . Documenting anomaly]

[Adapting . . . combining core Attributes]
[Custom Class generation is completed]
[You have gained the Death Smith class]

GRACE

The camp had turned from order into chaos in a matter of moments. Every Rifter felt the tremors in the air, the slight discomfort within their Rift-shards. The Rift-event was ending, and it wouldn't be long until it would turn unstable and finally explode outwards. The further away you were from the Rift-event, the less your chances were of surviving the return trip.

Grace had sent a runner out to retrieve the Rifters who had been out mining or hunting monsters. Still, no sane Rifter would ignore the clear signs of a Rift turning unstable. No one would want to linger where they were. Those within the camp were retrieving their equipment, reorganizing their backpacks, crates, and internal inventories.

We've lost six people, are missing resources, and will probably end up with wounded people on our hands if the others don't make it back in time, Grace thought, suppressing the desire to vent her frustration by burning something to cinders. A leader kept her cool, no matter her nature. Others looked at her and needed to see a calm face giving precise orders, lest this fiasco turns into something even worse.

She stopped when she reached Connor, Kira, and Louis, and noticed Kira patting Louis's back and whispering something to him. Louis looked several shades paler than she recalled, even after they had returned. "Mind telling me why this is happening, Connor?" Grace asked, her voice eerily calm.

"I don't know—" Suddenly, Connor was interrupted by a large stream of fire flying past and burning into a steel beam behind him. The metal grew bright red before it started dripping.

"You don't know why this event is closing? You don't know why a Rift-guardian suddenly died?!" Grace spat. Her eyes were wide with a rage that she tried fiercely to contain. She knew the other Rifters were looking at her, so she had to keep a lid on it for now. She moved toward him and placed her hand on his shoulder, her palm still hot enough to cause Connor discomfort.

"The minute we get on the other side of this Rift—and I mean the minute!— we're all going to have a long talk about what the hell happened here," Grace said. Although her voice had turned icy cold, her palm remained scorching hot.

She wanted to speak with them more, to learn more about the fate of the others, but knew that now wasn't the time. Her duty as a leader was to take care of the people under her command. So, she turned to them and began giving further instructions, trying to salvage as much as she could from this mess during what little time they had left.

LANCE

"Lance . . . please," Thomas said weakly as he struggled to locate his friend with his clouded vision.

Lance continued to maintain pressure on Thomas's wound, despite knowing it was too late. He didn't want to give up. He focused on the wound as he activated his Skill again.

[You have used Mend Wounds Lvl 1 at the cost of 10 Mana]
[Current Mana 17/125]

Only one more, Lance thought. He felt desperation and fear flood his mind as he kept his eye on his best friend. He noticed some color returning to Thomas's cheeks but knew that it was only temporary. The wound was simply too large to be closed by a weak Skill like this. There had been only one chance to save Thomas and he had failed. He blamed himself for not having gotten lucky and gained a healing Class. He wasn't sure what he had experienced when he had gotten his Class. His memory of that event grew hazier by the minute. The only thing he knew for sure was that he was now helpless to save his best friend.

"Everything is going to be fine," Lance lied. It was both for Thomas and himself. His mind was racing, trying to calculate how far it was to the camp and if he could reach it in time. In his heart, he knew it was futile, but he wasn't listening to that. He couldn't.

He suddenly felt a small nudge against his chin, demanding his attention. He saw Thomas's bloody right fist pressed against it as if he had tried to punch him. Seeing his friend's strength reduced to a mere tap nearly broke Lance as his eyes reddened further.

"Please . . . I need you to listen," Thomas said as he forced himself to lock eyes with Lance, demanding his attention. Lance had no choice but to nod as he felt Thomas's fist leave his chin and fall to the side.

"This place is ending . . . you got minutes . . . at most. You need to . . . make it out . . . alive," Thomas said as he forced the words out. He obviously was in a lot of pain. "I need you . . ." He stopped as he winced. The wound was opening again and undoing what little healing Lance had managed.

[You have used Mend Wounds Lvl 1 at the cost of 10 Mana]
[Current Mana 7/125]

"Stay with me, Thomas," Lance said as he poured the last of his Mana into his Skill. It invigorated his friend's body as the energy tried to close the wound.

As the blue light faded from Thomas, he stirred again, his eyes finding his friend and focusing on him. "I need you to take care of my family . . . Promise me," he said as desperation strained his voice. No doubt Thomas could feel his body weakening by the second. Despite Lance's attempts at convincing him otherwise, Thomas knew what lay in store for him. Lance could see tears forming as his friend struggled with the emotions that were no doubt raging through him. The fact that Thomas managed to keep himself together in that moment was a testament to his will.

"I promise. You don't have to worry about that," Lance said as he squeezed his hand and did his best to give a soft smile. He could see Thomas paling again. The wound was opening once more and draining the redhead of what little strength remained.

Thomas raised his hand as he smiled. Moments later he retrieved two items from his Inventory. His friend could see the items instantly forming in his dying friend's hand, taking the shape of a cheap lighter and a single cigarette.

"Too bad . . ." Thomas whispered. His eyes became unfocused as his hand shook. "I was . . . looking forward . . . to celebrating . . . with my . . . my best fr—" he said as his hand dropped. The items fell to the ground between them. They were stained red with blood.

Lance placed a hand on Thomas's neck, calling out his name as he desperately searched for a pulse. He saw his friend's empty stare, gazing into nothingness. He knew what it meant, even before a notification appeared above Thomas's body. Lance's voice transformed into an emotional roar that spoke of loss and despair.

"Thomas!"

As if mimicking his unstable emotions, the Rift joined him, the cavernous terrain trembling in unison as it grew more volatile.

Lance struggled to keep walking, carrying Thomas along with him. He wasn't sure how much time had passed since he had died. He could feel his knees burning from the additional weight of his friend, now slung over his shoulder. It paled in comparison to the mental weight of it all. He also knew that what he was doing would destroy any chance he had of making it out alive. Still, he pressed on, ignoring the pain in his body as he moved farther up the tunnel, towards the sound of running water. *I'm not leaving you,* he thought repeatedly as the words steeled his resolve.

He finally reached the cliff and fell to his knees, dropping Thomas in front of him. He tore his gaze away from his friend, not wanting to see that empty stare in his eyes. Instead, he focused on the ledge in front of him. Peering over it, Lance

could see the underground river flowing there. It looked violent, constantly clash-
ing against the rocks and stones that were directing it elsewhere.

Either this leads back to camp, or farther away from it, he thought as he remembered the flowing river near the camp. He hoped that if he survived not drowning that he could make it to the others in time.

Lance tried to stand up but fell back on his knees due to the instability that
flowed through the terrain, sending powerful tremors through the stone and dirt.
He didn't have time to stop and think about his chances of survival. He had to
go in now. So, he held out his right hand and retrieved an item.

[You have retrieved an item]

A moment later, his right hand gripped the handle of Thomas's banged-up
shield. He figured it would either drag him down to his death or increase his
chances of survival when faced with the jagged rocks dotted around the water.
Still, he needed to use everything he had at his disposal. He opened his status
screen and noticed the Level-Up notification, showing that he had reached Level
Ten and had Attribute points to spend. Having killed the Rift-guardian and the
smaller goblin, he had gained three Levels.

Nine points total, Lance thought, his chaotic mind wondering what might
improve his chances of survival in what little time he had left. He finally forced
all nine points into Endurance, figuring it was all or nothing.

[Endurance:] [25] (+9)

He could feel the changes within his body, strengthening his bones, muscles,
and skin. Compared to how it felt at the start of this Rift, he barely recognized it
now. The ache in his knees and shoulder lessened, the pain now only a sliver of
what it was mere minutes ago.

Now for the hardest part, he thought, steeling his heart before he shifted his
gaze towards his friend. Thomas's pale, unmoving frame tugged at his heart. He
could've put a thousand points into his Endurance, but the pain he felt when seeing Thomas like that would be just as emotionally damaging.

His gaze shifted from his still friend to that of the small notification above
him. It blinked now and again. It was similar to the one all Rifters had, informing them of when they could pick up an item such as a weapon or a piece of iron
ore. He had never seen it appear over a corpse until the moment he had reached
Level Ten and had gotten his Death Smith Class. As far as he knew, this was
unheard of in the world of Rifters. He didn't have to time to give it more thought
or figure out what his unique Class meant. For now, he focused his gaze on just
one thing.

[Would you like to store this item?]
[Yes] [No]

Gritting his teeth, he forced himself to look his friend in the eyes again before he accepted the action. A second later, Thomas dematerialized before his eyes, leaving behind his torn equipment.

[You have stored an Item in your Inventory]

Lance suppressed the urge to weep and/or throw up, ignoring the notification describing his dead friend as an "Item" as best he could. Instead, he grabbed Thomas's torn outfit and wrapped it around his arms and chest, hoping the additional layer of protection would allow him to survive at least one jagged piece of rock.

Lance then got up and gripped the shield tight in his hands before he jumped off the cliff. He felt gravity grab hold of his body and pull him downwards into the river. He hit the water hard and gracelessly. The freezing water quickly brought him to his senses as he felt his body get dragged down the river, slamming into the riverbed, the stone walls, and the occasional jagged rock that longed to cut into his flesh.

He could feel the steel shield grinding against the stone as the world around him vibrated more and more, a clear indication that the event was at its end. The tremors came faster and faster. Ignoring the pain and occasional cuts he got from slamming into the rocks, Lance swam along with the river, increasing his speed.

A part of him knew he wouldn't make it to the camp in time. Despite this, the sight of the enormous expanse of black energy suddenly rushing towards him took his breath away. It engulfed everything in its wake with an unnatural force. Lance barely had time to inhale deeply and hold the shield tight before plunging into the unnatural darkness.

CHAPTER TWENTY-SIX

Feeling Good

Outside Rift 7
Liverpool, England

GRACE

Grace suddenly felt disconnected from the black energy that had enveloped her. In an instant, her body came to a swift halt, her legs hit the ground. Before her eyes could adjust to her surroundings, she heard the roaring sound of objects slamming down around her. She heard people landing, rock peppering metal barriers, and protective cables being torn apart by fast-moving objects. Seconds later, a flood of whispers and cries erupted everywhere.

The Rifters' arrival had transformed the once-tidy and compact R.A.M. Rift site into something resembling a battlefield. No doubt shocked at first, the site crew quickly jumped into action, storming out of their mobile barracks as they organized.

It happened in the middle of the night, so most of the crew were in their sleep attire. The damp night air was icy on their skin, filled with the scent of unnatural elements that the Rifters had brought back with them. Some of these items littered the ground, having fallen out of broken containers.

"Rifters, report!" Grace yelled as she turned around to see if everyone had made it out alive. One by one, the Rifters reported they were intact. The Rift had flung those who had been farther away from the Rift-event quite far. The force had even launched some of them with enough force to tear apart the protective cables and nets that acted as a barrier around the Rift.

"Grace!" Jack Derby called out as he rushed towards her, concern clearly visible in his eyes. "What happened?"

"The Rift turned bad," she said, her eyes darting toward a massive hole in the protective net. She had no doubt that things they had brought with them had bombarded the surrounding area. Although this place used to be a construction yard, she feared there might still be collateral damage.

"How many wounded and how many dead?" Jack asked.

"Six dead. Five porters and one fighter. Beyond that, we have a dozen wounded, mostly minor," she told him, forcing out the words with no emotions. She hated herself for losing this many people. She shifted her gaze to the wounded Rifters. Most of the injured were Porters. She could see no life-threatening injuries at first glance.

"I'll contact GRRO and let them know we had a bad run. Anything above a 10 percent casualty range will warrant an advanced investigation. The best thing we can do is to be proactive about this. Anything I should know beforehand?" Jack asked. He noticed Grace scanning the holes in the protective nets before her gaze shifted over towards three Rifters in particular. There was a ferocity in her eyes.

Grace didn't answer him. Instead, she made her way over toward some of the seemingly unwounded Rifters. "Those not injured will help store and secure the items at a designated spot. I want no more injuries because of people tripping over sharp Rift materials," she ordered. The R.A.M. personnel had already set up a basic triage. Most of the injuries were minor, save for two who had suffered concussions and one with a broken arm.

She glanced backward and studied the Rift. It was less dense than it had been before, having shrunk since they had cleared it. She shifted her gaze and took stock of the injured Rifters, looking at each of them with concern until her gaze shifted back to Kira, Connor, and Louis. "Jack, follow me," she said as she started moving again.

Six dead. Where did it all go so horribly wrong? The people who died were under my command . . . my protection. What the hell do I tell their families? Grace thought as she reached the three Rifters. "You three, follow us. We're going to have a long talk about what the hell happened in there," Grace said as she pointed at a trailer that functioned as a break room.

LANCE

Lance groaned in pain as he woke up to the night sky looking down on him. A dirty blanket of rubble and dirt lay over his body, which was also covered in bruises, scrapes, and cuts. He lay there for a moment, letting the world spin around him. Everything seemed to pass by in a blur, but he didn't pay any attention to it. When he tried to wiggle the fingers on his left hand, they felt strange. He brought it up to his face only to discover that several fingers were bent out of place.

He gritted his teeth as he spoke to himself. "Dislocated—possibly broken as well." He used his right hand to steady the injured fingers before exerting pressure on them one at a time. Lance could hear them pop back into place one after another. He fought back some curses as he crawled to his hands and knees, feeling a sharp pain in his back as he did so. He could feel blood running down his side from a wound. Looking back, he noticed the steel shield embedded in the ground behind him. It had probably saved his life throughout the ordeal, but also nearly impaled him in the end. *I've probably lost a lot of blood,* he thought as he inspected the shield.

Blood covered the broken edges of the shield, showing that he had cut himself on it. *No doubt if Thomas were here, he would've shared a witty remark about it being a double-edged shield,* Lance thought, feeling a jolt of despair explode within his mind before he suppressed it. Instead, he focused on the task ahead as he activated his Skill.

[You have used Mend Wounds Lvl 1 at the cost of 10 Mana]
[Current Mana 59/135]

He realized some time had passed because some of his Mana had regenerated. "I must've been out for a while," he said out loud. He slowly got to his feet and felt the healing light pass through his body before it faded again. Lance then grabbed his friend's battered shield and stored it in his Inventory as he watched the blood and dirt that had clung to it fall to the ground.

He reached over and gripped a piece of debris to pull himself upright so he could lean against a nearby wall. Lance could see the Rift in the distance, suggesting that the force that carried him out of it must have been enormous. He could see the destroyed wall behind him and the impact marks on the dirt in front of him. He vaguely recalled the speed at which he'd exited the Rift, breaching the safety net. Lance had positioned the shield back in front of him to protect himself, but it had been a close call.

From what he could see, he had crash-landed in an old shed of sorts. He let go of the wall he was leaning on and tried to stand on his own feet. He swayed back and forth for a few seconds before managing to steady himself. *I'm lucky to be alive,* Lance thought as he massaged his left hand. He could see several emergency service vehicles in the distance near the Rift. Dozens of people were busy there, helping the wounded or securing the site itself.

He took a few steps forward, knowing that they could help him if he reached them. Lance stopped moving as he watched three figures make their way to a line of cars. Even amid this chaos, he instantly recognized them by their equipment, their build, and even the way they walked. There was no way Lance wouldn't recognize the people who had turned their backs on him and Thomas. The people who had left them to die.

"No!" he yelled as he watched all three of them get into a car. None of them appeared to be handcuffed. A part of him wanted to rationalize it, pointing at the GRRO logo at the side of the cars, knowing that they would probably be questioned. Still, that rational part of his mind failed to convince him. His traumatized state was far too unstable. "Why haven't they been arrested?" he asked out loud. His hands were trembling as he fought hard to control his breathing. He felt like he was mere moments away from having a panic attack. It was the first time he had seen those three again, and it had nearly broken him.

"I . . . I'll . . ." he paused, unsure what he wanted to say. It was more of an emotion that was forming inside of him, maturing with each passing second. He gritted his teeth as he activated his Skill three more times, sending bursts of healing energy throughout his body to lessen some of the damage he had sustained. His eyes narrowed to slits, and his mouth tightened as he watched the cars drive away. He felt his rage build up, pressing against his senses like a hammer upon an anvil. His body trembled with anger as he took a step away from the Rift and toward the car park in the distance. In that unstable mindset, he made up his mind.

A few minutes later, he climbed onto Thomas's motorcycle and turned on the engine as he adjusted his visor. Although he wasn't as proficient a driver as Thomas, he felt confident enough to operate it. Lance watched several GRRO employees and medical personnel arriving at the car park before heading towards the Rift. Some had observed him as they passed, but a wounded and bloody Rifter wasn't unusual that evening.

He had stayed away from the Rift site. Instead, he had collected his and Thomas's gear. The latter had resulted in him prying open Thomas's locker with the shield. Beyond needing the helmet and motorcycle keys, he took the rest of his friend's things. It hadn't felt right leaving them there so close to the Rift. There was too much commotion for people to realize who Lance was or that a person had smashed open a locker, not that he was clearheaded enough to ponder the consequences of his actions.

Lance knew he should've turned around, gone back to the others, and explained what had happened. Perhaps it might have hastened the investigation. Each time he felt the urge to do so, he checked his Inventory, seeing a broken shield, several black-shards, and the body of his best friend stored inside. It sickened him to see his friend labelled as an Item, but it was the brutal reality he now found himself in. How the hell could he explain what had happened to him and Thomas? What about his new Class, or that he carried his dead friend inside of his Inventory?

He had no answers to those questions, and a part of him knew he was growing more unstable by the minute. The many injuries, the blood loss, and the mental shock . . . all of it was building up. He needed some time to think things through, away from the others.

Focusing on an Item would usually bring up options, such as retrieving or combining it in a stack. This time, two new options were available: Repair item and Death Forge. Both stemmed from his new Skills at obtaining the Death Class. He had tried the repair option on Thomas several times, but the grayed-out option wouldn't work. He knew it was futile to get his hopes up, but each time it didn't work, he still felt a piece of his heart wither and die. Finally, in a wave of emotions, he pressed the Forge option.

[Item can be forged. Templates available: 1]
[Required Shards: 100. Do you wish to proceed?]
[Yes] [No]

Once he accepted it, he watched several black-shards get used up, along with Thomas's body. A countdown then appeared inside his Inventory. He nearly threw up right there and then, swallowing bile as he slammed his fist against the tank of the motorbike. Shortly after that he tasted fresh blood in his mouth. With what little clarity he still had left, he steeled himself to go home. He needed to figure out what this new Class meant, what he had done with Thomas's body, and what he wanted to do with the three people who had betrayed them. Most of all, he wanted time to process the loss of his best friend. The motorcycle jerked forward, taking him away from the Rift.

Lance groaned as he pushed open the door to his flat. His body ached after the long ride home. It was the searing pain in his left hand that bothered him the most. Another flash of blue light enveloped his body as it tried to mend his injuries. It was because of his Skill that he had gotten home in the first place and didn't pass out somewhere in a ditch due to fatigue and pain.

The light coming off his body illuminated the room and threw dark shadows in the corners. The apartment was old and on the smaller side. He had decorated his living room with a worn-out sofa and some plants in the corner that did their best to give some warmth to it all. A stack of clean dishes stood piled up in the kitchen, clearly forgotten by Lance before he had left for the Rift.

As the effects of his Skill faded from his body, he switched on the lights. He winced when he realized he had used his left hand. Old habits and fatigue had overridden his ability to prevent self-harm. He dragged himself to the kitchen to grab a bag of frozen peas from the fridge before collapsing on the couch.

Lance opened his Inventory as he inspected the state of the countdown before he withdrew his smartphone, letting it suddenly appear in his right hand. He tapped the broken screen and unlocked it. With the device back on Earth and suddenly near a mobile tower, it vibrated, showing missed calls, text messages, and other notifications. The last one was a missed call from Daniel. More missed calls would no doubt arrive later.

His mind was not yet ready to explain that he had survived and Thomas had not. The thought of him telling Thomas's family . . . his little brother . . . How could he even find the words? How could he explain to anyone what had happened?

He pressed the icy peas more firmly against his wounded hand, appreciating how the pain reduced his ability to lose himself in his somber thoughts. It wasn't healthy, but it would leave him emotionally intact for now.

[You have finished forging an item]

The status update immediately drew his attention. He had ignored the other messages about his low Health, Mana, and that he had Leveled Up to Level Eleven after surviving the Rift. He felt his throat dry up as he retrieved the unnamed item in his Inventory, ignoring the option to rename it.

[You have retrieved an item]

A moment later, a naked pale figure sat next to him on the couch, unmoving and unnaturally devoid of color. The body's once-red hair and bright blue eyes were now degraded to a shade of gray. It pained him to see his friend like that, sitting so eerily still and changed. Any hope he had of saving his friend left him at that moment. Still, the body appeared uninjured and didn't show the fatal wound that had stolen Thomas's life back in the Rift.

[You have stored an item in your Inventory]
[You have combined and retrieved an item]

Briefly, he removed the pale body from the couch, only to have it appear a few seconds later, now dressed in the battered, padded R.A.M. work clothes that had once belonged to Thomas. The badly-damaged clothes at least covered up its nudity. Even dressed, the it didn't move, nor react. The longer Lance stared at him, the more he noticed that the body never blinked or even breathed. It was almost statuesque in appearance.

[You have retrieved an item 2x]

Lance retrieved a single cigarette and lighter from his Inventory. He flicked open the lighter and produced a small flame, gazing into it for a moment before lighting the cigarette. After bringing it to his mouth, he inhaled deeply, letting the irritating smoke fill his lungs. Afterwards, he placed it between the lips of the pale man next to him, securing it in place. Lance fought back the urge to cough as he let the smoke stain his lungs, exhaling after a while. "There we go," Lance said, his gaze upwards. He stared at the ceiling as if that might hold answers to whatever he was feeling at that moment.

There was a stillness in his flat that went beyond mere silence. Lance simply sat there, injured, and covered in dirt and dried-up blood. The gray body to his side was perfectly still with a thousand-yard stare. The more Lance thought about the situation, the more he realized that this wasn't his friend.

The body's height, build, and even the small blemishes on his face were a perfect replica of his best friend, but it was missing whatever had made Thomas the man he had once been. Instead of the body having a white-shard, it now was a dull gray.

A few minutes passed like that, with both still and silent, the occasional bit of ash breaking off the cigarette and piling up in a single spot. "You know smoking is going to get you killed one day," Lance said, forcing his gaze away from the ceiling and towards his still companion. He noticed the cigarette was barely in place, trapped between unmoving gray lips. The sight might have looked funny, if not for the strange complexion of his companion and the fact that he had created it.

Instead, only anger lingered that evening. A type of silent anger that might undo a person if one wasn't careful. Lance's hands turned white from clenching his fist so firmly despite his injuries. The sack of frozen peas fell to the floor as he swore an oath right there and then.

"I swear to you, Thomas. No matter what, I'll get justice for you."

He then opened his email, and the file attached to it before hitting the play button on his smartphone. The file was a song that Thomas had sent Lance before. His friend had wanted to use it to celebrate when the two of them had reached Level Ten. A pained chuckle left him as he closed his eyes and listened to how the song made a sweet mockery of the situation.

The smartphone's screen showed both a reflection of a pale figure picking up a sack of frozen peas and the song's title displayed on the device: "Feeling Good" by Nina Simone.

Status Compendium

Name: Lance Turner
Level: 11
Class: Death Smith

Attributes

Endurance:	35	**Agility:**	26	**Wisdom:**	20
Strength:	26	**Perception:**	23	**Luck:**	20
Health:	650	**Mana:**	135		
Stamina:	215	**Inventory:**	25		

Traits

Taint of death:	Able to use Rift corpses as items	Prolonged use results . . . ~ERROR UNREADABLE!~
Shard instability:	~ERROR UNREADABLE!~	Prolonged use results . . . ~ERROR UNREADABLE!~

Skills

Mend Wounds	Lvl 1	Restores minor wounds	+10 Health +4 Stamina	−10 Mana
Death forge	Lvl 1	Allows (re)forging of death related items	+1 Item	−Raw materials −Black-shards −50% Stamina regeneration −50% Mana regeneration
Repair item	Lvl 1	Restores durability on items	+1 durability per 1 item per 1 minute	−Raw materials −Black-shards −25% Stamina regeneration −25% Mana regeneration

Ranking Rifts and Rifters

GRRO Manual, Part 14
Written by Samuel Jones
GRRO Chief Executive, London Branch

Greetings <insert_firstname>,
In this section, we will go over the way the GRRO classifies both Rifts and Rifters in terms of their measurable power. Take note that, although most of the world recognizes the GRRO standard, it still isn't universally accepted. Rifters going abroad might run into different classification systems.

Defining a Rifter's Level:
The GRRO recognizes a Rifter's Level according to their displayed number within their status. Withing certain situations, an external measurement might be required, but it is usually less secure compared to a Rifter simply stating their Level and Attributes. The GRRO recognizes and considers that there is a vast difference between a Rifter's Level and their actual combat strength. This is because of a multitude of factors that come into play, be it Skills, the distributed Attribute points, or the Rifter's natural affinity for combat and equipment, to name a few. The GRRO still holds the Rifter's Level as a benchmark for most Rifts since the Attribute baseline is universal.

Example: A Level 100 Rifter will always have a higher Agility Level than a Level 20 who spends all their points on Agility.

The Rifter's Ranking:

Level	Ranking	Recommended Maximum Rift Level
1–10	Survivor	3
10–100	Veteran	6
100–200	Expert	9
200–400	Elite	12
400–800	Master	15
800+	Legendary	Unrestricted

The GRRO maintains this structure because of the similarity between a Rifter's Class system, where each higher rank coincides with a change in their Class. In the past, this had been mandatory and strictly regulated, but with the increase in Rift occurrences and the abundance of higher quality gear, the GRRO has changed this demand into a mere recommendation. Privately-owned Rifts by companies or guilds might prefer different standards, but those monitored and under the administration of the GRRO will all be uniform.

A Rift Level:
We measure a Rift's Level or rank either by machines capable of monitoring the output of a Rift, or by Rifters that have the required Skills or Class to measure them. An example would be a person with a Seer Class or the Inspection Skill. In most cases, a standardized piece of machinery provided by the GRRO will determine the Level of the Rift.

A Rift's size and growth conveys little about its relative Level or the pitfalls that lay within. A rule of thumb is that the higher a Rift's Level, the higher the quantity or quality of the number of monsters and their equipment. Because of the varying nature between the quality and quantity, a Rift's Level can be deceiving. More than one party or guild has suffered casualties because of a Rift suddenly overwhelming them with a vast quantity of weaker monsters, or simply crushing them with a single powerful monster.

Beyond the strength of a Rift, there is also the nature of the environment inside. There are many examples of a weak Rift being far more dangerous because of poisonous flora and fauna, unbreathable air, an unstable flow of time, or simply the absence of fresh water.

The official GRRO policy is that a party's average Level should always be a few ranks higher than the Rift they are about to enter, and that proper research is to be done about said Rift beforehand.

<Link_index> <Link_next_page>

Rift-Shards

GRRO Manual, Part 21
Written by MSc Klara Sokolov
Author of 'The heart stone 224a-2'

Greetings <insert_firstname>,
In this section, we will analyze the peculiar nature of elements 2242-A and B, more commonly known as Rift-shards. Rift-shards are a curious element. One cannot find these shards anywhere on Earth, nor are they found in indigenous life-forms within the Rift. The only documented and recovered samples have been from Rifters and the entities that guard said Rifts. We describe the latter as "monsters." In essence, the Rift itself creates these shards.

The shards typically come in two variants: Element 2242-A, also known as a white-shard; and element 2242-B, known as a black-shard. We can find these white variants within humans or animals that have survived a Rift and returned to Earth. We find the black-shards within the monsters that lurk inside these Rifts. The monsters that are directly tied to the Rift itself are Rift-guardians. Typically, these variants of monsters have a black-shard with a red hue, but the reason behind that is still unclear. In this section, we will mostly cover the black-shards because of the complex nature of Guardian-shards and their ability to interfere with a Rift.

Properties:
Although rare documents exist of black-shards showing signs of damage, they are remarkably resilient. It is nearly impossible to damage them through conventional means. It has a rating of 11.2 on the Mohs scale, making it the hardest substance known to mankind, except for a white-shard. Beyond that, it is extremely heat-resistant, chemically inert, and does not conduct electricity. Analysis shows it is

radioactive, but research on what this radiation is and how or if we can harness this energy is still in its infancy.

What we have learned after several years is that there are no obvious signs of this radiation being malignant to organic life. The most accepted theory regarding this radiation is that it is a marker of how strong the monster had been. The field of Advanced Rift Chemistry and Minerals has come a long way, but there is still much to learn about this strange element. As far as we can determine, a white-shard is several times harder and more radioactive compared to the black-shards.

Location:
Typically, a shard is located within the chest area, although Rifters have recorded variation between distinct species. See the link for several documented variants.

<Link_document_#348-a>.
The flat surface of the shard protruding out of the body is smooth and uniform, resembling a crystal. The section of the shard embedded inside the body is chaotic and branches out in different directions, spreading farther into major arteries and nearby organs. Most theorists believe that this is by design and that it forces blood through the shard to get enriched by this strange radiation. Afterwards, the blood will spread it throughout the body using the intricate roadmap of veins and arteries. Doing so alters biological components and processes through radiation, allowing for the manifestation of strange abilities and the use of "Skills."'

Use:
Researchers have found little use for white-shards, beyond their ability to grind or cut into black-shards. Research has been slow, because of the scarcity of these shards and the obvious ethical aspects that surround them. The black variants are less scarce, and people frequently use these for crafting purposes. One such way is for a Rifter classed as a Smith or Crafter to use a Skill to repurpose these shards: a process that reshapes or fragments them, sometimes altering or destroying them entirely. This process is lengthy, but it maintains the stability of the material and the energy within it.

Machines and talented people can replicate this by using chemical processes and powerful lasers, but the result is usually far more unstable. This makes it better suited for generating energy or to be used in volatile processes.

Notable examples of items created from black-shards from Rifters: black-tipped arrowheads, encrusted shields, black-tipped ammunition, and flame-resistant coating. Some examples of non-Rifter created items: volatile black dust, overcharged Mana stones, and cloaking gems.

Price:

Depending on the size and the Level of a monster, a black-shard can be denser and more radioactive than others. These denser shards often result in better crafting recipes or results. Beyond that, Rifters frequently use these black-shards as a form of payment. This is due to the shard retaining its value and its status as a universal form of currency. It is hard to put an exact value on these black-shards, or to compare them to more earthly materials such as platinum or gold. This is because of the fluctuation between demand and the availability of these shards. Beyond Rifters there are other parties interested in these black-shards, from researchers, museums or even collectors.

Note: The GRRO encourages the sale of black-shards through official GRRO-licensed traders to ensure proper documentation and appraisal.

<Link_index> <Link_next_page>

About the Author

Osirium Writes is the pen name of author Joost Lassche, whose urban fantasy LitRPG series, Death Smith, was originally released on Royal Road.

DISCOVER
STORIES UNBOUND

PodiumAudio.com

Printed in the USA
CPSIA information can be obtained
at www.ICGtesting.com
JSHW022339140824
68134JS00019B/1584